CAPTIVATING THE HIGHLAND ROGUE

Highland Destiny
Book 3

by Michelle Miles

ARE YOU SIGNED UP FOR DRAGONBLADE'S BLOG?

You'll get the latest news and information on exclusive giveaways, exclusive excerpts, coming releases, sales, free books, cover reveals and more.

Check out our complete list of authors, too!

No spam, no junk. That's a promise!

Sign Up Here

www.dragonbladepublishing.com

Dearest Reader;

Thank you for your support of a small press. At Dragonblade Publishing, we strive to bring you the highest quality Historical Romance from some of the best authors in the business. Without your support, there is no 'us', so we sincerely hope you adore these stories and find some new favorite authors along the way.

Happy Reading!

CEO, Dragonblade Publishing

**Additional Dragonblade books by
Author Michelle Miles**

Highland Destiny Series
Desiring the Highland Laird (Book 1)
Loving the Highland Warrior (Book 2)
Captivating the Highland Rogue (Book 3)

Dedication

To my friend, Mark Karlik,
for her lovely Gaelic translations

CHAPTER ONE

SUN DAPPLED THE white sandy beach on the private island Brianna Sinclair enjoyed as a guest of the man she was currently dating. She stuck her toes in the sand, allowing the warmth to wash over her as she lounged back in the chair under the beach umbrella, a cold drink in her left hand, a large-brimmed hat on her head, wearing her favorite black-and-white polka-dotted bikini.

She stretched out her long sun-kissed legs, wiggling her toes deeper into the fine grains of sand and emitted a contented sigh. For years, she had worked as an underwater photographer, capturing the essence of the crystalline waters of the Caribbean, from dolphins to schools of fish. Until she caught the eye of one very rich, very handsome man who also happened to be a billionaire playboy. Grayson Radcliffe had invited her to his forty-foot yacht named *Fin and Tonic* one evening which was supposed to be nothing more than a business discussion. He wanted to hire her to go on deep-sea adventures with him and take pictures.

But as it turned out, she was wildly attracted to him and that business dinner had turned into a sultry night in his cabin.

Grayson had a reputation as a ladies' man who dated super models and A-list Hollywood actresses. She, being nothing more than a free-spirited nomad, was his girl du jour. She was fine with that. Her first unbreakable rule was *never get attached*. Once he was finished with her, she'd move on.

And that was fine with her. The sex was hot and she was living her best life without a care in the world. She maintained her independence by taking photography jobs whenever she felt like. Grayson was willing to let her travel with him on his yacht and stay in his white-washed mansion on the private island he leased from the Bahamas.

Things had not always been sexy billionaires, cocktails, and surf-and-turf dinners. When she was twenty-five, a car accident had claimed her parents' lives, leaving her two fifteen-year-old twin sisters alone. It forced her to pack up her beach life and head home to care for them as their legal guardian until they graduated high school.

Life was rocky then as she navigated probate for her parents who had left the world with no wills. She put up with a lot of shit from her teenage sisters while they finished high school all the while longing to return to her island-hopping life. For three years, she made sure they had a roof over their heads, clothes on their backs, food on the table, and everything else they needed to finish high school and graduate. Then she sold their parents' home, took her cut of the money, and left.

She hadn't heard from her sisters much since then, knowing the rift it had caused between them. When Chloe got her big-wig job in Edinburgh, Evie had called her to tell her the news. Brianna was happy for her. Happy she was living the life she always wanted. Evie begged her to come to Edinburgh with her, but she refused.

Why would she trade her perfect, beachy life for a place like Scotland?

She didn't know why she was thinking of all this now as she sipped her drink and gazed out at the azure water, watching the tide go in and out. Grayson used the morning to run on the beach. She saw him in the distance, his toned physique gleaming with sweat. He wore shorts and running shoes and nothing more. Afterward, he would dive into the shallow water for a quick dip, then head into the house behind her to shower. She'd follow him, they'd have a sexy romp and then sit at the glass table by the wall of windows in the dining room for a breakfast of poached eggs, French toast, and coffee.

She had everything she had ever wanted. When Grayson tired of her, she would pack her bags and be on her way. For now, though, she enjoyed his company and his money.

The morning sun made her drowsy, her lids drooping as she thought of the way her life turned had out and the choices she'd made. She was sure she had made all the right decisions.

Or had she?

As she dozed, her cell phone buzzed next to her. She cursed herself for even bringing it out to the beach with her, but she was expecting a call from a client. Glancing down at the screen, she noticed the strange number that appeared to be from the United Kingdom.

Odd.

"Brianna Sinclair," she answered.

"Hello, Miss Sinclair. This is Detective MacDougal from the police in Edinburgh, Scotland. I'm afraid I have some difficult news about your sister, Chloe." The male voice on the other end of the line had a Scottish brogue.

Startled, she sat straight up out of the chair, sloshing the drink over her hand. Her heart thudded wildly and her pulse raced. Despite the heat of the morning, icy pinpricks needled the back of her neck. Brianna clutched the phone so tightly her hand cramped.

"Is something wrong?"

"Aye, she's missing."

The blood whooshed out of her head, leaving her lightheaded. "What do you mean, missing?"

"No one has seen or heard from her for several days. Her job called to ask for a welfare check because it simply wasn't like her to miss work. Her director worried her disappearance had something to do with the attack on the museum during their fundraising gala."

"What attack on the museum?"

Worry pounded through her. Evie was supposed to go to Edinburgh to join Chloe for her big gala event. Brianna had declined to join them for the festivities, opting instead to remain in the Bahamas. Now regret shifted through her.

The detective explained a few nights ago—at the gala event—masked men with guns had invaded the museum. Though nothing was stolen, there was considerable damage. The museum was closed while they tried to sort everything out and get it back to normal.

"But your sister, Chloe, never showed up for work. The director asked us to do a welfare check. When we went to her flat, the door was bashed in and there appeared to have been a struggle."

Numb, Brianna listened, her breathing shallow as she stared into the glistening surf, trying to make her mind understand what he was telling her. The thing that bothered her the most was Evie was supposed to be at that gala, too. What had happened to her, then? The detective hadn't mentioned her.

"Have ye heard from your sister at all, Miss Sinclair?"

"No. What about Evie?"

"Evie?" he repeated. There was a faint shuffle of papers on the other end. "Och, aye, after the museum incident, Chloe was insistent her sister was still inside the museum but there was no trace of her. She filed a missing person report a day or so later."

No trace of her. Chloe missing. What the holy hell was happening?

Brianna clutched the phone tighter. "So, detective, you're telling me *both* my sisters are missing in your city. Is that right?"

There was a long pause on the other end of the line. "Aye."

"And what are you doing to find them?" she demanded, her mother instinct suddenly kicking in. She shot to her feet, pacing the small area in front of her beach chair.

"Well—"

"It sounds like a whole lot of *nothing* to me."

"Miss Sinclair, I assure you we're doing everything we can to find them. But there aren't a lot of leads—"

"Well, that's not good enough. They're my baby sisters and you're telling me they vanished without a trace?"

"I—"

"Save it. I'm coming to Edinburgh."

Her finger jabbed the end-call button with unsatisfying force, her chest heaving. She stared at the surf, the sunlight scattering across the waves glistening glass. Something inside her snapped, sharp and final, as she made the sudden decision.

The undeniable idea struck her like lightning. Go to Scotland. It wasn't a whim; it was a pull deep in her gut, an unshakable certainty. If she didn't go, regret would claw her forever, like it had when she ignored Evie's call begging her to come. That raw and relentless regret still ached. Like a wound refusing to heal.

She hadn't thought of Evie and Chloe until today.

Why now? Why today?

There wasn't anything significant about the date. It wasn't the anniversary of her parents' death. It wasn't anyone's birthday.

A shout broke through the rush of waves. Her head snapped to the left. Grayson sprinted up the beach, his hand lifting in a quick wave.

The unease didn't fade, even after making her decision to leave. It coiled tighter inside her chest, demanding she check on Evie and Chloe. She sucked in a shaky breath, willing herself to focus, but her thoughts scattered. Before she could gather them, Grayson appeared.

"Hey, babe," he said on a pant. When he realized something was wrong, his brows drew together. "You okay? You look like you've seen a ghost."

"I need to make a phone call."

Never mind she still held the phone in her hand as she spun and bolted up the beach toward the house, leaving Grayson behind without a second thought. Her feet pounded against the sand, her breath coming fast and sharp. She burst through the back door, barely registering the cool air inside as she dropped her icy glass onto the nearest table with a clatter. Sand scattered in her wake, but she didn't care.

In her guest room, she ripped off her wide-brimmed hat, tossing it aside without looking. Here, in the solace of her room, her stomach tightened as she scanned the screen—no missed calls. A sharp ache of dread pierced her chest as she jabbed Evie's number. It rang once, then went straight to voicemail.

"It's Brianna. Call me back!" Then she hung up.

Her hands shook. Why, she didn't know. But a sudden panic settled in her chest, making it hard to breathe. She dialed Evie's number again. Again, it went straight to voicemail.

She stared down at the phone as if it were the problem. She sent a text to Evie that simply read, *are you all right?*

She peered at the message for the longest moment, waiting to see if she would type back. Hoping the tiny three-dot bubble would appear.

Nothing.

She didn't want to call Chloe. They hadn't spoken in a long time and the last time they did they'd argued. But she *had* to call her. Opening her contacts again, she scrolled through until she found her and then punched the mobile number to dial.

It rang four times, then the voicemail picked up. "Hi! It's Chloe. Leave a message!"

Brianna hesitated. "Chloe...it's Brianna. Listen, I know you probably don't want to talk to me right now, but I feel like something is wrong. Are you okay? Where's Evie? I can't get her. Call me back."

She ended the call.

She was still staring at the silent phone in her hand when there was a faint knock on her door. Grayson stood in the doorway with a concerned look on his face.

"What's going on?" he asked.

She bit her bottom lip. "I can't get in touch with my sisters."

"Your sisters?"

She had never spoken of them, so likely it was a surprise to Grayson.

"The twins," she said, as if that elaboration would make him understand.

"You have twin sisters?"

"Fraternal," she clarified, distracted. "Evie and Chloe."

"I'm sure it's nothing," he said, sounding nonchalant.

He advanced into the room. Sweat gleamed on his naked torso. He reached for her, plucking the phone out of her hand and tossing it to the unmade bed. His hands slid around her waist as he leaned in for a kiss. She put a hand on his chest and pushed him away, unable to shake the feeling something was off.

"Stop." Her voice was sharp. He pulled back, releasing her, the surprise evident. She shoved out of his arms and reached for her phone again. "Something is wrong."

She tried calling Evie again. Again, voicemail. Then she tried Chloe. It rang but went to voicemail. She tried texting both of them.

"I'm sure they're all right—"

"No." She spun toward him as the detective's words came back to her, haunting her. "They're not all right. Something happened to them. A detective called me. He said—"

"All of a sudden you have sisters who need you. Sisters you've never told me about." Confusion followed by disbelief was clear on his face.

"I know it sounds weird, but—"

"Are you screwing some other guy?"

"What? No!" She quickly scrolled through the pictures on her phone looking for proof they existed. She came across the one photo she'd managed to keep—of the three of them on the twins' graduation day. She shoved the phone toward him. "Look. Me, Evie, and Chloe the day they graduated from high school."

Grayson stared at it for a long moment, then his gaze flickered back to her. "You expect me to believe this?"

"Yes."

The anger punched through the worry as she glared at him. She dropped the phone to her side. The need to go pounded through her. She spun in the room, looking for her bag. It was discarded on the other side, empty. When she unpacked, she thought she would be staying a while. She stomped to it and snatched it off the floor, then went to the dresser and flung open the drawer. She shoved what few clothes she had inside.

"What are you doing?" he asked, standing in the middle of the room looking befuddled.

"Packing," she said on a huff. She bent and found her suitcase stuffed under the bed. With a yank, she pulled it out, flung it on the bed and then went to the closet.

"You're…you're leaving?"

She pulled the clothes off the hangers, wadded them into a ball, and tossed them into the suitcase. Then she went to the bathroom and grabbed her toothbrush and other toiletries, as much as she could carry in her hands, and dumped them in the suitcase.

"You're leaving me," he said as though he was dumbstruck.

She paused in her frantic packing to look up at him. His handsome face contorted in shock. He was used to being the one to break it off with women. Not the other way around.

"I'm leaving, period," she said. Then resumed packing.

She shoved everything she could into the suitcase and zipped it closed. One glance down at her attire and she realized she had to put on real clothes. He stood and watched as she pulled white linen pants on over her bikini bottoms, then reached for a gauzy white shirt and pulled it on. She'd deal with getting dressed in real clothes as soon as she was out of the house.

The only problem was the only way off the island was by his private yacht. She slipped on her sandals and turned to him. He still stood in the center of the room, dumbfounded.

"I'm going to need you to take me to Nassau," she said.

"Now?"

"Yes, now."

"But…why?"

"Because I have to get off this godforsaken island and find my sisters. I think they're in trouble," she said. Then she took a deep breath, expelled it. "I'm going to Scotland."

"Scotland?" he repeated. Then he started to laugh like it was the best joke.

Fury pounded through her. "Yes, Scotland. That's where they are. I need to find them."

What was the point of telling him? He wouldn't believe her. He didn't even believe they existed. And that was on her. She was the one who kept everything locked inside, the one who never let anyone close. Concrete barriers around her heart kept her safe, sure—but at what cost?

She clutched her suitcase so tightly her hand cramped. If he wasn't going to take her off this island, she'd have to find another way. Huffing, she started for the door, shoving past him.

He grabbed her arm as she breezed by, halting her. She looked up at him, met his gaze gleaming with anger and confusion.

"Just like that? You're leaving?" he asked.

He didn't seem to comprehend the suitcase in her hand or the determination pumping through her.

"Yes, I'm leaving. If you're not going to take me to Nassau, I'll find another way."

His mouth twitched into a faint grin. "You will, huh?"

She jerked her arm free. "I've enjoyed your company but now it's time for me to go."

"For these phantom sisters of yours. Sure. Okay. I'll play." He folded his arms across his bare chest, his smirk like a knife to her patience. "When are you coming back?"

Her anger flared, scorching and uncontrollable. She took a step closer, her voice sharp enough to cut. "Coming back? Oh, I didn't realize you were worried about losing your favorite toy. Is that all I am to you? A distraction to pass the time?"

He frowned. "It's not like that, Bri—"

"Then what is it like?"

He was silent as he pressed his lips together, his gaze searching hers. As though he were looking for answers or the truth. The air whooshed out of her as her shoulders drooped.

"You don't believe me."

"How can I believe you when you never even mentioned sisters? You've never told me much about yourself except that you're from Texas. I don't even know your birthday or your favorite color."

He was right. Six months together, and she'd kept her life locked away, hidden behind walls he'd never even tried to breach. She'd given him bits and pieces—a few underwater photos, stolen intimate moments, sips of his expensive wine. But most of her time was spent on the beach, not in his house. She'd used him as much as he'd used her.

And that was intentional. Feelings were a liability, a weakness she couldn't afford. She'd built walls around her heart, brick by unyielding brick, each one a hard-earned defense. Letting those walls crumble for him? Never. He wasn't the settling-down kind. He was a playboy through and through, and if she stayed, he'd shatter her heart into pieces.

"I'm sorry, Grayson. But I really have to go."

She spun on her heel and headed for the door, the suitcase bumping along behind her. Everything she owned was crammed into that single case. Her whole life, reduced to a suitcase and a carry-on. The thought tightened her chest.

He didn't try to stop her as she made her way through the house, down the stairs, and to the front door. How the hell was she going to get off this island?

She flung open the door and stomped into the late morning sun, the warm Caribbean breeze fluttering through her long hair, lifting it from her shoulders.

The luxury car he drove sat in the driveway, gleaming in the morning sun. If only she'd thought to grab his keys, she'd be on her way to the dock. Then she could take his yacht to the port and get to the airport and get out.

As she stood there contemplating her next steps, a jingle of keys behind her caught her attention. Grayson stood in the doorway still wearing his swim trunks. But he'd pulled on a well-worn t-shirt and stuck his feet in flip-flops. A grim expression was on his face as he pulled the front door closed.

"Get in."

He walked around to the driver's side and pulled open the door. She was so stunned, she didn't move a step.

"Are you going to get in or what?" he snapped before he ducked and got into the car.

It was enough to spur her into motion. She hurried to the car and placed her bags in the backseat, then slid into the passenger seat. She buckled her seatbelt as he started the car and put it into gear.

"Thank you, Grayson," she said, her voice quiet.

He was silent as he pulled out of the driveway and headed away from the mansion to the dock.

CHAPTER TWO

B RIANNA SETTLED INTO the airplane seat and peered out the window at the wing while waiting for takeoff. Her gut clenched tightly as her hands shook. Years had passed since she'd left Nassau. Now she was facing the unknown. When she got to Edinburgh what then? She didn't have a plan. She needed a plan. What the hell did she think she was doing?

Aside from her nerves pounding through her, making her ill, it was awkward saying goodbye to Grayson as he ferried her back to the main island in the Bahamas. She was met with stoney silence when she tried to thank him for everything. She started to walk away from the car to hail a cab to the airport.

"Brianna," he called.

She turned to see him leaning across the passenger seat, the window down. Her chest tightened at the sight. His face twisted with raw, unguarded pain.

"I hope you find your sisters."

It was the last thing he said to her as he rolled up the window and drove away.

The worst part was she wasn't sad about that at all.

In the airport restroom, she managed to dress into something other than her bikini and cover-up. She dressed in faded jeans, a well-worn t-shirt, and sneakers, pulling her sun-kissed auburn hair back and tying it with a colorful scarf at the nape of her neck.

She stared into the mirror, her reflection unfamiliar. Dark

shadows clung beneath her pale gray eyes, making them look hollow, haunted. Lines carved deep across her sun-kissed forehead, each one a reminder of too many years baking under the Caribbean sun, too many nights lost to rum and music. She looked brittle, worn thin, like the life she'd built had taken more from her than it had ever given back.

Now, settling into her first-class seat, she leaned back and slid on her Bulgari sunnies, shielding more than her tired eyes. Her body ached with exhaustion, and the thought of the long flight ahead—with layovers in Miami, then London—made her shoulders sag. Still, a flicker of relief stirred in her chest. She was finally on her way. She would finally get answers.

TWENTY HOURS LATER, Brianna landed in Edinburgh. She was not prepared for the weather. Though it was mid-September, the temperature was certainly not what she was used to—warm Caribbean breezes and sultry afternoons. Her lightweight clothes were not going to work and she looked as out of place as a clown at a TED Talk.

She hadn't thought much ahead when she boarded the plane. She had no place to stay. So when she was herded through the airport to the taxi line, she hadn't a clue what to tell the driver. A quick search on her phone yielded numerous hotels in the area. She picked one closest to the museum where Chloe worked.

At the hotel, she garnered a few strange looks at her summer attire, but she ignored them. After settling into her room, she decided her next order of business was to find proper clothing. She made a significant dent in her credit card on Princes Street as she purchased everything from jeans and sweaters to scarves, hats, and a coat.

By the time she was finished shopping, hunger pains cramped her stomach. Her last meal was in the Nassau airport before takeoff. She really had no sense of day or time. She only knew what day it was by looking at her phone.

Carrying her packages, she made her way through the Royal Mile looking for a place to eat when a strange little shop caught her eye. She stopped in the middle of the sidewalk to peer at it from across the street. Gold lettering over the door announced the name of the shop as Mystic Treasures. It was nestled between a cigar merchant and a shop specializing in cashmere and lambswool.

It looked out of place and yet not.

The shop called to her, a silent whisper threading through the air and wrapping around her soul. A hum vibrated beneath her skin, an electric current that seemed to pulse in time with her heartbeat. It wasn't mere curiosity—it was something deeper, a pull that felt woven into her very being. *Destiny*, a voice in the back of her mind whispered, though she tried to dismiss it. She didn't believe in fate or mysticism, but the sensation refused to fade. It coursed through her veins, insistent, impossible to ignore. The shop wasn't just a place; it felt alive, waiting for her.

Before she realized she'd made the conscious decision to move, she crossed the street, making a beeline for it. Juggling her packages, she shoved open the door and stopped short as the bell chimed her arrival.

The antique store overwhelmed her senses. Trinkets crowded every surface, furniture loomed in every corner, shelves sagged under the weight of old books. A wall of glass cases gleamed, filled with jewelry that caught faint glints of light. The air was thick with the dusty scent of forgotten attics and musty basements, mingling with the comforting aroma of aged paper and brittle parchment. She froze, her breath hitching. Memories surged—her grandmother's house, warm and cluttered, where books ruled every room. Dusty shelves had groaned under their weight, each spine faded and cracked with age. Her grandmother would never part with a single one. Those books were treasures, just like this place, every corner alive with echoes of the past.

"Hello!" a woman called from the back.

It startled her out of her reverie.

The woman weaved her way through the crowded store to greet her with a smile. Long, silver hair was in a thick braid hanging over her shoulder. Her sparkling bright blue eyes glinted with friendly warmth and yet there was something otherworldly, something ancient, lining her ageless features that indicated to Brianna she was someone worthing knowing.

"How can I help you today?" Her voice was warm, flowing, hinting at a faint Scottish brogue.

"Oh, I—" she started, then pressed her lips together.

It would sound odd even to her own ears if she told the woman she was drawn here by some strange force.

The woman gave her a quick once-over. "You look a bit out of sorts."

Brianna flushed hot to the roots of her hair wishing she'd taken time to change into her new Scotland friendly clothes. "I landed today."

She didn't know why she said it. It was a lame excuse but it was the only thing that came to mind.

"Good thing, too. I've been expecting you." She smiled, showing off the one dimple in her cheek.

Sharp, unexpected surprise jolted through her as she stared at the woman grinning at her with eager anticipation. Words tangled in her throat, her muddled thoughts scrambling to make sense, to form a reply.

"I'm sorry?" she finally said.

"I'll let you have a look around while I tend to some business in the back."

The woman hurried away, leaving her alone surrounded by musty old furniture and the strangest feeling creeping through her. She didn't understand what was happening. Maybe too many hours in the sun had addled her brain.

Brianna shoved aside the strangeness of the interaction. Juggling her packages, she moved deeper into the shop, her gaze alighting on all the vintage and antique objects.

Then a strange power thrummed through her, vibrating her senses. She halted to look around, trying to pinpoint where it was coming from. Her gaze landed on a glass case on the other side of the shop, the one that appeared to hold jewelry and other trinkets.

She made her way over to it, that thrumming igniting her senses and making the hairs on the back of her neck stand on end. When she reached the glass case, she paused to look over all the objects resting on glass shelves.

A dagger with a gilded hilt. A sapphire and ruby brooch imbedded in Celtic knotwork glittering under the garish light. A silver kilt pin in the shape of a clan crest. Several old coins that appeared to bear the visage of a woman. Perhaps Mary, Queen of Scots? A small ornamental knife with a carved handle of a stag horn.

A jagged piece of stone with strange markings on it.

As soon as her gaze landed on the stone, the thrumming deep inside her intensified. She stared at it, wondering if that was the thing she was drawn to.

"Och, I see you found it."

Brianna jumped. The woman appeared at her side as though she'd materialized out of thin air. She noticed the nametag on her crisp white shirt read *Moira*. She had a pleasant look on her face as she if she were delighted Brianna stood there in front of that case.

"Found what?"

"The stone. Would you like to see it?" Moira asked.

Her mind screamed *no* but her mouth said, "Yes."

Pleased, Moira opened the glass case and retrieved the piece of stone. Brianna dropped several of her packages at her feet and held out her hand. Moira placed the stone into her palm. The moment she did, there was a warming sensation that flickered through her from the center of her palm all the way up her arm to her shoulder.

A flash of something strange and vivid ripped through her

mind—a woman standing tall on a craggy hill, her fist raised to the stormy sky. Light spilled through her clenched fingers, fierce and otherworldly. Beside her stood two more women, their stances unyielding. Before them stretched an army so vast it sent an icy bolt of fear straight through Brianna's chest.

Her breath hitched, sharp and shallow, as the vision dissolved. Her gaze snapped back to Moira. The warm, pleasant expression was gone, replaced by something heavier, more serious. The weight of it pressed against her, making her pulse stutter.

The air around them shifted and suddenly the woman standing next to her was different. More ethereal. More otherworldly. There was an ancient glint to the depths of her eyes.

"Wh-what was that?"

"*That* is your future. And your past," Moira said, her tone even and clear.

Brianna's brows drew together. "I don't understand."

"Find your sisters, Brianna."

Her breath caught, the words slamming into her like a physical blow. "What?" she gasped, her heart hammering in her chest. "How do you know my name? How do you know about my sisters?" Her voice cracked, rising with each question, raw with desperation and fury. "Did you have something to do with their disappearance? Who the hell are you?"

"Without you, all will be lost," she said.

"All what will be lost?" Brianna shook with the force of emotions she couldn't contain—fear, anger, and a growing, terrible dread.

"The future and the past."

"I-I—"

"There isn't much time," Moira said, her voice stern and her expression grim. "Evie and Chloe need you. Now more than ever. Without you, chaos cannot be corrected. Without you, the future will never come to pass."

Moira reached for her hand, then, and closed her fingers

around the stone. "Take it."

"But—"

"Find them. Help them."

"I don't know how to find them," Brianna said. "I don't know where they are."

"You *will* know," Moira insisted. "Take the stone but never let it out of your sight. *You* are its guardian now. Go. Rest. All will be clear in the morning light."

And just like that, the air shifted around them once again. Moira's expression was back to a pleasant one, an expectant one as if she'd asked Brianna a question and she hadn't heard her.

"I'm sorry. What?" Brianna asked.

"I said would you like me to package it up for you?" She nodded to the stone still resting in her palm.

Brianna blinked the confusion from her eyes. A moment ago, the woman had closed her fingers around it. But maybe she'd imagined that? Was she also imagining that humming of the stone?

"Ah, yes, please."

Grinning her delight, Moira plucked the stone from her palm and walked to the middle of the store. Brianna scooped up her packages and followed. By the time she was at the counter, Moira had the jagged piece of stone in a blue velvet bag.

"Here you are," she said, handing it over to her.

Brianna juggled her packages again to reach for her wallet. "How much?"

"Free of charge."

She halted. "Free?"

"Aye, lass."

She noticed the picture of the castle on the wall behind her. The castle towers reached for a blue sky while behind it the sunlight glistened off the calm waters of a loch. As soon as she looked at it, a strange déjà vu rippled through her, as though she had stood in that same spot once before staring at that same castle. She couldn't quite grasp when.

"What is that place?"

"Dundale Castle in the Highlands," Moira replied. "Home of Clan MacLeod."

Brianna stared at it another long moment, trying to shake the feeling. She took the bag from the shopkeeper. "Thank you."

"Enjoy your visit to Scotland, Miss Sinclair."

As Brianna stepped out of the shop, a chill prickled down her spine. She froze mid-step, the realization hitting her like a cold slap. She hadn't given the woman her name. So how the hell did she know it?

CHAPTER THREE

AFTER HER ORDEAL at the antique shop, Brianna picked up takeout and returned to the hotel. As soon as she was done eating, she passed out as exhaustion overtook her.

The dream started instantly, bursting through her mind with a force for which she wasn't prepared. She rode toward the castle with a man dressed in a kilt with dark auburn hair and eyes the color of spilled ink. When he smiled at her, dimples dented both cheeks. Though she should be wary of him, she wasn't. There was something about him that put her at ease. He took her hand in his and kissed it.

"Yer safe here, lass. Dinnae fash yerself," he said.

She fell into his arms and they kissed, a daring but sweet kiss that sent her senses reeling.

Now, morning pressed against Brianna's closed eyes as the dream faded and she awoke, alone, in the hotel room bed. She stared at the drab ceiling, remembering the vivid dream like she was there. She touched her lips, certain she'd felt his kiss.

The castle, of course, was that of Dundale, the same castle she saw in the painting over the counter in the antique store. It must have been why it appeared in her dream.

But the man? She hadn't a clue who he was. She had never seen him before. Her rational mind tried to tell her she'd likely seen him somewhere—in the airport or on the Royal Mile—and he imprinted on her subconscious. However, there was an all-too-familiar feeling that swept through her when she remembered, with clarity, the way he looked, the way he smiled at her.

She pushed aside those thoughts as she sat up, slid out of bed to stand and stretch. She didn't know a soul in this city. She wasn't even sure where to start searching for Chloe and Evie. Maybe she'd start with the local police and then head to Chloe's place of business, the museum. She might be able to get answers there.

But first, she needed a shower and a jolt of caffeine.

She took a step toward the bathroom, but a low humming noise caught her attention. Turning, she expected to see her phone buzzing, but it was silent. Next to her phone was the blue velvet bag Moira had given her in the antique store. Curious, she picked it up and felt the vibration through the material of the bag.

How strange.

Opening the drawstring, she dropped the small stone into her palm and stared down at it. Smooth on one edge, the other two were jagged as though it were part of a bigger piece or pieces. The lines across the stone were faded but still visible: One that looked like an arc. Another that seemed to be part of a circle sweeping through that arc. It emitted that low hum and a vibration that warmed against the skin of her palm.

What was it about this stone that was so intriguing? Why did Moira want her to have it?

As she stood there, staring at it, memory slammed into her with such force she sank to the edge of the bed.

Find your sisters, Brianna. They need you. Now more than ever. Without you, all will be lost.

It was Moira's voice that flickered through her mind. Moira who had told her to find her sisters and that they needed her.

She recalled the woman saying that to her in the antique store, but afterward the memory faded away as though it was nothing more than an illusion or a dream.

But it had really happened.

Cold pricks of dread and worry settled over her. She dropped the stone back into the blue velvet bag and pulled the drawstring tight.

She had to find her sisters.

MUCH TO HER dismay, the hotel didn't have regular black coffee. All they had were coffee machines offering fancy lattes and cappuccinos. She'd never developed a taste for that. Dismayed, she settled for a glass of orange juice and a dry pastry.

Once she'd eaten, she headed out; it was a short walk from the hotel to the museum stretching before her. The wind bit through the layers she'd bundled herself in, and despite the proper clothing she'd bought, a shiver snaked down her spine. She tugged her coat tighter, her teeth clenching against the cold. The Caribbean heat had spoiled her. Even the faintest chill cut through her like ice now.

Before she left her hotel room, she'd stuffed the strange little stone still in the bag in the front pocket of her jeans. And despite it buried inside the layers of velvet and denim, she still felt the weak vibration as it continued to hum.

She kept her hands shoved deep into her pockets and her head down to shield her face from the stinging wind, so she never saw the man until he rammed into her shoulder. The moment she bounced off his hardened exterior, her head snapped up, ready to lash out at him.

He looked genuinely shocked he'd bumped into her. He reached out to her, placing hands on her upper arms to steady her as she stumbled backward. Brianna jerked her hands out of her pockets and pushed him off her as she took a step back.

"Watch it," she snapped.

"Och, lass, I dinnae mean to do that to ye. Are ye all right?"

His Scottish brogue was so alluring she almost forgave him. Almost.

He was tall with a head of thick, wavy black hair and steely blue eyes that met hers without flinching. His face was all hard angles.

"I'm fine," she said at last.

She didn't spare him another glance, her focus fixed on the path ahead. Hands buried in her pockets once again, she quickened her pace, the museum looming closer with every step. Once she got there, she'd find the director and get answers about Chloe.

The Tower entrance welcomed her with its heavy doors and the faint hum of activity inside. Her gaze swept the space until it landed on the information desk—a logical starting point. She approached with purpose, her nerves humming in concert with the stone in her pocket. Behind the desk, a young woman greeted visitors with a polished smile, her nameplate declaring her role as Visitor Experience Assistant. The name tag pinned neatly to her blouse read *Alex*.

"Hi, Alex. I was hoping to speak to your director about an urgent matter," Brianna said.

"I can see if she's available." The girl picked up the phone and dialed. After a moment, she spoke with someone—who seemed to be the director's assistant—and then hung up. "I'm sorry she's not available."

"My name is Brianna Sinclair. I'm Chloe Sinclair's sister. My sister is missing." When her statement was met with a blank stare, Brianna added, "My sister who works here. Tell her that."

With reluctance and annoyance flickering over her face, Alex picked up the phone again and dialed. She relayed the information to the other party and then cast a nervous glance at Brianna.

When she hung up, she said, "The director said she could spare a few minutes."

"Thank you."

Brianna moved off to the side to allow the other patrons of the museum to book their tours and buy their tickets. It wasn't long before a young woman arrived.

"Miss Sinclair, I'm Jane, the director's assistant. I'll take you to her office if you'll follow me."

Brianna fell in step behind Jane, who led her through the museum to an office with the door slightly ajar. Jane gave a quick rap and then pushed it open and stood aside.

The museum director's office was a blend of antique charm and professional austerity. Bookshelves stuffed with historical volumes and dusty artifacts lined one wall. An oversized wood desk was in the center. Behind it, a polished woman in her late fifties with sharp eyes and salt-and-pepper hair rose to her feet. The moment she saw Brianna she came around the desk and extended her hand.

"Miss Sinclair, I'm Director Greaves. Please have a seat. Would you like tea or water?"

"No, thanks." Brianna took the chair in front of the desk.

"That will be all, Jane." Director Greaves slipped behind the desk and eased down into her leather executive chair, lacing her fingers and placing her hands on the desk in front of her. "I'm sorry about your sister. It's been quite a shock to all of us."

"Thank you. I admit it's been a shock to me, too. I don't want to take much of your time, but I would like to know everything that happened the night of the gala," Brianna said, cutting right to the chase. "I understand there was an incident?"

The director's expression changed from concern to sorrow.

"A horrible night, that. Aye, there was an invasion. They came in and forced everyone on the ground. One of the men seemed particularly interested in one of the guests. Your other sister, I believe."

Her breath caught. So, Evie *was* here with Chloe that night.

"Evie," Brianna said, her voice weak.

The woman nodded. "Yes, I met her briefly. She was visiting for the gala. I seem to recall one of the men chased her up the stairs to the second level."

Alarm pounded through her. "Why?"

She shrugged. "I don't know. As far as I know, the police never found the men or the motive to the attack."

"No?" Brianna asked. Hope bloomed in her breast. Maybe Evie was hiding out somewhere in the city. "Did they find Evie?"

"Not that I know of. They've had no leads. The strangest thing of all was nothing was stolen. Then a few days later, Chloe went missing," Director Greaves said.

"Do you have any other information you can share with me?" Brianna asked, hope rising in her chest. "Anything at all about Chloe or Evie."

"I'm sorry, I don't. I do sympathize with your situation, Miss Sinclair, but as I told the authorities, Chloe's disappearance has nothing to do with the museum. It's a personal matter. I suggest you let the police handle it."

Not to mention Evie's disappearance. Why would the invader chase her up the stairs? Why her and no one else? Brianna didn't like how the woman had suddenly turned aloof.

"A personal matter? The museum was invaded, Evie is missing, and Chloe's flat was broken into. You don't think all that's connected?"

"I don't know how it could be."

She leaned back in her chair, the leather crunching with her weight. There was an obstinance about the woman and a sudden unwillingness to help, if she even could.

"I do wish there was something I could offer you about your missing sisters. If that's all, I have other pressing matters to attend."

Brianna didn't like the dismissive tone of the director. Even so, she got to her feet. She'd gotten nowhere with the standoffish woman.

"Thanks for your time."

Brianna left the woman's office and wandered out in the main gallery of the museum. She was impressed by the soaring white pillars and the glass roof that bathed the space in warm sunlight. She stood off to the side of the atrium and tried to imagine what the night of the gala was like. Why would men invade the museum and steal nothing? Why would one of the men chase Evie up the stairs?

In her pocket, the stone continued to hum and vibrate.

Ignoring it, Brianna decided to retrace Evie's steps the night of the gala. There was a staircase within sight that led to the next level. As she started across the atrium, she sensed someone heading toward her.

The man with steely blue eyes walked toward her with a purposeful stride. The moment their eyes locked, she recognized him as the man she had run into on the sidewalk. He granted her a knee-melting smile as he approached.

An eerie sensation went through her. Had he followed her?

"Hello, again," he said, his voice deep and thick.

Brianna stared at him, suspicion skipping through her. "Are you following me?"

He chuckled. "Not at all, but I'm glad to see you. Are you quite all right, miss?"

Her eyes narrowed. "I told you I was fine. I meant it."

Without waiting for a reply, she started for the staircase again. Much to her dismay, he fell in step beside her.

"Glad to hear it, lass."

Brianna halted, huffing out a breath, and turning toward him. "Look, I don't mean to be rude, but what do you want?"

He looked abashed. "I wanted to make sure ye were all right. That's all. And it appears I've been rude." He stuck out his hand then. "John MacDonald."

She hesitated a moment before shaking his hand. "Brianna."

"Pleasure to meet ye, Brianna. Where ye headed?"

"Why do you care?"

He laughed. "Dinnae fash yereself, lass. I mean no harm. It's clear ye're visiting my country and I thought I could show ye around a wee bit."

"The museum?" she asked, lifting a brow.

"If ye like. Do ye fancy a tea? The rooftop terrace has a lovely view."

It was against her better judgment, but she nodded. "Tea sounds nice."

They headed to the elevator where they took it to the top floor. All the while, the cursed stone in her pocket continued to hum and buzz. She tried to ignore it, but it was getting more difficult as the humming and buzzing grew louder.

The balcony café had several tables that allowed patrons to sit and view the atrium. Brianna wasn't sure why she allowed John MacDonald to buy her tea but she was weary from her travels and worried about her sisters.

"The terrace is one more level up. I'll meet ye there with the tea." He motioned to the elevator.

Nodding, she said, "All right."

Minutes later, she stepped onto the terrace off the elevator. John was right. The view was breathtaking. It had a lovely panoramic view of the city, including Edinburgh Castle in the distance.

But it was hard to enjoy the view with the continued buzzing in her pocket. She removed the blue velvet bag from her pocket and then dropped the stone in her palm. The faint lines across the stone were glowing, the buzzing continuing. When the stone hit her palm, a dizziness swept through her. She staggered a bit as her hand closed around it. Then she felt a strong hand on the middle of her back.

"Woah, there, lassie." John's voice was strong and sure behind her.

She glanced up to see him holding a paper cup in one hand. His other was still on the center of her back.

"Thanks," she muttered as she took the cup from him. It didn't escape her notice he had nothing for himself. "No tea for you?"

"Och, no. I was glad to buy ye one, though."

A tentative sniff determined the scent was a heady bergamot. She allowed the steam to warm her nose and cheeks. In her other hand, she clutched the buzzing stone that refused to be silent.

"You're right. The views *are* stunning," she said.

"Aye," he said slowly.

He turned to her, his arm wrapping around her as he eyed her in a way that sent a shiver up her spine. His demeanor suddenly shifted, his gaze predatory. His arm tightened around her.

Her breath caught as her pulse pounded a rapid beat. He'd trapped her in his embrace, this stranger who leered at her.

"Now, lass, ye'll be handing over that buzzing stone in yer hand."

Confusion flickered through her as her heart drummed a wild beat against her chest. How did he know about the stone?

"What?"

"The stone." He nodded to her clenched fist. "It calls to me. Give it to me."

She tried to pull from his embrace but he turned toward her, his other hand wrapping around the wrist of her fisted hand. She still held the scalding paper cup in her other hand.

"Let me go." Her tone was one of warning.

"Open your hand and give me the stone and I will." There was an evil, determined glint in his eye.

Moira's warning burst through her mind.

Never let it out of your sight. You are its guardian now.

Brianna did the only thing she could think to do. She flung the scalding tea in his face. He screamed, releasing her and putting his hands up as it splashed over him. He was an idiot to give her the cup so he deserved that. It also gave her enough time to stumble away from him.

Her heart was in her throat, the panic mounting as she made for the elevator. Her gaze flickered over the terrace looking for stairs—a quicker way out. But she saw none. The elevator would take too long. Once he regained his composure, his anger would drive him to her. His determination to get the humming stone out of her hand was written in those glittering blue eyes.

Footsteps pounded the ground behind her. A quick glance

back to see he was closing the gap between them. He would get to her in seconds.

She opened her hand a bit to see the lines on the stone pulsing a bright white. It was mesmerizing as she peered down at it. Seeing it sent a pang through her and something told her to swipe her finger over the lines. Intuition maybe? She wasn't sure.

Brianna halted and spun to face him. He came to a halt, his face red and blistered from the tea she'd flung in his face.

"Hand it over and I won't hurt you," he said through clenched teeth, holding out his hand.

She backed away, the pulsing light growing brighter and brighter.

"I don't know who you are or why you want this stone, but I'm not giving it to you."

"Fool," he spat.

Then he lunged toward her as she swiped her fingertip over the glowing lines.

In a breath, the world dissolved around her. Tiny bright white pinpricks exploded against her eyes and her head throbbed with a sudden pain. As John lunged toward her, his hands trying to grab her, the ground fell away from beneath her feet and then she was tumbling through space. Instinctively, her hand clenched around the stone, clutching it tight in her grip as a cold wind sucked the breath out of her lungs. For a moment, she felt as though she were drowning. She no longer saw the terrible face of John MacDonald and she fell into a free fall.

And then there was nothing but blackness.

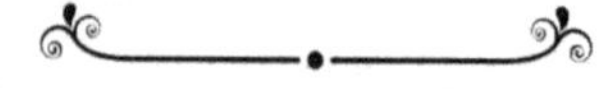

CHAPTER FOUR

JAMIE MACLEOD STOOD in what had become known as the tapestry room staring at the woven wall hangings with a sweeping feeling deep in his gut. The third Sinclair sister in the enchanted tapestry emerged days ago in a white gown with her hair billowing to the side. Since then, Jamie had visited daily as he healed from his injuries to watch and wait for a sign she traveled back in time to join them.

He'd stalked the tapestry room every day to see if the third Sinclair sister appeared. Brianna, they called her. This morning, his patience had finally paid off.

It was an admission he'd made to only himself that he was jealous of his two older brothers finding true love in the arms of the two Sinclair twins. The last few months were strange and wonderful with the addition of the women—they filled their home with love and laughter and warmth. It was clear Evie and Chloe adored his brothers, Callum and Malcolm.

He wanted that, too. He wanted someone to love and adore him. He'd tried to make things work with the MacDonald lass, but she was nothing more than a cold, detached woman who wasn't interested in him, despite their handfasting. Returning her to her father was the catalyst that had started the war between their two clans and the reason he'd left the country to travel with their uncle.

That lass was not for him, nor was she as bonnie as the one

staring back at him from the enchanted fabric with her wintery eyes and her auburn hair blowing in the breeze. The white gown she wore hugged her every curve and billowed to the side like her hair.

Lo and behold, here she was in another tapestry separate from the one of her standing on the craggy hill in the white dress with her hand lit up as though she were ready to do battle. This one was different. Her image morphed within the enchanted fibers depicting her arrival in their time. The space around her was split open as she fell through time and space.

In the tapestry, a strange light flickered over her face as she tumbled through the opening. Her hair was a mess around her. But it was her eyes that caught his attention. Pale gray and piercing. They were the most unusual eyes he'd ever seen.

"Oh, hi, Jamie," Evie said behind him, startling him out of his dreamy thoughts.

He turned to see her standing in the doorway, light framing the small round swell of her belly. As she entered the room, her gaze landed on the tapestry. Her eyes widened a bit as she stared at the new fully formed image.

"'Tis yer sister, aye?"

He kept his gaze on her to watch her expression change from surprise to wonder. She moved closer to the tapestry, reaching out to run a finger down the fringed edge.

"Brianna. I was coming to see if it had changed yet to show her arrival. I see it has. I wonder when it happened?"

"She appeared today," he said. "This morn, in fact."

"Today?" Her gaze snapped to him as she lifted a brow. "How long have you been watching?"

He flushed, not ready to admit his secret obsession. He had come here under the guise he needed to exercise his injured leg to regain his strength. He'd never made the conscious decision to end up at the tapestry room, but the first time he did, he was mesmerized by the magical weavings. And then it had become a habit turned obsession.

"Jamie MacLeod, do you have a crush on my older sister?" she teased with a grin.

"Och, no." He turned away from the tapestry and Evie so she wouldn't see he was lying.

"I haven't seen her in years," Evie mused. "Truthfully, I'll be shocked if she steps foot in Scotland."

"Why is that, lass?"

"Well, Brianna is a bit of a free spirit."

Unsure what she meant, he cocked his head to one side in question.

"That means she lives a much different life than me or Chloe." Evie turned back to the tapestry, again reaching for the material. "She loves the beach. The warmer weather. Brilliant afternoons under a blue Caribbean sky. I always imagined her sunning herself with a mai tai in her hand. I can't imagine how she'll do in Scotland." She chuckled at the thought.

"Well, mayhap she'll surprise ye and Chloe when she arrives. And it looks as though she will arrive."

Evie peered at the newest image. "It seems as though it will happen. The tapestry has never been wrong."

It was more of a hopeful thought than a certainty.

"Aye," he agreed. "Ye both are here. Ye both have two pieces of the keystone. 'Tis only a matter of time before the third piece and yer sister arrive."

She nodded. "If the prophecy is to be believed, yes."

Jamie had grown up with tales of the prophecy his entire life. It was said the mystical keystone was forged by the gods and believed to hold Time itself. It was entrusted to the Triple Goddess. His da, Hamish, insisted that one day, three pieces of a keystone would come to their clan for protection. Those three pieces of stone would be carried from the future to the past by three sisters from the clan Sinclair.

So far, two of those pieces had arrived in the hands of Evie and Chloe.

It was only a matter of time before Brianna arrived with the third.

"Well, I should find Chloe and tell her this new development. She'll want to see it, too."

Evie headed for the door. Jamie fell in step beside her.

"I told Callum I'd ride out to check the perimeter," he said.

"Are you sure you're ready for that?"

She glanced down at his injured leg, which he favored as he walked. He wasn't sure the limp would ever go away.

"I cannae be an invalid forever." He flashed a smile with more confidence than he felt. "There's no knowing when MacDonald will strike again using the power of his great axe."

Next to him, she visibly shuddered. They'd seen the power the man wielded with his shimmering great axe, how he could rip the fabric of time itself and create a portal. There was no movement from the MacDonalds for the last several weeks, leaving them all tense and on edge.

Climbing into the saddle would be difficult with the dull pain still throbbing in his calf: A gift from the MacDonald when he tried to escape their captivity. He was shot in the leg with an arrow. Dougal had managed to dig out the arrowhead and stitch him up, but he was left with lingering pain. His wrists had healed from the rope burns, but those scars would never quite go away.

One thing he never told either of his brothers was how the MacDonalds planned to keep him a prisoner for as long as possible. Not only a prisoner, but they intended to get their revenge on him for jilting Margaret MacDonald.

Malcolm had once jabbed him that he hadn't tupped her properly or at all. He hadn't realized how close to the truth he was, which only served to make Jamie irate. Every time he'd tried to touch her she'd pushed him away.

The truth was, their handfasting was never properly consummated. When Jamie decided to give up trying was when he returned her to her father, Rory MacDonald.

"I've wondered how he managed to get such power," Evie said as they walked into the great hall.

"Does Chloe not know?" he asked.

Chloe's piece of the keystone was the power of the past. She had visions of the first battle between their ancestors when MacLeod fought MacDonald. That was when the prophecy was born—the Night of Shadows.

She shook her head. "I don't think so. Or if she does, she hasn't spoken of it. Those visions of the past were fairly distressing to her." When they halted in the great hall, she turned to him, stood on tiptoe and kissed his cheek. "You be careful out there."

Then she hurried off to the kitchen to see Roslyn.

Jamie left the great hall and headed to the stables where he saddled his horse and headed out the gate. His leg ached, but he managed to push through the pain and ignore it as he rode. The cold wind bit through him. He pulled up his tartan to wrap around his shoulders.

Checking the perimeter was his way of escaping the castle for a few hours to ride through the Highlands. It was a balm to his tired, injured soul and gave him time to reflect. He hadn't been a good person—he knew—and he regretted his actions of rejecting Margaret MacDonald. He'd never intended to start a clan war.

He told himself the clan war would have started anyway once the lassies arrived with the pieces of the keystone, the pieces the MacDonalds were so determined to get that they kidnapped both Chloe and Evie.

As he trotted away from Dundale, the flash of light in the west caught his eye. He pulled his horse to a halt and watched the air in front of him split in half, creating an opening. Through it, he saw a strange world. He thought he saw Edinburgh Castle in the distance, which didn't make sense.

Then someone tumbled through it—a woman. The moment she landed on the ground, the opening sealed shut and the light was gone.

Both Callum and Malcolm had told him when Evie and Chloe arrived, there was a brilliant flash in the sky.

With his heart pounding, he kicked his horse into a gallop. As he approached, he saw it was indeed a woman with a fall of auburn hair. Her clothing was similar to Chloe's and Evie's when they'd arrived. She was unconscious.

He dismounted and hurried over to her, kneeling by her side. Her beautiful face, with high cheekbones, full lips, and pointed chin, was in repose. Freckles dotted the bridge of her nose and the high part of her cheeks. Her lashes were long, dark and curled upward. Golden strands were intermingled with her dark auburn hair.

Just like her counterpart in the tapestry.

Her hand was limp by her side. In it, a small object. With a gentle touch, he pushed open her fingers and saw the keystone against her burned palm. The lines had left an imprint just like Evie's and Chloe's.

Brianna and the third piece of the keystone had arrived.

CHAPTER FIVE

BRIANNA AWOKE WITH a raging headache and a bone-chilling cold. The last thing she remembered was falling and the frigid wind sucking the breath out of her lungs. She did a mental inspection. It didn't feel like she had any broken bones. Mostly she was cold and sore.

Her eyes blinked open to a wintery sky overhead. Groaning, she rolled to her side and sat up. The moment she did, pain exploded through her. She winced, placing a hand to her head, and groaned.

"Good morrow, lass. 'Tis good to see ye awake."

Her eyes flew open at the sound of the man's voice. He stood across from her, leaning against his horse with his arms folded over his chest and a tartan pulled up to cover his head and shoulders. He wore brown breeches and scuffed black boots. He was young and handsome and smiled at her as though he knew her and stood there waiting for her to wake up. His chiseled face was rugged with hard angles. His eyes, a deep doe-brown, twinkled.

Her breath pooled in her chest as a sense of familiarity drifted through her. It was a strong sense of déjà vu, as though she had seen him before—not in passing, but in some distant, half-forgotten dream lingering out of reach, teasing the edges of her memory.

A quick glance at her surroundings and she realized she was

no longer on the museum terrace. She was no longer in the city. She was surrounded by mountains and ridges with a beautiful untouched landscape.

"Oh, God."

Her voice was raw and raspy. Her hand flew to her throat as she looked up at the man standing across from her, still smiling.

"Where am I?"

"Och, lass, I think the question ye should be asking is *when* are ye." There was a sparkle of mirth deep in his eyes.

Panic shifted through her as her heart picked up speed. She didn't like where this was going. Her mind was a frenzy of questions as her brows drew together. What did he mean by *when* instead of *where*?

"James Alexander MacLeod," he said. "But ye can call me Jamie. And ye are?"

MacLeod. The familiar name flickered through her mind. Where had she heard it before?

"Brianna," she managed.

"Sinclair, I'd wager."

"How did you know that?" Her heart skipped a beat as panic swelled.

"I ken a lot more about ye than ye think." He winked in a charming sort of way that made her want to swoon.

Confusion shoved aside the panic.

He pushed off the side of the horse and stepped over to her, holding a hand down to her. She hesitated, staring at his hand with suspicion. She had trusted John MacDonald and he'd tried to attack her and take the—

Frantic, she glanced around searching for the piece of stone Moira had told her not to let out of her sight. When she did, she noticed her hand was burned with the imprint of the stone's lines.

"Looking for this?" Jamie held the silent stone out to her. It rested against his palm, the lines no longer glowing. The stone no longer humming.

She snatched it from him, closing it in her fist and holding it against her chest protectively. She glared at him.

"Ye dropped it," he said. "Ye'll be wanting to keep that safe, aye?"

"Who are you?" she demanded, her voice stronger, though it still felt raw. She placed the small piece of stone in the front pocket of her jeans.

"I told ye my name." Again, he held his hand down to her. "Come with me, lass. I can take ye to someone who can answer all yer questions."

Still, she was wary of her rescuer. "Why should I trust you?"

"'Tis a good question. But I can tell ye, on my honor, I willna hurt ye. I only want to help. I dinnae think ye wish to remain here, alone, in the wild, do ye?"

That was enough to spur her into action. She reached for his hand, allowing him to help her to her feet. His palm was calloused, as though he were a working man. Yet his hand was warm as his fingers closed around hers. When she stood, she fell forward, her legs weak as a dizziness swept through her. He caught her, held her close in his strong arms. He smelled of leather and heather, which was quite the opposite of what she was used to in the men who had held her as close. They usually smelled of ocean breezes.

Their eyes met, his soft and wonderous as he held her. His body was rock hard, yet soft enough to make her want to sink against him. It was a dangerous thing to want.

"Careful, lass. Ye've had a bit of a shock, aye?"

The deep timbre of his voice rumbled through his chest against her. For a moment, she wanted to close her eyes and allow the feelings of need and want to overtake her. But she quickly shoved all that away. What was wrong with her?

A smile tipped the corner of his mouth. He wrapped an arm around her shoulders and led her to the horse. She noticed he walked with a slight limp, favoring one of his legs.

"Can ye ride?"

"Yes," she said.

It had been ages since she sat a horse—the last time she rode was with one of her rich boyfriends who stabled horses and liked to ride on the beach. She used to be quite the horsewoman, but she was a bit out of practice. At least then she was able to ride with confidence.

Jamie stepped into the stirrup and settled in the saddle first. Then he held his hand down to her. She took it, hoisting herself up and onto the horse behind him. She wrapped her arms around his waist as he took up the reins.

It was hard not notice the solid feel of him against her. More solid than any of the soft, rich bachelors she tended to pick.

He kicked the horse into a gallop. As they rode away, the wind whipped through her. She ducked her head, pressing the side of her face against the soft material of his tartan. She was grateful she still wore the coat she'd acquired in Edinburgh, but she shivered nonetheless. It was a far cry from the beach paradise she had come to love.

Certainly she was still in Scotland? At least, it seemed that way. Jamie had a lovely Scottish brogue, much thicker than John MacDonald, who had tried to take the stone from her. Jamie *had* taken the stone from her while she was unconscious but willingly handed it over when she demanded it.

Who was he? Why was he so willing to help her? Why would he *want* to help her?

It did occur to her that his manner of dress was far different from any modern man. She hadn't come across any man in Edinburgh wearing a kilt or a tartan.

He'd said she should ask *when* she was, not where, which didn't make any sense to her at all. What did that mean?

She lifted her head long enough to see a castle rising up in the distance perched on a craggy cliff. Its towers rose up behind the curtainwall, reaching for the sky. Behind it, a glistening loch reflected the sunbeams that managed to break through the clouds.

"Where are we going?" she asked.

He turned his head to reply. "Dundale."

Another bell of recognition clanged in her mind. "Dundale Castle?"

"Aye, that's it."

She chewed on her lower lip, trying to recall where she'd heard about Dundale.

And then it struck her.

Dundale Castle in the Highlands. Home of Clan MacLeod.

She'd seen this castle in a painting behind the counter—in the antique shop. It was Moira who told her it was home of Clan MacLeod. And here she was, riding a horse, clinging to a man named Jamie MacLeod heading right for that castle.

It confirmed one thing for her—she was still in Scotland. But she had somehow traveled to the Highlands.

When she was, he had said.

Those words trickled through her mind again. Hot pinpricks erupted through her as understanding dawned.

Jamie was right. It wasn't about *where* she was. But *when*. And she had a distinct feeling she had somehow traveled back in time. But how? Why?

The closer they got to the castle, the more apprehension shifted through her. He rode through the portcullis and trotted toward a building that looked like a stable. A young man ran out to meet him, reaching for the reins as he came to a halt.

"Fergus," he greeted. "Is my brother about?"

"He's with Dougal, my lord."

Nodding, Jamie dismounted. She didn't wait for him to help her. She swung her leg over and jumped down from the saddle. He looked impressed.

Fergus took the horse and led it away into the stable.

"Come, lass. Ye'll want to meet the laird and his wife."

"The laird?" she repeated.

"Aye."

He motioned her to follow. Clutching her elbows, she fell in step behind him. They entered through a heavy oak door with iron hinges that groaned, announcing their arrival. She stepped into a grand, imposing room with a soaring, intricately carved beamed ceiling. The massive stone walls were draped with tapestries and heraldry showcasing Clan MacLeod. Tall, narrow-arched windows fitted with stained glass windows filtered the faint sunlight, giving it a warm glow. All around the room, candelabras blazed. A massive, ornate fireplace was on one end hosting a roaring fire to warm the room. In the center was a long, wooden table big enough to host twenty with chairs on either side.

Sitting at the table were two men. Both looked up when they entered. One rose to his full height. He had sharp, bright-blue eyes and long dark hair with two plaits on either side. He peered at her with interest and curiosity and then his eyes widened as though he recognized her. The other man gave her a curious glance.

"Dougal," the taller one said. "Would ye fetch my lady wife?"

"Aye, of course."

Dougal hurried off to do his bidding while she and Jamie paused in front of the imposing Highlander who looked her over.

"I was checking the perimeter like ye asked," Jamie said.

"Aye," the man said. A dark brow lifted toward his hairline as he waited for Jamie to explain her presence.

"I found her," he said, then turned to her. "This is my broth-er, Callum and laird of Dundale."

"And ye are, lass?" Callum asked.

She opened her mouth to answer when a feminine gasp erupted to her left. Her head snapped in that direction. The young woman stood inside the doorway, her hands pressed to her lips and her eyes wide—familiar soft brown eyes—as she stared at her. For a moment Brianna thought she was seeing things.

The young woman staring back at her was Evie.

CHAPTER SIX

B RIANNA GAPED ACROSS the great hall at her younger sister. The last time she had seen her was when she and Chloe graduated high school and that was years ago. But this was not the youthful girl she remembered. Her braided fiery red hair hung over one shoulder, the end tied with a scrap of tartan. This was a full-grown woman who had come into her own, who looked regal and older than her years.

As Evie rushed to her, she noticed her round belly and realized with some shock that she must be Callum's "lady wife" and she was pregnant.

Evie embraced her in a fierce hug. "I knew you'd come."

"Knew?" Brianna echoed.

Evie pulled back, holding her at arm's length and grinning at her with a bright smile. Tears of joy glittered in her eyes. "There is so much to tell you. You won't believe it."

Brianna glanced at Jamie, who still stood to her side grinning as though proud of himself for bringing her here.

"*This* is the someone who can answer my questions?" she asked.

"Aye, lass." He looked well-pleased with himself. A smug grin creased his face.

Evie took her by the hand. "Come on. We have to find Chloe. She'll be surprised to see you, too."

A wave of apprehension shifted through her as Evie dragged

her away through the great hall. The last words she'd had with Chloe were less than favorable. She wasn't sure how the other twin would handle her arrival. As Brianna was led away, she stole a glance over her shoulder at Jamie, who never took his gaze off her.

Once they were out of earshot of the others, Brianna pulled her sister to a halt.

"Wait. What is going on here, Evie?"

Evie spun to face her. "What did Jamie tell you?"

"Nothing."

"Nothing?" she repeated, surprised.

"That's right. Nothing. What the hell is going on? Where are we?"

"Well, that's a bit difficult to explain." She reached for her hand, the one that had the strange imprint of the lines from the stone. Holding it in one hand, she traced the lines with her fingertip. "The keystone brought you here."

"The keystone?" Brianna repeated. She fished in the pocket of her jeans and pulled out the small stone. "You mean this?"

When Evie's gaze landed on it, her eyes widened. Releasing her hand, she reached into the pocket of her gown and brought out a similar piece of stone. She pressed it against Brianna's. One side fit perfectly. The lines of Evie's stone matched up with Brianna's but there was clearly a missing third piece.

"Yes, I mean that."

Frustration edged through her. She huffed out a breath as she pocketed the stone once again. Evie did the same. "Are you going to tell me what's going on or what?"

"I am. Let's go see Chloe."

A piece of her wanted to refuse. There was friction between her and Chloe, long-standing friction she wasn't ready to face yet. Evie, though, was easy, more laid back. Though they'd had their differences, she always made a point to get along with her no matter what, even when their parents died and there was so much stress and strife between all of them. When Evie was headed to Edinburgh to join Chloe for her museum gala, she'd called her and begged her to come.

What did she do? She'd refused.

Finally, Brianna said, "I'm not sure Chloe wants to see me."

"She does," Evie said. "She'll be glad you're here."

"Are you sure about that? We've never gotten along."

"I'm sure. And we have a lot to share with you. Come on." Evie took her by the hand again. "For me?"

She could never deny those big brown eyes of hers. Reluctantly, Brianna nodded agreement. They started off again, heading for a curved stone staircase that led up to the next level. It was so narrow they had to go single file.

At the top of the stairs, Evie turned left and headed down a long, drafty hallway lined with the same arched, stained-glass windows as the great hall. Was she in a real medieval castle? She had never actually stepped foot in one, but she'd read enough history to know what one looked like.

At a door, Evie paused and lifted her hand to knock. Before she did, she turned back to Brianna. "Maybe let me do the talking first."

She wanted to ask why but kept it to herself as Evie knocked on the door. Moments later it opened. A man stood on the other side. He was tall, like the other two, with dark hair and sea-green eyes. His gaze landed first on Evie, then Brianna where he stared at her, openly, for a long silent moment. So long that it made Brianna shift from one foot to the other.

"Hi, Malcolm," Evie said with a bright voice.

"Ye'll be wanting Chloe, then," he said, his voice gruff. "She's in the garden with Roslyn."

"Oh," Evie said on a breath. "We'll go find her there, then."

She turned away from the door, but Malcolm remained there, his gaze still fixed on Brianna.

"Is this…?" His words trailed away.

"Brianna," Evie said, sounding so happy and proud. "Our older sister." She practically beamed.

Malcolm looked her over with interest as he took a step out of the bedchamber. "She has the look of Lady Sinclair."

"Who's Lady Sinclair?" Brianna asked.

Evie took her hand again. "I'll explain that later. Thanks, Malcolm."

She tugged her away from the door and headed once again for the staircase. Brianna had many questions. One of them was to ask who Malcolm was, but Evie was in a hurry.

Back down they went to the great hall where they crossed it. When they entered, there was Jamie again. The moment they stepped foot into the great hall, their eyes locked. A curious swooping went through her gut, which had never happened before.

It went beyond mutual attraction. It was as though there was a sensuous light that passed between them. As though they were meant to find each other. But Brianna shoved that thought away because she didn't believe in that sort of thing. She'd had many suitors over her single years, but never one that made her feel as though she were the most beautiful woman in the world and the center of his universe.

She pulled her gaze away and followed Evie as they crossed the great hall, through another corridor, and ended up in the kitchen. It was abuzz with activity. Pots boiled on one end over an open fire. A maid chopped vegetables. Another cubed meat. They all looked up as she and Evie passed through, giving her a curious sidelong glance. Evie paid them no mind as she made her way to the open door on the other end.

Cool air spilled into the kitchen which made Brianna glad, once again, for the coat she wore. Evie seemed unconcerned by it as she stepped into the late morning into the back garden. Here, plants grew wild and fragrant. On the other end of the garden, a woman kneeled on the ground while Chloe stood next to her with a basket in her hand laughing at something the woman said.

As they neared, Brianna's heart clawed its way to her throat. Why was she so nervous? It was ridiculous.

They were almost to the two of them when Chloe glanced their way. Her smile faded from her face and was replaced with shock as she saw Evie leading Brianna toward her. The basket slipped from her hand and landed on the ground with a muffled thud. The woman kneeling on the ground glanced up and followed her gaze to Evie and Brianna. She rose to her feet, wiping dirt from her hands on her apron and granted her a welcoming smile, as though she already knew who she was.

She and Evie halted in front of Chloe and the other woman, who must be Roslyn.

"I dinnae believe my eyes," the woman said.

She stepped forward and embraced her with a tight hug, surprising Brianna. She had no choice but to hug her back. It was the warmest hug she'd had in quite some time and, strangely, reminded her of her mother. When the woman stepped back, holding her at arm's length, she smiled with tears pooling in her eyes.

"Ye've arrived at last."

Brianna cut a questioning glance at her younger sister, whose face gave away nothing.

"What does that mean?" she asked.

"Roslyn, will you excuse us please?" Evie asked.

"Forgive me, my lady. 'Tis a fine thing to see the lass here, though. I'll leave ye to explain." She picked up the basket Chloe had discarded and headed back to the castle kitchen. When she entered, she closed the door behind her.

"My lady?"

Brianna lifted a brow as she assessed the young woman standing before her wearing her medieval garb. Who was addressed as *my lady* and the wife to the laird of Dundale Castle.

Chloe also looked older and wiser. Deep emerald eyes assessed her with aloof skepticism. The anger and fury emanated off her in thick waves. While Evie seemed happy to see her, Chloe's pinched expression said otherwise. Her auburn hair was not braided like her twin's. Instead, it was wild and free around her face, her face that had aged with lines of fatigue smudging under her eyes. She was dressed like her sister, too, in a heavy woolen dress.

They stood in silence. Brianna shifted from one foot to the other as her nerves jittered through her.

"She's here," Evie announced, a smile in her voice, as though this was a news flash.

"I see that," Chloe replied tersely. "I can say with absolute surety I'm surprised."

"Chloe—"

"Why do you say that?" Brianna interrupted.

"Because you've disappointed us before. Why not this time, too?" Chloe brushed by them heading down the footpath to the castle.

That explained the anger she harbored. Chloe was always the one to hold grudges while Evie was the peacekeeper.

"Chloe, don't be like that," Evie said, her tone pleading.

"Honestly, I don't know why she came," Chloe snapped and turned to face them again, folding her arms over her chest. "I mean, she's never once supported us in anything. Why start now?"

"That's not true and you know it, Chloe," Brianna said, her ire rising.

"Sure, it is. You were only interested in doing the bare minimum after Mom and Dad died. The fact you ended up in Edinburgh is a shock to me," Chloe said. There was so much venom in her words, Brianna winced. "How *did* you end up in Edinburgh, anyway?"

Even Evie flinched. "Chlo, don't. Now isn't the time."

"When *is* the time, then, Eve?"

Brianna clenched her hand into a tight fist, frustration edging through her as she glared right back at Chloe. "I got a call from the Edinburgh police telling me *you* were missing."

Her eyes widened with astonishment before she quickly recovered. Her surprise was quickly replaced with wariness. "Did you? And you charged to Edinburgh to see if your little sister was all right. Is that it? Whatever motivated you do to that?"

"Chlo—"

Fury flashed through her. "I tried calling you both but only reached voicemail. I knew Evie was in Edinburgh. She told me she was going to your gala. When I was unable to get in touch with either of you, I knew something was wrong."

Chloe remained stiff and silent as she clenched her jaw. Guilt flashed over Evie's face as she glanced between the two of them.

"You told her?" Chloe said, turning her heated, accusatory gaze on Evie.

"I invited her to come. You worked so hard, Chloe, I thought—"

"And yet you *didn't* come." Her ire swung back to Brianna.

"I did. I came when I thought you might be in trouble."

"Clearly, it was too late." Color rose high in her cheeks.

Brianna huffed, losing patience. She didn't want to fight with Chloe and changed the subject. "Maybe you two tell me what the hell is going on here."

"She doesn't know, does she?" Chloe asked Evie. And then she emitted a nervous laugh. "She doesn't know where she is or why."

It was like old times—the two of them sharing some secret between them, some inside joke they never let her in on. Once again, she was the outsider. A pariah in her own family. She shoved those feelings aside for now to get to the truth.

"All I know is somehow this little piece of stone brought me here. But where is *here*?" Brianna asked.

Evie and Chloe exchanged a knowing glance, one that still did not give her the answer she wanted.

"Tell me!" she demanded.

Chloe pressed her lips together into a thin line and looked to Evie to make the explanation.

"You're in the Highlands of the past," Evie said. "Specifically, 1357."

Brianna gaped at her as though she'd grown a second head. Hot pinpricks of disbelief went over her. Jamie's words came back to her. He'd alluded to the fact she was in a different time period, something he seemed to know but didn't share. He wanted to bring her to her sisters and let them tell her. Even so, it was difficult for her to believe she was transported through time.

"You're joking."

"I'm not," Evie said, deadpan.

"Yes, you are. This is some elaborate hoax you two have managed to pull on me to get my attention. Or something. Well, I can assure you, you both *have* my attention. I refuse to believe this jagged piece of rock brought me into the past."

"Brought all three of us," Chloe corrected.

She pulled something out of the pocket of her dress and held it out to show Brianna. It was a piece of stone similar to the one Evie had. It looked like the missing third piece.

Brianna stared at the little piece in Chloe's scarred palm, a scar that looked hauntingly familiar to the burn on her own hand. When she glanced at Evie, she held up her hand and showed her she had the same brand. Brianna glanced down at her own, saw the red, angry imprint on her palm and understood then that it was never going away.

"Your hands…"

"Like yours," Evie said. "You clutched the stone in your hand when you fell through time."

Brianna stared down at her hand, remembering. She stood on the terrace. She held the humming stone with the pulsing lines in her hand. John MacDonald had attacked her and tried to take it from her. She'd panicked and ran.

"There was a…flash of light," Brianna said.

"Yes," Evie agreed, giving her an encouraging nod.

"And a cold wind that seemed to suck the air from my lungs," she added.

"That, too," Evie encouraged.

"Then I was falling and then…" She shook her head. "I don't

remember much after that."

"You blacked out," Chloe said. "I'll bet Jamie was there when you woke up."

Brianna flushed as she recalled the way he'd stood against his horse, his arms folded, looking devilishly handsome. "Yes."

"It's how I met Malcolm," Chloe said.

"Who's that?"

"Brother to the laird of the castle and my husband," she said.

"You're married?" This was all too much to believe. She leveled her gaze at Evie. "And you're married, too, I assume? Especially since you appear to be pregnant."

Evie flushed, her cheeks turning pink. "Yes, Callum is my husband and the eldest and laird of this castle. And yes, I'm pregnant."

This was strange and hard to believe. Here were her sisters, married to men of the past. She pressed a hand to her head where the headache pounded.

"And…Jamie?" she asked, her voice shaking a little.

"The youngest brother of the three," Evie said.

Brianna smirked. "Who is he married to?"

"No one, yet," Chloe snipped as she looked her over.

Evie met Chloe's gaze, ignoring her sharp tone. "Chlo, it's all coming true."

"What's all coming true?" Brianna demanded. There was still more information neither of them was telling her. She felt like she was in a nightmare with more questions than answers. It was hard to quell the panic that wanted to erupt.

Evie took a deep breath, expelled it. "It may be difficult for you to hear right now. I know all of this is a shock and hard to believe."

"You're damn right it is. Shock is a bit of an understatement." She clutched her hand around the stone once again, then shoved her fist into the front pocket of her jeans.

"The three of us coming back in time—you, me, Chloe—we were meant to be here."

"And that means what exactly?"

"For God's sake, Bri, stop being so dense," Chloe snapped, her patience gone. "What Evie is trying to tell you is that there's a prophecy that foretold of our arrival here. We were destined to be here. All three of us."

Brianna stared at the both of them as disbelief pounded through her. Then she did the only thing she knew to do. She ran for the kitchen door.

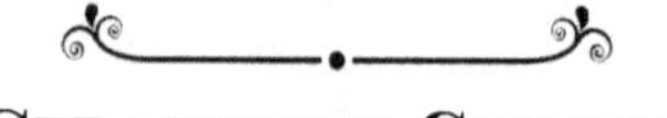

CHAPTER SEVEN

Brianna burst through the kitchen, startling the maids and the others who were working there. Tears clouded her eyes as she ignored their gaping stares and ran to the other side, through the door, and found her way into the great hall. Jamie and Callum were still there, sitting at the table and conversing when she made her sudden appearance.

Jamie shot to his feet, but she ignored him as she made for the door. Without stopping, with her heart ramming against her chest and her feet pounding the strange straw-mat flooring, she barreled through the great hall door and back into the late afternoon.

The cold wind bit through her, stinging her cheeks and eyes. She paused there, her gaze scanning the area, looking for a way out. There were no cars within sight. Fine. She'd ride out of here. She ignored her stinging eyes and made for the stables. She ran across the greenway until she came upon the building, falling through the doorway and gasping for breath. She startled a poor stable boy who was grooming one of the horses. His head shot up, his eyes wide.

She swiped the tears from her frigid cheeks as she stumbled inside the stable. The air was thick with the smell of hay, leather, and musk of horses, a familiar smell that soothed her agitated soul.

"You," she snapped. "Can you saddle me a horse?"

Mute, he nodded and dropped the brush he was using. He set about saddling a gray horse in the far stall while Brianna tried to collect herself. Her sisters were insane, and she was getting out of here. She was going to ride back to the nearest city and rent a car. Then she'd go back to Edinburgh and catch the first plane back to Nassau. As soon as she got back on that sunny beach with the crystal-blue water, she was never leaving. She would spend the rest of her life there, living alone. She didn't need anyone or anything. She didn't want anyone or anything. All she wanted was solace.

"Going somewhere, lass?"

Jamie's voice behind her made her spin to face him. He leaned against the doorframe, one ankle crossed over the other and his arms folded over his chest showing off his thick forearms. His dark auburn hair was not quite as long as Callum's but long enough to brush his shoulders. When the firelight from the interior torches hit it just right, glimmering golden strands intermingled with the dark red.

"Yes. I'm leaving and I'm not coming back."

"Are ye?" He tipped his head to the side in amusement. "Where are ye going then?"

"I'm going to find the nearest town and then call a cab or rent a car. And then I'm going back to Edinburgh," she said, strong and confident as she tried valiantly to ignore his rugged good looks. "When I get there, I'm booking the first flight back to the Caribbean."

"I dinnae ken this place, nor do I understand what these things are ye mentioned," he said. "The only way to Edinburgh is by horse. But are ye sure ye want to be riding there alone?"

Horse? Fine. She'd ride all the way there if she had to. She was good in the saddle.

"Yes," she said, her voice terse.

The stable boy walked the horse to her, saddled and ready to go. She gave him a nod of thanks, then reached for the saddle, ready to step into the stirrup.

"Are ye sure about that, lass? 'Tis a fifteen-day trek, at least."

"Fifteen!" She gaped at him.

There was a quirk of a smile on his lips. "Och, aye. It's no easy ride traversing the terrain on horseback. And then there's the weather. Rain, wind, snow."

"Snow?" Her confidence faltered. She wasn't prepared for snowy weather.

"Aye. Not many inns between here and there, either. Ye would have to camp in the wilderness. Do ye have provisions?"

Her shoulders sagged as she realized her idea to ride to Edinburgh—alone—was a terrible one. There was no way she would be able to navigate the rugged landscape alone, without food or water, facing the elements.

The reality of the situation settled deep within her. She glanced around the stables, saw nothing but horses and tack. A few stable hands were busy tending the stalls and the animals. There were no cars. No taxis. No airplanes. No way to get back home.

A sick feeling clenched the pit of her stomach as the reality became clear. Evie and Chloe were telling the truth. She *was* in the past.

Holy hell.

"No," she said at last.

"They told ye, did they?" he asked, moving closer.

"Told me about what?"

"That ye time traveled to the past," he said.

"You make that sound like it's a normal everyday occurrence," she huffed.

He chuckled, a sound resonating deep in his broad chest. "I witnessed the two lasses arrive here in the last few months, so, aye, it is."

Her gaze met his. When it did, her stomach flipped. It was hard not to notice how handsome he was. It was also hard not to notice that he seemed a bit younger than her.

"And you believe that? You believe that we—the three of

us—are from the future?"

"I have no reason no' to believe it, lass."

The wind whipped through the stables, making him shiver. He pulled up his tartan to cover his head and wrapped it around his shoulders. Brianna turned back to the horse, her hand still on the saddle. Indecision flashed through her. Riding to Edinburgh was likely out of the question. If she made it there, then what? There were clearly no airplanes that would take her back to the Bahamas. That was, if she were truly stuck in the Middle Ages, and she was starting to understand that this was her new reality. She was going to have to come to grips with that new reality at some point.

She took a deep, steadying breath. "If you knew I was from the future, why didn't you tell me?"

"Would ye have believed me?" he asked.

It was a valid question. She considered that for a long moment, thinking back to waking up on the cold ground with him standing there gazing at her as if her arrival was expected. No, she would not have believed him if he'd told her she was no longer in her future. He'd given her the stone as though he knew she was supposed to be the keeper of it.

Finally, she shook her head. "I suppose not."

"I thought it best the news come from someone ye trusted."

Her sisters, of course. And he was right. Though she trusted them because they were her blood, she still did not quite believe their story about a prophecy foretelling their arrival.

He pushed off the stable wall in a slow, languorous motion that reminded her of a graceful lion. There was something about him that was alluring in every way—aside from his good looks. He appeared to be a hardened warrior, someone who knew his way around a battle and how to use a sword. The muscles in his hands and forearms were evidence of that. She found she was drawn to him in a way she had never been drawn to anyone else.

He moved deeper into the stable, his gaze never leaving hers and it sent a shiver of delight right through to her very core. It was not wise to allow herself to get caught up in the charming young Highlander.

Jamie reached for the nose of the horse she still stood next to and patted it.

"Since ye already have the horse saddled, we may as well go for a ride." He made a motion for the stable boy. "Fergus, my horse."

"You mean, ride like in the grounds?"

"Och, no. I mean outside the gates."

She almost refused but then stopped herself. Here was a handsome young man asking her on a ride. It was impossible to say no.

"Is it safe?" she asked.

He chuckled, that smile lighting up his eyes. "Aye."

Fergus brought his horse and handed over the reins. Jamie took them and mounted in one fluid movement. Her heart beat wildly as she hoisted herself up into the saddle of the gray horse she'd tried to commandeer. Together, they trotted out of the stables and toward the portcullis. As they headed through the bailey, she caught a glimpse of Evie stepping out the door. Their eyes met for only a moment as Brianna looked away. She didn't want to deal with her sisters right now.

They exited the castle grounds with Jamie in the lead. Brianna followed closely behind and for the first time in her life, she felt a sort of freedom that made her heart light. She'd spent her adult years as a nomad, moving from place to place and seeking solace in the arms of rich men who weren't interested in long-term relationships. That worked for her at the time, especially after a marriage that had lasted only a year to a man who was emotionally unavailable.

That failed marriage had caused a rift between her and her parents. The twins were young at the time and had no idea of the heartache and hell she went through. She'd bottled that up and buried it deep inside to never think of again.

Jamie led them away from the castle to a cluster of trees

swaying in the late afternoon breeze and beyond that, the loch where the last remnants of sunlight flickered over the waters. He came to a halt there under the trees and dismounted. She did the same.

He turned to her, reaching a hand out, which sent her heart thudding harder against her chest. It was a simple gesture but one that made her melt. When she took his hand, he laced their fingers. Together, they walked from the trees to the loch.

"It's beautiful here," she said and meant it.

She had never seen the likes. Frothy waves spilled over the craggy shore with that soothing rhythm she'd come to adore about living beachside. But this was no beach she was used to.

"Aye," he said.

He lifted their clasped hands to examine the burned imprint of the stone on her palm. With a gentle touch, he traced the outline of the lines, sending delicious shivers rippling through her.

"Does it hurt?" he asked.

"No," she said.

Even so, he lifted her palm to his lips and pressed a kiss in the center. A breath shuddered out of her at the unexpected tenderness. Butterflies erupted in the pit of her stomach, a feeling she had not had in so many years, she almost didn't recognize it. Her pulse quickened, thrumming under the surface. But she knew it for what it was—raw, undeniable attraction.

"Jamie, I—"

"Mayhap I shouldna have kissed ye, lass, but I cannae resist."

She blinked, surprised by the admission. "You don't even know me."

A hint of a smile played upon his lips. "I've watched and waited for ye to arrive."

At that, her heart thudded hard against her chest. There was something endearing about the way he said it. Something that made her pulse race in concert with the fluttering that had taken up residence in her gut. Even so, there had to be a real explanation for that.

"Because of my sisters. They told you I would come?"

"Nay." He shook his head.

"No?" The butterflies continued to flutter. She resisted the urge to press her hand against her stomach to calm them.

"When ye first appeared in the tapestries, I couldna wait to see yer face." His gaze flickered to hers, locking with hers.

For a moment, she was stunned into silence. She had no idea what he meant by these tapestries, but she was more than intrigued. And what did he mean, she *appeared* in them? It didn't make sense to her. She drew her brows together.

"What tapestries?" she asked.

"Did yer sisters no tell ye about them?"

She flushed hot with her chagrin. "I'm afraid they didn't tell me much before I stormed out."

Regret pounded through her as she recalled her reaction to the news she was destined to travel back in time. And something else about a prophecy. She hadn't stuck around to find out what that meant. She didn't believe in destinies or prophecies. She believed in free will and choice.

"What did they tell ye?" he asked, curious.

"That there was some prophecy that brought us here." She snorted derision and shook her head.

"Ye dinnae believe it?"

"Should I?"

He laughed. "Oh, aye, I think ye should."

She tugged her hand from his and walked toward the edge of the loch. "I have never believed in such things. Destiny and prophecy are intangible. Just as I don't believe in soulmates. They make you believe something that isn't real. And drive you to make bad decisions."

"And yet ye hold the third piece of the keystone. The piece that represents the Future."

She snapped her head at him. "I don't understand."

He heaved a sigh and ran a hand over his chin. "I should leave it for yer sisters to explain."

He turned away and started for the horses. Brianna grabbed his arm and pulled him back to her.

"Tell me, Jamie. What does it mean my piece represents the Future. I'd really like to know."

A tawny brow lifted. "Are ye sure, lass?"

She nodded.

"Very well then. Evie's stone represents the Present. Chloe's the Past. Yours the Future. The keystone controls all of Time."

"*All* of Time?" she asked.

This sounded too far-fetched for her.

"Ye dinnae believe it?" he asked.

She considered it. Perhaps if she threw out all logic and accepted the fact that these small pieces of rock could actually send them through time, she'd believe it. If that were the case, then why did they all three end up in the same place, in the same year? Why not scatter them across various eras of time?

"Aye, I can see ye dinnae believe it."

"It's not that, it's…"

"Did yer sister no tell ye about the prophecy?"

"Well, she mentioned it but—"

"Then I will, though I dinnae think it to be my place," he interrupted.

Brianna blew out an annoyed breath. "Fine. Then tell me about this 'prophecy.'" She put the word *prophecy* in air quotes, then crossed her arms over her chest.

"*When the stars align and the shadows of chaos eclipse the sun once again, the time will come to unite a warrior's heart and a maiden's grace. Together, they'll reunite the pieces of the keystone and protect it, to safeguard it for time eternal. Three pieces of stone. Two ancient bloodlines. One divine destiny.*"

He had clearly memorized this as he said it with confidence.

"A warrior's heart and a maiden's grace," she repeated, amused. "You the warrior, me the maiden?"

He nodded.

She wanted to laugh. She hadn't been a maiden in several

years.

"Do ye no' see? Y're here to reunite the pieces of the stone. *You*, Brianna, have the third piece. Three pieces of stone—Past, Present, Future. Two ancient bloodlines—MacLeod and Sinclair." When he said his surname, he thumbed at his chest. When he said hers, he motioned to her. "One divine destiny—all of us together."

Gooseflesh erupted all over her skin. She dropped her arms and squared her shoulders as she locked gazes with him. He was deadly serious. There was no snarky grin on his face. He wasn't kidding around. He meant everything he said—he spoke of the prophecy as though it were something to be revered. He believed the words with his whole heart.

"Well, then," she muttered. "I guess that means I'm screwed."

CHAPTER EIGHT

BRIANNA CLUTCHED HER elbows as the wind whipped past them, making her shiver.

"We should go," he said, waving toward the horses.

"Jamie, there's one more thing I need to know." When he gave her a quizzical look, she continued. "Something you said. That you've been waiting for me. That I appeared in the tapestries. What did that mean?"

His cheeks flushed as he glanced away, fixing his gaze on the loch. "'Tis hard to explain. It would be best if I showed ye."

"Show me."

"To do that, we have to ride back to the castle."

"Then let's go."

It was a short ride back as the sun dipped toward the horizon, leaving the sky blistered with a fantastic sunset in gold and pink and orange. It was hard not to notice the breathtaking beauty. Once back at the castle, they wasted no time returning their horses to the stables and then headed back into the great hall. It was empty by the time they returned.

Brianna expected Chloe and Evie to be there waiting for her, but they weren't.

It was just as well. She was tired, but she wanted answers. Then she would decide what to do next—staying here was likely her only option. She had nowhere else to go.

Jamie led her through the great hall, down a corridor and to a room with the door standing open. Firelight from candelabras flickered along the floors and wall of the chamber that had one oversized four-poster bed, a fireplace that was cold and dark, and a chair beside the hearth. Along the wall were several tapestries with images on them the likes she had never seen. As she approached them, her heart pounding a wicked beat and her breathing shallow, she knew immediately they were something special, something enchanted even.

She paused at the first one, staring at the image of the three women standing on a craggy hill. The woman in the middle had silvery hair billowing out to the side with something clenched in her fist and light seeping from around her fingers. Upon closer inspection of the woman in the center, recognition slammed into her with such force she sucked in a sharp breath.

The woman in the center was the shopkeeper in Mystic Treasures who had given her the piece of keystone.

"Moira," she whispered.

The next tapestry was of the same three women with swirling, dark clouds behind them. The ground was lit by bolt of light. The wind still whipped around them. Below them, an army approached with weapons held high and in the center of it all was a man holding aloft a glowing great axe.

She swore she saw the images moving. She looked away, shook her head to clear it, but when she looked back, the images were still moving in what appeared to be super slow motion.

The third tapestry made her gasp and clutch her throat. There was a woman with fiery red hair laying on the ground in a black dress and one arm out to the side. She was unconscious. The sky above her looked as though it had a rip in it.

"Is that…Evie?" she asked, peering closer at the image.

"Aye. When she arrived here," Jamie said.

She stole a glance at him over her shoulder to see him leaning one shoulder against the doorframe watching her as she examined each tapestry. He pushed off the frame in a slow, languid movement and then stepped into the room, joining her. His gaze was focused on that first tapestry with the three women.

"This is the Night of Shadows." He pointed to the first one. "This is what we call The Shattering." He pointed to the second.

"Who are the women?"

"The Triple Goddess. They shattered the keystone into three pieces to protect it."

His response made more questions surface in her mind. She started with the simplest one. "From whom?" she asked.

"The Clan MacDonald." He pointed to the army advancing on the Triple Goddess.

Brianna noticed the wall hanging next to Evie then. There, she saw a familiar face—Chloe. And behind her, a man. Like the wall hanging showing Evie, this one had a rip in the space around Chloe and the man, as though they had tumbled through it. Through the rip, she thought she saw a city.

"Who's the man?" she asked.

"Bruce MacDonald. He followed her through time."

MacDonald.

The man she'd met on the street in Edinburgh said his name was John MacDonald. Was he related to this Bruce? He had said something about the stone calling to him and that's why he tried to get it from her. The only person who would know the answer to that was Chloe. She made a mental note to ask her about it later.

The final tapestry nearly made her heart stop. She moved closer to inspect it, to make sure she was seeing what she was seeing.

There she was, standing on a craggy hill with her hair billowing around her wearing a white gown. One hand was clenched and glowing. The other reached for something or someone. At the edge of the moving picture, she saw an image. Perhaps a hand reaching for her? It wasn't clear.

What was clear was that she was in that tapestry. Just like her sisters.

She pressed cold, shaking fingers to her lips. "It's me."

"Aye," he said, his voice low. "And this one, too."

He pointed to the tapestry next to that one. There, woven in the enchanted fibers, was another image of her falling through time. Just like the one with Evie and Chloe, there was a rip in time around her. And through that she saw what appeared to be the city. She'd used the keystone when she was on the terrace of the museum.

"I ken ye were going to arrive when yer image fully appeared."

This is what he meant. He was waiting for her to fully appear in the tapestry. He'd said he was waiting to see her arrival. Hot pinpricks danced along her spine as heat flashed over her. She unbuttoned the coat and ripped it off, dropping it on the floor and stepping closer to examine the shimmering thread of the woven fabric. The images truly were moving.

"You knew I was going to arrive," she repeated. "You knew because you saw it foretold in this tapestry."

"Aye," he agreed.

"That's why you were there when I woke up."

"I dinnae ken it would be today."

She turned to face him. "So, you just happened to be in the right place at the right time."

He stepped closer to her. There was no mistaking the burning desire deep in his eyes. His gaze was like a soft caress, leaving a tingling sensation in the pit of her stomach.

"'Twas good luck." He grinned, one corner of his mouth pulling up which was so familiar now she found it endearing.

"And did I meet your expectations?" The words spilled from her mouth before she was able to stop them. She knew what she was doing—but flirting with this young Scotsman seemed harmless.

"More than ye can ever know."

His voice was low and soft, rumbling around in that magnificent chest of his. He stood a breath from her. She hadn't realized he was so close until the moment he reached for her, cupping her face. Nor had she realized he was much taller than her. So tall, in fact, she had to tip her head back to look up into those devastating eyes that had such depth she thought she could fall in and never pull herself out.

When his lips met hers, she did not expect to feel anything other than a simple kiss, the brush of his lips on hers. What she felt, instead, was so much more. Her heart exploded with a fiery passion she thought long dead. Her arms slid around his waist as they fell into each other, his body rock hard and solid against hers. He was not like the men of her time—the men of her time who were soft and weak.

His mouth was tender and sweet and experienced, which surprised her. He certainly knew what he was doing when it came to kissing and she certainly liked kissing him. A mewl vibrated in her throat. Then he was trailing kisses across her jawline.

A part of her screamed at her to push him away, to stop this nonsense. But the other part—the part so starved for this type of affection—refused to do that. That part of her wanted more and more and more. That part of her wanted this to never end. That part of her wanted him to go on kissing her forever.

How long had it been since she felt like this? How long had it been since a man kissed her as though she was something precious? Something to be cherished. Instead of something to be used and discarded when he was done with her.

The answer was she could not recall a moment in her life when she felt so light, so free, so adored. And she was powerless to resist.

It was a heady and wonderful sensation. She never wanted it to end.

But then she came to her senses and pushed out his arms, stepping away from him. She needed air and space between them before she totally lost her head. It would be far too easy to fall into bed with Jamie MacLeod.

"Is there something wrong?" he asked. "Did ye no' like my kisses?"

A weak laugh shuddered out of her. That kiss was everything and it would be hard to forget. "Oh, I liked it quite a lot."

"Then why did ye move away?"

He took a step toward her. She took a step back, trying to maintain distance between them. She bent to pick up her coat from the floor.

"I think you know why. I'm tired and I'd really like to rest. I should find Evie."

It was too soon to be kissing this young Highlander. Too soon for warming thoughts pounding through her.

"Why?" he asked.

"Well, she seems to run the place," she said. "I figured she'd give me a place to sleep."

His gaze never left her face, his compelling eyes riveting her to the spot. Then, that casual smile appeared.

"Ye can stay with me," he said.

She lifted a brow. He was a bold one. She was not so naïve that she couldn't read between the lines. She understood an invitation to bed when she heard one.

"With you?" Desire pounded through her. Oh, how she wanted to say yes.

"Aye." His eyes twinkled with hope.

His charms were bold, enticing, and endearing, pulling at her in a desperate way. Part of her wanted to say yes, but she knew better. She knew what would happen if she climbed into bed with him and even though he was handsome and willing, she wasn't ready for that type of intimacy. Besides, he was far too young for her.

She smiled slowly and reached a hand to him, brushing his cheek.

"I do appreciate the offer, but I think it would be best for me to sleep in my own room." She glanced at the bed with the thick coverlet and curtains on each post. "This will do."

Disappointment flooded his features. "Are ye sure, then, lass?"

She nodded. "I am."

It was for the best. She was in a weakened state and far too vulnerable. She needed to keep her distance, especially from the handsome Highlander.

He reached for her hand, took it in his, and kissed it. Her heart fluttered at the simple gesture.

"Good night, lass."

"Good night."

He left the room, pulling the door closed behind him, and sealing her inside the silence.

CHAPTER NINE

F OR A MOMENT, Brianna remained in the room, her gaze fixed on the peculiar tapestries, which seemed to possess an almost lifelike quality, their intricate details captivating her attention. She watched them, mesmerized by their slow movements depicting the strange scenes. What an odd thing to have in the castle.

She didn't know much about this prophecy. Only what Jamie had shared with her. In the morning, she would find Evie and Chloe and demand answers to all her questions. If she were stuck here in the past, representing the Future, she deserved to know why.

With a sigh of fatigue, she toed off her shoes. She reached into her front pocket and brought out the piece of keystone, placing it on the bedside table. How was something so small responsible for so much power? And did she really believe that a piece of rock controlled all of Time? It seemed farfetched.

She shucked her jeans and shivered. The room was cold, the hearth devoid of a fire. But since she didn't see any spare wood, there was no way to build one. She moved around the room, snuffing out the candles and plunging it in darkness. Feeling her way back to the bed, she slipped under the blankets, pulling them to her chin, shivering.

She hated being cold. She was much more suited to warmer climes.

But exhaustion overtook her, and it was only a matter of

minutes before she was fast asleep.

Then the dream came, bursting through her unconscious mind.

Like in the tapestry, she stood on the craggy hill. The bone-chilling wind pummeled her, billowing the white gown around her legs. She tried tucking a wayward lock of hair behind her ear, but the wind ripped it free, snaring her auburn, sun-kissed locks.

Before her, a vast army the likes she had never seen. Before it, a crusty old man with a faded beard wielding a shining great axe sneering at her with murder in his eyes.

"You are the key to the future and the past," the woman next to her said.

She hadn't realized the woman was there. It startled her. "Who are you?"

"I am Athea, the Goddess of the Future. One of the Triple Goddess."

"What do you want?" Brianna asked.

"Behold the army before you." She motioned outward with her hand to the men on horseback and foot. "They want what they cannot have. What you cannot give them. For if they claim the keystone in its entirety, it will doom generations to come."

She glanced down at her hand to see the keystone—now whole—resting against her scarred palm.

"How so?" Brianna focused on the man before her, the one who was the leader with this glowing great axe.

"I will show you."

Athea reached for her, holding her hand out to her. Brianna hesitated a moment before finally placing her hand in hers. Then Athea swept her other hand outward, encompassing the encroaching warriors and showed her.

Rory MacDonald cleaved the air in front of him with the great axe, opening a portal to the Realm of Chaos that allowed in all manner of dark and dangerous creatures. Horned creatures with hideous faces, claws, and leathery wings. They swarmed the opposing army who had come to fight MacDonald and his men. At the head of that army were the three MacLeod brothers. They charged with their claymores held high as they bellowed a war cry.

"Do something, Bri!" Chloe said, emotion clogging her throat. She stood next to her, fear evident on her face.

"Use the stone," Evie urged. She was on the other side of her.

"I don't know how."

Brianna choked out the words, glancing down at the whole keystone in her hand, the lines glowing and pulsing. A sense of helplessness rammed through her as she stood there on the craggy hill. She did not know how to make it work. She did not know how to save the MacLeod men from the onslaught of disgusting creatures. She did not know how to stop Rory MacDonald from charging up the hill on his destrier with malice creasing his face, his great axe held aloft, and a war cry ripping from his throat.

She sucked in a breath. Evie and Chloe stumbled back away from him. He was after one thing—the keystone. And if she didn't give it to him, she would die.

Brianna cried out as she sat up, staring into the gloomy shadows of the strange and unfamiliar bedchamber. Her heart raced with a frantic beat as she clutched the bedclothes to her chest and tried to get her breathing under control.

"It was just a dream. Only a dream," she said into the darkness.

Was it?

The female voice fluttered through her mind. She snapped her head in the direction of the tapestries and saw the one with the Triple Goddess illuminated, the golden threads shimmering and emitting an ethereal light.

Brianna shoved out of bed, her feet hitting the cold stone floor, sending a shiver prickling up her entire body. She clutched her elbows as she edged toward the wall hanging. When she looked closer, she realized it was not the Triple Goddess at all within the woven fabric, but her and her sisters.

BRIANNA HAD A fitful sleep the rest of the night. She was haunted by images of death and destruction and dark creatures of the night. Of a rip in space and time. Of a man who used a glowing great axe to kill all those who tried to stop him.

By the time morning came, and sleep was out of grasp, she shoved off the blankets and sat on the edge of the bed. She raked a hand through her tangled hair. She was more exhausted now than when she arrived. The dream was disturbing and clung to her mind like a spider to its web.

She glanced at the tapestry to see if she had dreamed seeing the three of them as the Triple Goddess. But no. The image hadn't changed. The piece of stone on the bedside table was cold and silent.

With effort, she dressed, stuffing the stone back into her front pocket, and left the bedchamber. She needed to find Evie. She had questions. The first one being why she was here and what she was supposed to do with this jagged piece of stone she was carrying around in her jeans pocket. The next was how was she supposed to get home?

Thinking of *home* seemed abstract. Once she returned to the future, then what? Where would she go? How would she live? She'd long since burned through her inheritance. She would be forced to get a real job, something her mother had always hounded her about. Or find another rich bachelor who wanted her.

Thinking that gave her pause as she pulled open the chamber door. She halted in the doorway, the light from the corridor slashing across the threshold behind her. What kind of person did that make her? A horrible one, that's what. Did she really want to whore herself out to the highest bidder for room and board?

The answer to that was no. Which shocked her. She didn't want to go back to that life. And yet, she didn't have a purpose, or a place. No one would miss her or even care she was gone. In the hours she had landed in the Scotland of the past, she'd fallen into the arms of a Highlander who seemed to want her more than anything.

But he didn't know her. He only knew what he saw in a magical tapestry. He was infatuated. Nothing more.

Still…none of the men she'd been with had made her stomach flutter as it did now when she thought of Jamie. She pressed her hand against her gut, willing those feelings to go away.

"Bri, you okay?"

It was Evie's voice that pulled her out of her thoughts. Her sister stood in the corridor, a curious look on her face. Brianna hadn't realized she had appeared.

"Did you sleep here last night?" Evie asked.

"Yes," she said. "It was late when Jamie and I returned, and I didn't want to disturb you."

Evie lifted a brow. "Where did you go? I saw you riding out with him."

She wanted to tell her she intended to run away, back to Edinburgh. But Jamie had squashed that thought when he told her it was a fifteen-day trek over rough terrain and camping in the wilderness. She wanted to tell her she hated everything about being here, in the past. She wanted to tell her Jamie had hit on her, inviting her to his bedchamber with a sensual gleam in his eyes but she refused him.

She wanted to tell her all of this but didn't.

"Yes, I rode out with him to the loch."

"Have you…always known how to ride a horse?"

It likely would come as a shock to her that, yes, she'd learned when she was young. She'd started riding when she was six with the hopes of making it onto the Olympics equestrian team. When the twins were born, she and her parents had moved to a bigger home—to give them all a better life, her father said—and that meant giving up her horses.

Because there simply wasn't enough time or money for that

anymore.

"What are you doing here?" Brianna asked, a bit more sharply than she intended.

Evie winced. "I come to the tapestry room every day."

"The tapestry room?"

"That's what we call it." Evie motioned to the open door behind her. "To see if anything has changed."

"Something *has* changed." Brianna stepped aside to allow her entrance.

Excitement gleamed in her eyes as she hurried through the doorway and headed right for the tapestries. She halted in front of them, staring at the one with the changed image, her shoulders stiff and back rigid. Brianna easily read her body language and knew she was processing what she was seeing.

"This image is..." Evie's voice trailed away. She turned to look at her. Her face drained of color. She pressed a hand against her abdomen.

"It's us," Brianna said.

Even saying it aloud made her stomach churn.

"You're in the center. Where Moira once stood."

"I replaced Moira?" Brianna moved to stand next to her, peering up at the image. "What does it mean?"

Evie shook her head, her scrutinizing gaze on the woven textile. "I don't know."

"What do you know about these tapestries?" she asked.

"Not much, actually," Evie admitted, her gaze still on the wall hangings. "Hamish was the one who first told me about them. He's the one who showed them to me. He said they always had images on them. But lately, they've been changing and the images on them have been coming true."

"Who's Hamish?"

"Their father." Sorrow tinged her voice.

A signal that something must have happened to Hamish.

Evie added, "He was killed."

"You knew him?" Brianna asked.

"Only for a short while." She turned to her then, reaching for her hands and clasping them in hers. "When I first came, Hamish was the one who told me about this prophecy. He begged me to convince Callum it was real."

"And does he believe now?"

She smiled. "He does but it did take some doing." She glanced back at the wall hangings, her gazed fixed on them. "The Triple Goddess had to split the stone into three pieces to keep it out of the hands of Brodie MacDonald." She released her hand to point to the one wielding the glowing great axe.

"That's his army?"

"Yes." She turned back to her then. "Chloe was gifted the piece of the Past. She had…visions."

That caught her attention. "Visions? Like what?"

"Like she saw the Night of Shadows in her vision. That's where it all started. There were three goddesses representing Past, Present, and Future who protected this keystone that holds all of Time itself. Sometimes it's called the Chronos Stone. Others tried to steal it and breach the barriers between the mortal realm and the Realm of Chaos. That became known as the Night of Shadows. So, the three goddesses decided to break the stone into three pieces and hide it to keep it out of their hands. The Shattering."

The Realm of Chaos.

"Your stone is the Future, Bri," she said on a whisper.

Her dream with Athea flooded back to her. What message was Athea trying to send to her with the dream? Was that a vision of the future? Of what was to come?

She contemplated telling Evie about the dream, but she wasn't ready to do that yet.

"So, what are we supposed to *do* with these pieces of stone? Put them together? And then what?"

Evie shrugged. "I don't know. All I know is that we—the MacLeods and the Sinclairs—were tasked with being the protector of it."

"*Three pieces of stone. Two ancient bloodlines. One divine destiny,*" she said, remembering what Jamie told her.

"Yes." Evie nodded. "Jamie told you."

It was not a question, but Brianna nodded anyway.

They lapsed into silence as Brianna gazed at the three of them in the tapestry. Her in the middle and the twins flanking her. Her relationship with Evie was better than the one she had with Chloe.

Evie wanted a harmonious family. Hence the reason why she'd called Brianna and asked her to come with her to the gala in Scotland.

Chloe tended to bristle when she was around, giving her the hairy eyeball and keeping her at a distance. Hence the reason why Brianna refused to go with Evie to Scotland.

Something she regretted now. If she had gone, would things have turned out differently for them? Would they still be in the past? Would their fate be decided?

"Why does Chloe hate me?"

Evie glanced at her in surprise. She hadn't meant to ask it aloud, but the words spilled out before she halted them.

"She doesn't hate you," Evie said, her voice soft. Then she straightened and reached for her hand again. "Come on. Let's find something to eat. I'm starving."

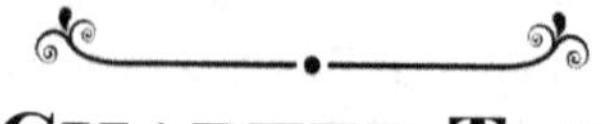

CHAPTER TEN

BRIANNA FOLLOWED HER out of her room knowing full well she had changed the subject because she didn't want to deal with the question of Chloe.

Neither of her sisters truly understood her. How could they? There was a ten-year age gap between her and the twins. They'd had a very different childhood than she did—almost charmed. As the older sister, she had been expected to be more responsible, levelheaded, dependable. While the twins—who were late in life children—were allowed to run wild and free.

Brianna admitted now, looking back, there was a certain amount of resentment toward them. When the girls were young, she'd often felt invisible. It had fueled her bad decisions. It had encouraged her to rebel against her parents. Which in turn had garnered their attention.

Not exactly the attention she'd wanted, either.

When they entered the great hall, all those dismal thoughts of her previous life fled her mind. Jamie was there. The moment he saw her, his face lit in a bright smile, showing off his deep dimples. He got to his feet as they entered.

Callum and Malcolm were there, too.

And Chloe, whose sharp emerald gaze bored into her.

But Brianna only had eyes for Jamie. She did her best to ignore her sister's dagger eyes.

"Good morrow, lass," he greeted. "I trust ye slept well."

"Well enough."

Brianna took the seat nearest him while Evie sat next to Callum. He gave her adoring looks, and it was clear they were mad for each other.

In front of her was a trencher of what appeared to be some type of porridge or oatmeal. Next to it, a stack of oat cakes. It was quiet in the great hall as the men finished eating. Callum kissed his wife's cheek.

"I have duties to tend."

She nodded and watched as he headed for the door.

"As do I."

Malcolm was the second to abandon the great hall, following Callum out.

Tension shifted through the room. Jamie was the last to get to his feet. "I… have horses to tend. Mayhap ye come to see me after? We can have another ride, if ye like."

He granted her a weak smile as he scurried out behind his two older brothers, the door banging closed behind him, sealing the three of them inside.

It all seemed too convenient for Brianna. Unease flickered through her as she picked up her spoon. Her stomach was suddenly in knots.

Silence.

Chloe glared at her as though she'd committed some heinous crime.

Evie broke the silence first. "The tapestries have changed."

Chloe's curious gaze slid in her direction. "Oh? How?"

"We are represented as the Triple Goddess," she said, as though it were the most natural thing to say. She stuck her spoon into the porridge and took a bite.

"What do you mean represented as the Triple Goddess?" Chloe asked.

"I mean, the images have changed. Instead of Moira, Bridget, and…" She faltered.

"Athea," Brianna said, filling in the name. "The Goddess of

the Future."

The goddess she represented. They both looked at her in surprise. Eventually, she was going to have to tell them both about the strange dream she'd had.

"You know this?" Evie asked.

Brianna nodded.

"How?" Evie asked.

Chloe interrupted with her impatience. "What do you mean we are represented as the Triple Goddess?"

"I mean, the three of us are positioned like the Triple Goddess in the tapestry of the Night of Shadows," Evie said.

Chloe's gaze snapped back to Brianna, her eyes narrowing. "Brianna, too?"

Before Evie could reply in an attempt to keep the peace, Brianna answered.

"Yes, me, too. Just what is your problem with me?"

"I'll tell you what my problem is. You—"

"Chlo—"

"Don't try to shush me, Eve. She has it coming."

"I have *what* coming? You don't even know what I went through for you two."

Brianna dropped the spoon, her flight instincts rising. She didn't want to fight her sister. She wanted to bolt. But then, she also wanted to clear things up with Chloe if she'd listen. The problem was, she doubted she'd listen.

Chloe scoffed. "Oh, please. After Mom and Dad died it was so obvious you were only doing your duty."

Brianna remained mute, pressing her lips into a thin line as she stared across the table at her sister. Evie's face drained of color once again. She sat ramrod straight and perfectly still in her chair, her eyes wide and her spoon hovering over the trencher. Brianna waited for her to intervene, but she said nothing.

She took a deep breath to calm her ragged, raging nerves. "You have no idea what I was going through when Mom and Dad died."

"Yes, I do. You were living it up in Puerto Rico. I doubt you were 'going through' anything stressful." Chloe put the words *going through* in air quotes and rolled her eyes.

Red rage clouded her vision. She clenched her hand into a tight fist, her nails biting into her sore palm. She realized, too late, it was the one with the brand from the rock.

"You think you're so smart with your fancy degree and your international museum job, don't you? But the truth is, Chloe, you don't have a damn clue about me or my life." Chloe started to object, but Brianna forged on. "Let me finish. You're going to hear what I have to say and you're going to keep your mouth shut while I say it."

Evie's eyes widened at the sheer venom in her voice. Chloe clenched her jaw, the anger lines in clear display around her mouth.

"I was going through the divorce from hell when Mom and Dad died. Not only did I have to pack up and leave *my home*, but I also had to come back and deal with the probate court and all the shit the goes along with two people who died without leaving wills. Not to mention dealing with two moody teenagers."

Evie sucked in a sharp breath of surprise. Chloe's eyes widened a scant inch.

"That's right. They had no wills. Do you know what a giant pain in the ass that was? Meanwhile, not only did my ex-husband decide to clean out my bank accounts, leaving me in financial ruin, but he also took everything I ever had except for the clothes I came back with. So don't be so quick to judge me with your high and mighty self, hmm?"

And with that, she shoved back from the table, her chair scraping along the floor, and stomped out of the great hall. The door slammed behind her. She stood a moment there, the cold breeze fluttering over her burning cheeks as she closed her eyes and took a deep, calming breath. Tears threatened behind her eyes, but she refused to let them fall.

Brianna had done everything possible to shield Evie and

Chloe from the hell she had been going through with her parents' deaths and her messy divorce. Maybe she'd shielded them too well and it had clouded Chloe's vision about who she was and her motivations.

"Lass? Are ye well?" Jamie's voice was like a soothing balm to her soul.

She opened her eyes to see him standing near her, concern creasing his features. She shook off her anger and her despair and managed to smile.

"Yes, thanks. Just a bit of strife with my sisters."

His gaze flickered to the closed door behind her. Deep understanding furrowed his features.

"Och, siblings can be difficult, aye?"

She stifled a giggle. "They can."

He held his hand out to her. "How about that ride?"

"I'd love that."

The invitation was much too difficult to refuse. She placed her hand in his. He closed his warm fingers around hers and led her to the stable. And for that moment, there was only her and Jamie and nothing else mattered.

But on their way to the stables, she shivered in the cold wind. She didn't have her coat. "I forgot my coat."

"Dinnae fash," he said, giving her winning smile.

He unfastened his own cloak and handed it to her. She stared at the offering, her heart doing a quick ka-thud.

"Oh, I couldn't." She shook her head, but he walked around and placed the cloak on her shoulders.

"Ye can."

The cloak was still warm from his body heat. She pulled it tighter around her frame, enjoying the feel. In this century, chivalry was still alive and well. She could get used to that.

She followed him to the stables. She couldn't help but notice his limp. It seemed worse today than it was the day before as though the pain was more intense. In the stable, the horses were saddled and ready, as though he expected her to arrive at any moment. That was endearing, really. She loved that he wanted to be with her.

Jamie called out to his brother that he was going to check the perimeter. He winced a bit as he climbed into the saddle. Clearly, the ache in his leg pained him. Once they were ready, they trotted through the bailey and out the portcullis. She kept pace with him as they headed away from the castle. He pulled his horse up next to hers and slowed to a walk.

"I dinnae ken what this trouble is with ye and yer sisters, lass, but I do ken Evie has been waiting for ye to arrive since ye first appeared in the tapestry."

She appreciated his attempt to make her feel better. "I have a better relationship with Evie than I do with Chloe."

"Why is that?" It was a genuine question of curiosity.

"I think Chloe thinks I've had a charmed life."

He gave her the side-eye while smiling. Those dimples deep in his cheeks showed. It was starting to be her favorite thing about him. "Have ye?"

When she realized he was kidding, she laughed. "Hardly."

She mulled over what to tell him as they took their time to walk around the perimeter of the castle. The sky was dotted with thick, gray and white clouds. Only a break here and there allowed slashes of morning light through. Being here in the Highlands, though, Brianna appreciated the wild, untamed, yet beautiful, landscape. Even if it weren't for her. She longed for her sunny beaches and her warm ocean breezes.

"When our parents died, I was the one who took care of Evie and Chloe until they were able to make it on their own," she said. "It was a hard period of my life. I was going through a bad relationship breakup at the time, so I probably wasn't the most fun to be around."

After the failure of her marriage, she decided she'd never marry again. She was done with that. As soon as she was able, she'd returned to Puerto Rico to finalize her divorce. He'd already found a new girl and was living in their apartment with her. That was the moment that had changed everything for her. The moment she'd decided she would throw herself into her business. The moment she'd decided casual relationships were better than commitments.

"I'm sorry for ye," he said.

"Oh, don't be. I brought a lot of trouble on myself." She tried to say it with good humor.

"Mayhap ye should talk to them both to reconcile."

Truthfully, she had thought about it more than once since they'd departed on poor terms. She couldn't seem to bring herself to do it. When Evie called to invite her to the gala, she'd ignored the olive branch and tossed it aside. She should have taken it. She should have accepted her invitation. Maybe then, none of this would have happened. Or, maybe, things would have happened differently.

"*Teothaidh an fhuil ris an fhuil.*"

The sound of his native Gaelic language was lyrical as it lilted on his tongue. She tilted her head to one side. "What does that mean?"

"*Blood warms to blood.* Family will always support each other, no matter the reason."

A modern phrase leapt to her mind. *Blood is thicker than water.* Perhaps Jamie was right. Perhaps she would find a way to clear the air with Chloe. She would consider it.

"Are you saying I should find a way to reconcile with her?" she asked.

"I'm saying that sometimes family is more important than anything else."

He sounded like an authority on the subject.

"I'll consider smoothing things over with her. But that's enough about me, I think. What about you?"

She looked over at him to see thoughtful contemplation crossing his face. "I had a bad relationship breakup, too."

"Oh?" That intrigued her.

"My da wanted me to marry MacDonald's daughter. We

were handfasted but it dinnae work out."

"No?" She titled her head to the side, her curiosity piqued.

He cut her a glance. "Are ye familiar with handfasting?"

She shook her head.

"When a man and woman wish to wed—or pledge themselves to each other for a time—their hands are bound together with a length of cord. It shows their lives are now entwined. They speak their vows witnessed by their kin, and for a year and a day they live together as man and wife. At year's end, they can part, if they wish."

His words whispered around her, warmth curling through her chest. Handfasting—an unbreakable bond, a promise sealed with a knotted cord. The thought slipped in before she could stop it. Jamie's hands covering hers, the rough brush of his calloused fingers, the steady weight of his gaze as they spoke the vows.

Ridiculous. She barely knew him. And yet, the idea lingered, unsettling and impossible to shake.

"It sounds like an old-fashioned wedding. That's kind of beautiful, actually. What happens if they don't wish to part from each other?"

"Then they are bound together for all eternity, making a true lasting marriage."

It sounded like a fairy tale—dreamy, romantic, the kind of vow that actually meant something. Not like the farce she'd lived through, standing under the flickering neon glow of a Vegas chapel, a rhinestone-studded Elvis declaring her married. Her stomach twisted. She refused to let that man's name stain her thoughts, not even for a second. That part of her life was dead and buried.

But the thing that scared and surprised her the most was…she wanted the fairy tale with Jamie. For once in her life, she wanted that dreamy romantic vow.

"Is that how my sisters were married? They were handfasted?" she asked.

"Aye."

Why did a pang of jealousy stab her? She quickly shoved that aside.

"You said it didn't work out. I assume you two parted ways?" she asked, still interested in hearing the rest of his story.

"She was a cold, frigid bitch so I returned her to her da and broke the handfasting."

It sounded like he had gone through his own version of divorce. It seemed they had something in common.

"Her da dinnae take too kindly to that. 'Tis one reason our clans' feud. That and he wants the wee keystone."

"So, breaking up with this woman started a war between your families?"

"More or less," he said, sheepishly.

She laughed, suddenly feeling a little better about her situation. At least her divorce hadn't started any wars.

JAMIE WASN'T SURE why he'd felt free to tell her about Margaret MacDonald. But seeing her eyes light up and hearing her melodious laugh made it all worthwhile.

He was unwilling to go back to the castle yet. He enjoyed her company far too much. When he finished his perimeter check of the castle, he continued to keep her close to him. She followed without question, seemingly content to ride side by side.

She'd looked so sad standing outside the keep, he was compelled to do something to make her smile. He'd shown her the borders of their land and talked a lot about growing up with his older brothers. About losing his mother when he was born and his sister succumbing to a fever. About his da being killed in battle with Rory MacDonald.

"After I returned Margaret to her clan, my da was so furious he packed me up and sent me on travels with my uncle."

"Where did you go?" she asked.

"We spent time in France. Calais, Rouen, Paris."

"Do you speak French then?"

"*Oui, mademoiselle. Tu es la plus belle femme du monde.*"

She flushed, her cheeks turning a pale pink. "I don't know what that means but it sounds like a compliment."

"Aye," he said, pleased with himself.

He didn't tell her he got into some romantic trouble in Paris where he, quite literally, was caught with his pants down in a compromising position with a French noble's daughter. It was the final straw for Uncle Argyle, who immediately set sail for Scotland. His uncle then returned to clean up the disaster he'd left in his wake. Guilt swept through him, remembering his abhorrent and less than chivalrous behavior.

After that, he'd made a silent vow to be a better man, to stop chasing the lassies—no matter how bonnie—and to be more gallant. And then he'd set his eyes upon Brianna. While he still intended to be the valiant man he aspired to be, he could not resist chasing her, charming her, or wanting her.

She focused her wintery gaze on the sky, which was heavy with gray clouds that threatened rain. "Maybe we should head back."

"Aye, we should."

It was getting late in the day. He'd enjoyed their time together far too much. Though he'd known they would have to return at some point, he still wasn't ready to do that. Reluctantly, he nodded and turned his horse back toward the castle. She did the same with such ease, it was as though she'd done it all her life.

"Ye are a much better rider than yer sisters," he observed.

She flushed again, her cheeks turning a pretty pink. "Thanks. I used to ride a lot when I was younger. Where I come from, we have a horse competition that involves a rider and horse jumping obstacles. I was in training to do that."

He had never heard of such a thing and was instantly fascinated. "Aye? Jumping over logs?"

"You might say that," she replied with a smile. "It was a

timed competition. So the faster you and your horse completed the course, the better your score." She gave him a surreptitious glance, a mischievous grin on her face. "Want to race?"

"Ye wish to race me back to the keep?" he said.

She gripped the reins tighter in her hands. "I do."

Before he agreed, she kicked her horse into a full gallop and took off, leaving him in her dust.

CHAPTER ELEVEN

THE RIDE BACK to the keep was exhilarating. She hadn't felt that alive and free in a long time. The wind whipped through her hair leaving it in tangles as she galloped along, the cold biting through her clothes. But she didn't care because it was wonderful to be on the back of a horse again, even if she was stuck in the Middle Ages.

Jamie caught up to her before they made it to the gate. He gave her a wicked grin as he encouraged his mount to go faster. A laugh escaped her throat as she tried to follow, but he pulled ahead of her and reached the portcullis first. He reined in his horse, coming to a halt, leaving a shower of dirt clods in his wake.

When she came a halt near him, she was grinning from ear to ear as was he.

"Ye lost, lass."

"This time," she said with a grin.

"Will there be a next time, then?" There was a twinkle of mirth in his eyes as he smirked, showing off those two deep dimples.

"Of course, there will."

Together, they trotted back to the stables. The stable hands were busy doing their tasks when they arrived. As Brianna dismounted, she wondered if it was possible to care for the horse. She wasn't ready to go back into the keep and face her sisters.

"How about I remove the saddle and brush her down?" Brianna offered.

Surprise flickered over his face. "Ye wish do to that yerself?"

"Yes, if that's all right. It's been a while since I was able to care for a horse. I miss it."

Jamie said nothing as he stepped down from his mount. One of the stable boys rushed over to take the reins and lead his away. When a second arrived to do the same for her horse, he waved him off.

"If ye wish, lass. I'll show ye the stall."

He motioned forward. Clutching the reins, she followed him to the last stall on the left, which had thick wooden planks as a half-wall divider between the other stalls. She led the horse inside. The floor was packed earth covered in hay. Faint sunlight filtered through the narrow slits in the stone wall. On one side of the stall was a bucket of oats. On the other, a water trough with fresh water.

Jamie remained in the doorway of the stall and watched with a curious eye as she unbuckled the girth strap. The horse shifted once the strap hung loose, adjusting to the sudden freedom. She moved to the horse's left and grabbed the pommel and the cantle, ready to lift off the saddle off the horse. When she tried, though, she realized this was no modern-day Western saddle. This was a lot heavier.

Jamie moved into the stall, his feet shuffling the hay. She sensed his presence behind her.

"Allow me?" he asked.

She turned her head and met his gaze. He was looking at her intently. A heated flush crept up her cheeks. She took a step away and allowed him to lift the saddle without effort. He placed it over the low half-stall wall.

Brianna removed the saddlecloth and draped it over the wall. Then she ran her hands over the back and sides, feeling for any sign of chafing or soreness.

"Ye really do care for them, don't ye?" There was wonder in his voice.

"I do. When I took riding lessons, I loved helping. Brushing her, bathing her, or whatever needed to be done. I even mucked the stalls."

It was a time in her life she hadn't thought about in so long. A memory long buried.

"Why did ye stop riding?" he asked.

She inhaled a deep breath, expelled it. "When Evie and Chloe were born, things changed. The house we lived in wasn't big enough. My parents wanted to move. We'd be too far away for me to take lessons anymore. So, I had to give it up."

It was hard to hide the twinge of sadness in her voice.

"I'm sorry ye had to give it up."

"Me, too."

She unbuckled the bridle, but the horse jerked its head as she tried to remove it, causing the buckle to jerk out of her hand. The rough edge of the buckle raked across her scarred palm, leaving behind a gash and well of blood. She sucked in a sharp breath, releasing the bridle.

"Och, ye're hurt. We best go wash that out."

She clutched her wrist as she cupped her hand. "It's not bad."

"Come on then. The stable hands can handle the rest."

He clutched her by the elbow and led her out of the stable back to the keep. In the great hall, he pointed to one of the chairs.

"I'll be back," he said.

She perched on the edge of a chair, holding her hand palm up in her lap and waited in the silence. It was a relief to be to be in the great hall without her sisters. She heaved a sigh, knowing she had likely further damaged her relationship with Chloe.

Jamie returned a moment later with a bowl, a pitcher, and Evie on his heels. Her face was pinched with worry as she carried long strips of linen.

"Let me see your hand," Evie demanded. She placed the strips of linen on the table and took the seat next to her, holding out her hand.

Brianna gave her a sidelong look. "Since when did you get so bossy?"

Evie pressed her lips together, holding her hand out, waiting for Brianna to comply. "Since I had to be in charge of things. Show me."

Huffing out a breath, she placed her hand in Evie's. She peered down at the small cut with a critical eye as if looking for something. It had already stopped bleeding.

"Did you touch the keystone when you cut your hand?"

What an odd question. "No."

Evie's gaze flickered back up to Jamie, who stood there still holding the bowl and the pitcher.

"I can take it from here," she told him, dismissing him.

Without a word, he placed them on the table and then walked away. But he cast a longing look at her as he departed. Brianna kept her gaze on him as he moved through the great hall to the staircase that led to the upper floor.

"Why did you dismiss him? He was trying to help," Brianna said.

"I need to tell you something."

She paused as she gathered her thoughts. Then she held out her scarred hand for Brianna to see. She clearly made out the lines from her piece of the keystone. But there, across the scar, was a faint silvery scar. Like something had slashed across her palm.

"You cut yourself, too?"

"Yes," she said slowly. "It's what powers the stone."

Brianna's gaze narrowed as she looked at her younger sister. "What does?"

She lifted her gaze from her hand and met Brianna's. "Blood."

"Really, Evie, if this is some riddle or something—"

"It's blood magic. That's what she's trying to tell you." Chloe's voice echoed through the great hall as she stepped into the room.

Brianna pulled her hand out of Evie's grasp and placed it back in her lap. Chloe paused next to Evie and showed Brianna her palm. She had the same type of scarring on her palm—a brand from the stone as well as a silver slash.

"You both cut your hands? Why?"

The twins exchanged a glance as silent communication passed between them. It was something they'd done a lot when they were younger, as though they had telepathy and always knew what the other was thinking. Chloe gave her a nod of encouragement.

"We have a lot to tell you," Evie said. "But first, we should clean that wound before it gets infected."

TWO HOURS LATER, Brianna sagged against the chair. She still sat at the great hall table, utterly drained from listening to the two of them tell the story of how they had both ended up in the past, how they had both cut their hands and used the blood magic and the stone to see into their respective time.

Evie had the power of the Present. Apparently, she had the ability to create a time bubble, to slow down time, and see all the possible outcomes of immediate choices. She'd used this to see the battle Callum had faced with Rory MacDonald. She'd seen his death in several different scenarios if she hadn't intervened.

Chloe had the power of the Past, giving her the ability to extract memories from people as well as uncover ancient truths. Like Evie, she'd had visions of the past showing her the history between clans Sinclair and MacLeod, how the Night of Shadows had come about and how the Triple Goddess had shattered the Stone and proclaimed both clans protectors.

Brianna held the power of the Future. None of them yet knew what power that would give her. Evie, though, was determined to find out. She stared at the small piece of stone on the table in front of her. Next to it, a dagger. The candlelight winked off the sharp blade.

"You're telling me if cut open my palm and I bleed on the

stone, it will give me this power?" Brianna asked. She wasn't sure she believed in any of this.

"Yes," Evie said.

"You know this for a fact?"

"Yes," Evie replied.

Brianna looked to Chloe, who had remained mostly quiet during Evie's tale. "And it worked for you like that?"

"Not at first," Chloe said. "It was only later after Malcolm and I—" She pressed her lips together. She was unwilling to tell her what she and Malcolm had been doing, but Brianna knew. "I discovered I had to touch Malcolm and the stone to invoke the power."

"Why?" Brianna asked.

She shrugged. "Maybe because we're connected."

"But it wasn't like that for me," Evie said. "Only when Moira sliced my hand did I gain that power the night of the battle."

Brianna stared at the dagger next to her piece of the stone. She glanced down at her hand freshly bandaged hand in her lap, wondering if she was insane to even consider what Evie wanted to do.

"The only way we'll know what power of the Future you hold is if we do this," Evie urged.

She peered at her little sister. The one who was always so quiet and reserved. The one who seemed to be a bit of a pushover, the one who never stuck up for herself. Now, she was a different person. She was strong and insistent. A born leader who had become the lady of the castle. The wife of a laird and soon to be a mother.

She took a deep breath, expelled it, and made her decision hoping it wasn't one she'd regret.

"All right. Let's give it a try, then."

Chapter Twelve

E VIE REACHED FOR the knife resting on the table, clutching it in her hand. Brianna unwound the bandage. The well of blood in the shallow cut had stopped. She held it out to Evie, who wrapped her fingers around her wrist.

"So, how does this work?" she asked.

"You'll want to be holding the stone," Evie said. "When I slice your hand and your hand starts to bleed, place the stone in it and clench your fist."

"That's it? Then what?"

"Then we see what happens," Chloe said.

"Are you ready?" Evie asked, the tip of the knife hovering over her palm.

She took a deep breath, expelled it. "As I'll ever be."

Evie placed the tip against her skin, hesitating only a moment. Then she swiped it down her palm, slicing open her skin. The stinging pain lasted only a second. Brianna took her piece of the stone off the table and clenched it in her hand as Evie instructed.

Nothing happened.

Silence descended on the great hall for several heartbeats. Evie gave her an expectant look, but Brianna shook her head.

"Well, it was worth a try—"

"Wait," Brianna said.

A sudden hum vibrated through her hand. It was low at first, then louder. Evie's eyes widened as she reached into the pocket of her gown and brought out her stone. It was humming. The lines were glowing. Brianna looked up at Chloe to see she held hers, too. It was also humming and the lines were glowing.

"What's happening?" Brianna whispered.

The moment the words left her mouth, a piercing pain shot through her arm up to her shoulder. She staggered to her feet, wincing as she sucked in a sharp breath.

"Bri, are you—"

It was the last thing she heard when the world seemed to tip on its axis. It was as though she were shoved through a keyhole in time, then everything blurred around her as it zoomed by. As though she stood still but everything else was on fast forward.

Ahead of her, she saw the army marching toward her. The man in front held a glowing great axe. He was flanked by other men who rode alongside him. The massive army followed as though they had all the time in the world.

Evie stood to her right. Chloe, to her left. And in her hand, the glowing keystone. When she opened her fingers to look down at it, she saw that the stone was whole. All three pieces were fused together once again.

The power is within you.

The voice lilted through her mind. Soft and sweet.

Use the stone to stop the coming war, Brianna. If you do not, all will be lost.

She opened her mouth to ask who was speaking, but nothing came out. A cold piercing wind swept through her. She realized she wore a white gown as it billowed around her.

The army marched on. From her left another group of men approached. It was another army coming from the north led by Callum, Malcolm, and Jamie. On her right, from the south, more men heading in their direction led by two men she did not recognize. The leader had a fierce look on his face and eyes the color of a winter morning. A strange sense of familiarity flickered through her, almost as if she knew this man or had seen him before.

Before her, the leader with the glowing great axe glared at her with a fierceness that jangled her insides. She knew this was the MacDonald army.

The battle for Time had arrived.

With a flash of his great axe, MacDonald created a rift in time. The air before her pulled apart, light flickering from whatever was beyond.

Then she woke up.

Brianna opened her eyes and stared up at the concerned face of her sister. Her body ached from head to toe. She realized, dimly, she was on the floor and beyond Evie's face was the wood-beam ceiling.

"Are you all right?" Evie asked.

"What happened?" she croaked, her voice weak and rough.

"You collapsed," Chloe said. She sat on her knees opposite Evie.

She shoved to a sitting position, the nausea taking hold of her as her stomach cramped. A blinding pain pounded the backs of her eyes. She groaned as she put her head in her hand, squeezing her eyes closed.

"I feel sick to my stomach."

"That's the blood magic," Evie said. "Chlo, help me get her up. She needs to rest."

But Brianna shrugged them both off. "I'm fine."

Though she wasn't fine, she managed to get to her feet under her own power. On the floor, next to her feet, was her piece of the keystone smeared with blood. She bent to pick it up and then inspected her sliced hand. Her palm was smeared with blood.

"Let me bandage you." Evie motioned toward a chair at the great hall table.

Brianna stumbled toward it, falling into it. She rested her cut hand on the table, palm up.

"Is that what is was like for both of you?" she asked.

"Yes," Evie said.

A glance at Chloe who nodded. "It left me so weak, I slept for hours."

As Evie bandaged her hand with strips of linen, she asked, "What did you see?"

Brianna dragged her lower lip through her teeth. She wasn't sure how to explain what she saw. "There was an army led by a man with a glowing great axe."

"Rory MacDonald," Evie said, nodding encouragement.

"And two other armies," Brianna continued. "One led by Callum, Malcolm, and Jamie."

Chloe sucked in a breath at hearing her husband's name. Evie stilled, her face draining of color.

"The other army was led by someone I don't know but he had eyes the same color as me."

"Sinclair," Chloe said, her voice but a whisper.

A strange feeling crept through Brianna. "As in…our ancestor?"

"We think so," Evie said. She tied off the bandage. "There. That should stop the bleeding. You need to rest now."

"No," Brianna snapped. "There's more. In the vision, the three of us stood on a hill. I held the keystone. It was one piece."

They both stared at her in silent shock. Evie's eyes were wide and round.

"What do you mean one piece?" she asked.

"It was put back together," Brianna explained. "And the lines—the Celtic symbol on it—was glowing."

Chloe sat down hard in the chair next to Evie, as though her knees buckled and gave out. Brianna placed her piece on the table in front of her. Evie and Chloe did the same. Evie nudged them together but kept them apart, just enough to see the connecting lines across the three stones. All three pieces were silent and unlit.

"Yes. It looked like that," she said.

Brianna glanced between her sisters' shocked faces.

"What does it mean?" she asked.

Evie shook her head slowly. "I don't know. The only one who would know is Moira."

"I heard a voice in my head, too," Brianna said. "A woman's.

She said to use the power of the stone to stop the coming war or all would be lost."

The silence hung thick in the air between them. None of them moved or said a word. Evie looked perplexed, trying to work out the meaning. Chloe looked terrified, her face ashen.

"We need to know more about this prophecy," Chloe said. "There has to be more than what we've been told."

"Maybe Jamie or Malcolm will know," Evie said.

"Will ken what, lass?" Jamie's voice lilted over them as he entered the great hall.

He stopped short when he saw Brianna with her bandaged hand still resting on the top of the table. His disapproving gaze flickered between all three of them.

"Och, lass, what did ye do?"

Evie jumped to her feet. "We needed to see if the blood magic would work for her, too."

He scraped a hand over his face as the blood drained from his cheeks. His lips formed a thin line. Distress flickered through his eyes.

"And did it?" he asked.

"Yes," Brianna replied, her voice quiet. It took a monumental effort to push to her feet. "And you're right, Evie. I need to rest."

"I've prepared a room—"

"I'll see to her needs," Jamie interrupted. He stepped closer and wrapped a protective arm around her shoulders. "The two of ye have done enough."

Brianna sensed a bit of anger against them as he led her away. Truthfully, she was grateful for his strength as she leaned on him. Once they were at the curved stone staircase, though, he nudged her in the lead. She took the steps slowly, her legs burning as she ascended. At the top, she leaned on the wall, trying to catch her breath. It was a testament to just how out of shape she was.

Without a word, Jamie was at her side, wrapping his arm around her shoulders once again. Then, before she realized what he was doing, he swept her into his arms and stomped the rest of the way down the hall.

"I don't need you to carry me." It was a weak protest.

He kept his gaze firmly ahead. "Aye, ye do, lass."

He kicked open the door to a bedchamber. When he was inside, he used the heel of his boot to shove it closed. Then he walked to the oversized bed and lowered her down. She expelled a sigh once her tired body hit the feather mattress. He pulled the blanket up to cover her and then went to stoke the dying fire. Moments later, he had a blaze going.

"Why did you come back to the great hall after Evie shooed you away?" she asked, unable to squash her curiosity.

"I had a feeling she was up to no good. I was right."

"She's just determined," she said around a yawn.

"Aye, at your expense. Rest, lass."

Brianna, still fully dressed, snuggled under the warmth of the blankets. A dreamy sensation came over her and before too long, she was fast asleep.

$$\text{CHAPTER THIRTEEN}$$

Chapter Thirteen

When Brianna awoke, it took several minutes for her to remember where she was. Then, with the throbbing of her palm, it all came flooding back to her.

Jamie.

He'd come into the great hall and quite literally swept her off her feet. She assumed she was in his bed. Why did that give her warm fuzzies all over? It was silly. She was not the type of girl to swoon over something so simple.

Not only did her palm throb with a fierce pain, but her entire body hurt. She groaned as she rolled to her side and opened her eyes. Jamie stood at the hearth and turned to meet her gaze when he heard her movement.

He held a pewter tankard in his hand. He placed it on a tray and then walked to the bed, perching on the edge.

"How do ye feel?" he asked, concern creasing his youthful, handsome features.

"Like death," she groaned. As she said it, her stomach rumbled with hunger.

"Come eat. I brought a tray of food." He waved to the tray sitting on a table between two chairs in front of the hearth.

The simple gesture sent a pang of...what? It was such a foreign emotion, she wasn't sure what to call it. He was sweet and thoughtful and she was fairly certain she didn't deserve any of that. But she shoved off the blankets and put her feet on the ground. She still wore her shoes. He hadn't bothered to take them off when he'd placed her on the bed and covered her with the quilt.

Now, she toed them off. She pushed off the bed and stood.

And immediately sat again as a wave of dizziness accosted her.

Jamie was at her side, though.

"Are ye all right?"

"I'm a bit lightheaded, that's all," she said.

He held his hand down to her. She stared at it for the longest moment, trying to make her unwilling brain accept that this man wanted to help her in every way. Tipping her head back, she looked up into his dark eyes. He grinned, showing off those deep dimples that did funny things to her innards.

She was ridiculous. Even as she thought it, she placed her unbandaged hand in his. He helped her to her feet and, holding her hand, led her to the chair next to the fire. She eased her tired body down and leaned back with a heavy sigh. God, she was exhausted.

Jamie picked up a pewter plate and loaded it with bread, cheese, sliced meat, and fruit and then handed it to her. She took it from him, watching him intently as he poured another tankard of a dark brew and placed it on the tray in front of her. Then he turned to the hearth and added another log to the fire.

"Thank you," she finally managed to say.

She placed a slice of cheese on a piece of bread and popped it into her mouth.

Still kneeling by the hearth, he looked up at her, their eyes meeting. That curious swooping feeling went through her again. She swallowed her bread and cheese as her mouth turned to ash.

"Tell me what happened when ye sliced open yer hand," he said.

She reached for the tankard and sipped. It smelled like weak ale. She took a healthy swig and then placed it back on the try. It was definitely weak ale and nothing like what she was used to drinking.

"I ken there is blood magic," Jamie added.

"Blood magic." She scoffed at the words, shaking her head.

"Ye dinnae believe in it?"

"I don't know what to believe, honestly." She picked up a red grape and popped it into her mouth.

"But something *did* happen, aye?" he asked.

"Yes." She pushed a piece of dried meat around on her plate. "I'm not sure I can explain it."

He moved from the fire, sitting in front of her and looking up at her, the light from the fire flickering through his eyes, illuminating them with golden light.

"Try," he said in an encouraging tone.

She told him about the vision she'd had when she'd touched the stone, how all three of their pieces were humming and glowing. How she was facing the MacDonald army with the whole keystone in her hand. And how the woman's voice in her head told her she had to use the stone to stop the coming war.

He was silent as she spoke. His face was impassive and devoid of all emotion. Then he sat back on his heels, his hands on his thighs as he turned his head to gaze into the fire. The light flickered over his face, accentuating his handsome features.

"*When the stars align and twilight fades, a maiden from the future comes. Through time's veil, her path she will find, with heart and courage, to mend all Time.*" His voice was quiet as he spoke.

Icy pinpricks danced up her spine. "What does that mean?"

He gave her a spectacular grin and shrugged.

"You don't know." Deflated, she sat back in the chair.

"'Tis part of the prophecy. My da used to say this to us when Malcolm and I were wee laddies." Thoughtful contemplation crossed his face as he gazed at the fire.

"*A maiden from the future,*" she repeated, thinking over what he'd said. "One maiden. Not three."

"Aye," he said slowly, his gaze moving from the fire back to hers. "Ye think it means something?"

"I'm not sure. Maybe that I arrive with the third piece of the keystone. And then you said *her path she'll find, with heart and courage, to mend all Time.*" She thought about this last bit a long, quiet moment. And she didn't like the implications one bit.

As she said it, dread crawled through her. To mend all Time could mean something along the lines of her being the one to fix…what?

"Jamie, tell me about the Night of Shadows and the Shattering."

"I told ye all I ken."

"But there has to be something more. Why did the Triple Goddess break the stone into three pieces?"

"To keep it out of the hands of MacDonald. There was a great battle the Night of Shadows. Clan Sinclair and Clan MacLeod fought Clan MacDonald."

Now they were getting somewhere. "Why?"

"Because MacDonald tried to use his glowing great axe to open the Realm of Chaos."

"For what purpose?" she prodded.

He peered at her, the lines furrowing his forehead as he tried to recall. He tapped a finger against his chin.

"Did your da tell you anything about this?"

"Nay," he said. Then his gaze fixed on hers. "But Chloe did."

"Chloe," she said on a breath. "Her vision."

"Aye. Her vision of the past was the Night of Shadows. She saw the battle between them. As though she was there that night. MacDonald tried to open the Realm of Chaos. That's why Moira and the other two split the stone. She said they used the power in the three stones to mend the rift, but it was only stitched back together."

And if it was stitched back together, perhaps her vision showed the rift was opening once again with the help of MacDonald's glowing great axe.

"And tied our two bloodlines together?" she asked.

He nodded.

She glanced down at her throbbing bandaged hand. Though

she could no longer see the scar from the imprint of the stone, she knew it was still there. And now she suspected she had a part to play in this strange world. She had a terrible feeling she understood what that meant.

Through time's veil, her path she will find, with heart and courage, to mend all Time.

She came through time's veil. That much was true. She may not have gone to college like Chloe, but she was still smart enough to use deductive reasoning and figure out what this cryptic message meant. Wasn't that how all prophecies worked anyway?

In her vision, the keystone was whole. And in her hand.

Oh, shit.

"Jamie." She said his name slowly and on a quiet breath, which got his attention. "In my vision, the keystone was whole again. The prophecy says 'her path she'll find with heart and courage to mend all Time.' That can mean only one thing."

His hands curled into tight fists. "Do ye have a theory, lass?"

"I do." She nodded "I think I'm the key. I'm the one who has to mend Time."

What did that mean for her, then? Her death? Or something else? She had no way to find out.

Or did she?

Could she use the stone and the blood magic to have another vision and find out? The moment the thought flickered through her mind, her hand throbbed with a sharp pang.

He remained silent as he stared at her, his hands in fists.

"I think we have to know," she said, her voice a quiet whisper in the room.

"How do ye intend to find out, lass?" he asked. Worry lines creased his face, as though he understood what she intended to suggest.

She held up her bandaged hand with a stain of blood on the linen. He shook his head immediately.

"I cannae allow it."

Brianna lifted a brow. "Since when are you in charge of me?"

"Since I brought ye here to rest," he said, his voice hard. By the firm expression on his face, he wanted no argument out of her, either. "I intend to care for ye."

He looked away as he said the last. His face was flushed, either from the fire or his emotions, she wasn't sure which. And yet, she was touched by his admission. Her heart fluttered, making her want to melt into a puddle. That he wanted to care for her. No man in her long, sordid history had ever wanted to take care of her.

"That's kind of you, but I can take care of myself. I have been for a long time now."

When he looked at her, there was such caring in his expression, such a softness about him that she almost swooned. "Ye dinnae have to anymore," he said softly.

She blinked, sudden hot tears pricking her eyes. Why was he so sweet to her? She had only known him for a short time and in that short time, he had managed to endear himself to her. He held a hand out to her then. She didn't hesitate when she took it. His fingers gently closed over her bandage, his thumb scraping across the linen. He focused his gaze on their intertwined hands.

"Do ye think it is the only way?" he asked.

"I think it's one way," she said. The blood pounded against her palm. In order to use the blood magic again, she'd need her stone. "I left my piece of the keystone on the table."

He stood then, reaching into his sporran and pulling out something. He held his hand out to her. Resting in his palm was her piece of the keystone smudged with her blood.

"While ye slept, I retrieved it for ye."

"You are full of surprises, Jamie MacLeod." She plucked it from his hand.

"Aye." He grinned when he said it, showing off that deep dimple that was quickly becoming her favorite feature. "Now, if ye wish to use it, let me be here with ye when ye do."

"So you can catch me when I fall?" She said it in jest.

He nodded. "Aye, lass. And I will."

Her stomach fluttered. She wasn't sure what to say to that. The emotions rolling through her were almost too much to handle. She needed to focus on one thing—the stone and finding the truth. She held up her bandaged hand.

"Will you untie the bandage? I'm afraid I can't do it one-handed." It was a lie, which he probably knew, but it was the only way she could think of to get him closer to her, to feel his touch against hers.

"Ye wish to do this now?"

"Why not? My hand is still bleeding. Might as well take advantage of that."

He hesitated, his fingers hovering over the knot. "And…what do I tell yer sisters should anything happen to ye?"

That was a good question. She bit her lower lip. "Tell them I insisted. That I wanted to seek the truth about my vision. None of that will be necessary, though, because I'll be fine."

He looked less than convinced but went about untying the knot on the linen bandage anyway. With a slow and careful touch, he unwound it. The cool air of the chamber hit her wound, making her suck in a sharp breath. The slice in her palm still oozed.

"Chloe said when she had her vision, she and Malcolm were touching. Perhaps that would help keep me grounded."

She rose to her full height and placed the stone in the center of her bleeding palm. "Take my hand, Jamie."

He did, lacing their fingers. Her hand closed around the stone and then they waited.

Nothing happened. She counted her heartbeats as she waited, listening, holding her breath. Her gaze flickered up to his intense one. She had almost given up when the stone began to hum against her palm.

"Something's happening," she whispered "I think—"

The world spun into nothing but blurred motion and light, smearing along the edges of her vision. In the air directly in front of her, a stream of light shimmered as though the very space ahead of her was pulling apart. Light seeped through the crevices.

She stood on the craggy hill with her sisters. In her hand, the keystone, whole and glowing and humming. Before her, the horde of men with their swords and spears and other sharp weapons. At the head of it, MacDonald holding aloft his glowing great axe.

"Ye cannae think to defeat me, lass," he shouted from his mount. "I come to finish what my ancestor started. I will summon the darkness and take over these lands."

He slashed his great axe through the air where the light glittered, cleaving through time and space. Sparks burst, like fireworks in the sky, and then the seam exploded with light and opened. All manner of dark creatures poured out into the world. Winged ones. Fanged ones. Horned ones. Evil ones.

The army charged. Jamie and his brothers went into action. She watched, helpless, as all three of the MacLeod brothers rushed toward the swarm to attack.

"Do something, Brianna!" Evie said.

But what? What could she do?

They never made it to attack MacDonald and his army. They were all three slaughtered by the creatures of the night.

A scream ripped from her throat. Next to her, both Evie and Chloe cried out with their distress.

"Now you see the future," the woman said. It was the same voice who had spoken to her before.

"Who are you?" Brianna demanded.

"Athea is my name. I am the Goddess of the Future."

She lifted her arms out from her sides, her palms upward toward a sky shrouded in darkness. When she did, everything around the two of them slowed, the blurring motion coming to a crawl.

"I have the power of the Future, as do you."

"What does that mean?"

"It means, Brianna of Clan Sinclair, you have the power within you to shift the timeline, to prevent or bring about certain destinies." She motioned to the strange creatures continuing to pour through the rip in time. "You can change this outcome, now that you've seen it. You know *what MacDonald will do. And you know how to prevent it. For if you do not, you will all die."*

"I don't—"

Athea turned back to her, clutched her by the shoulders. "You do. Never forget that. You are prepared for what is to come. Fight the darkness. Save the land."

The vision ended. Brianna groaned with the pain lancing through her from head to toe. When she opened her eyes, she realized she was cradled against Jamie's chest and they were on the floor by the hearth. The tray had been knocked off. Food scattered along the floor. Ale pooled in a puddle.

"I've got ye." He clutched her tight.

So tight. Being in his arms made her feel safe. She reached up with her good hand, clutching his tunic in her fist. He smelled of leather and heather.

"Are ye all right, lass? What did ye see?"

"I saw…your death."

CHAPTER FOURTEEN

A N HOUR LATER, Brianna sat curled in the chair by the great hall fire, her legs tucked underneath her. She held a steaming mug of something that smelled a lot like weak herbal tea between her cold hands. The steam rose from the cup, curling around her nose and warming her face.

After her second vision, she was inconsolable. Her tears had long since dried but her throat was raw. Mostly, she was embarrassed she had fallen into such distress in front of Jamie. She would never live that down.

Jamie didn't know what else to do with her, so he scooped her up and carried her to the great hall where the others were having their evening meal.

Evie took one look at her and scurried off to the kitchen. Chloe sat mute and ashen next to Malcolm with her hand on his, peering at her with large, round emerald eyes, as though she hadn't a clue what to say to her. Truthfully, Brianna wasn't sure what to say, either.

Callum sat at the head of the table. Calm, quiet, stoic.

They all waited for her to speak with expectant looks on their faces.

"Well?" Chloe finally said. "Are you going to tell us what this is all about? Or is all this drama for nothing?"

"Chlo." Evie's tone was one of warning.

Brianna flashed her sister a glare but said nothing.

"She had a second vision," Jamie said.

He'd parked himself beside her, one hand on her shoulder to comfort her. She liked it there.

"Another vision?" Evie drew her brows together.

"Of the future." She managed to croak out the words.

"If I dinnae ken any better, I'd say the lass was in her cups," Malcolm said.

"She wasna drinking the ale," Jamie said, defending her.

She dropped her feet to the floor and placed her cup on the table with a thump. "I saw the future. In that future, we all die."

Her tone was matter-of-fact, as though she were reporting on nothing more than the fine weather. Her gaze alighted on each and every face. As she did, she reached for Jamie's hand, lacing their fingers together. In her weakened state, she drew her strength from him.

"Tell us, Brianna, about your second vision." Evie was calm, controlled, as she sat next to her husband with her hands folded in her lap.

So she did. She told them everything about how the world seemed to blur around them—the three of them standing on the craggy hill facing the MacDonald's massive army. When she described the glittering seam in the space in front of them, Chloe snapped to attention.

"That's what I saw in my vision of the past," she said. "A temporal rift in space. MacDonald wants to open a portal to the Realm of Chaos."

"Yes," Brianna agreed. "And he does. When he does, dark creatures spill into our world. He wants to use them to take over the lands. He wants to control all of the Highlands."

Callum made a noise of disbelief. "I will be dead before he conquers my lands."

"And that's exactly what he wants," Brianna said, pinning him with her best stern look. "He wants you and your brothers dead. The only thing standing in his way right now are three pieces of stone."

"You said in your vision the stone was whole again," Chloe pointed out.

She nodded. "I did. And it was. Which means, we have to find a way to put it back together."

But she was uncertain what would happen once they did that.

She also didn't mention to them Athea seemed to think she was the one who had the power to shift the timeline. It was hard to forget those words ringing through her mind. Every time they came back to her, her stomach cramped with a wave of sickness.

She didn't want to be that person. And though the goddess told her she had the power within her, she hadn't a clue how to use that power.

"There has to be more to this prophecy than we know," Evie said. She turned to Callum. "Did Hamish mention anything else about it?"

He shook his head but it was Jamie who spoke next.

"There is more to it, brother," he said. "Ye dinnae care to remember." Then he glanced at Malcolm. "But we do."

Malcolm looked deep in thought as he tried to recall the words. "All I remember is something about a maiden."

"*When the stars align and twilight fades, a maiden from the future comes. Through time's veil, her path she will find, with heart and courage, to mend all Time.*"

As Jamie said it, his gaze met Brianna's. In that moment, her heart leapt into her throat to beat a wicked beat. He granted her a knee-melting smile. She sank back into the chair by the fire, her strength drained.

"You need to eat something, Brianna," Evie said in her mothering tone.

"Aye, eat, lass." Jamie pulled a chair next to her. He handed her the cup.

Taking it, she took a sip, letting it warm her.

"I'll fetch you some pottage." Evie started to rise, but Callum put a hand on hers.

"I will," he said and gave her a stern look that said she'd done enough for one day. He pushed from the table and left them to head to the kitchen.

Unease shifted through her as she was aware of all eyes on her, as though waiting for her to say something profound.

"I'm too tired to eat," she said. She reached a hand for Jamie.

He took the signal and helped her to her feet.

"Bri—" Evie objected.

"Later," she snapped.

Jamie led her back up the stairs and to his bedchamber, where he closed the door with a snap. He helped her to the chair by the fire, stoking it to make it come alive once again.

"Yer sister is right, lass. Ye need to eat to keep yer strength."

He bent to pick up the mess she'd left behind when she had her second vision. He righted the table between them and slid the tray back on top of it.

"I know, but I...I needed away from all those prying, expectant eyes. I should help you clean that up."

"Nay." He scooped up the discarded food and dropped it on the tray.

It appeared he or someone had already cleaned up the spilled ale. When he stood straight again, there was concern deep in his eyes.

"I'll fetch ye the food. Then we can talk more."

He picked up the tray with the old food and slipped out of the room and closed the door behind him, not waiting for her reply. She expelled a breath, the energy leaving her as she gazed into the fire. She didn't want to talk about the visions anymore. She didn't want to talk about the damn keystone anymore. All she wanted was to be left alone.

And truly, she wanted to return to her life in the Caribbean. She was not cut out to carry such weight. She was not the one to alter destinies or shift timelines. As these thoughts consumed her, she realized with some discomfort she had left her piece of the keystone behind once again.

Jamie returned and placed fresh food on the table in front of her. It was a steaming bread bowl of something that smelled delicious. Next to it, fresh baked bread. He poured two tankards of ale and took the chair opposite her.

"Eat," he insisted.

"I can take care of myself." She frowned, pouting into her bread bowl.

"Aye, I ken that. Now, eat." There was the glint of annoyance in his eyes. "Or I'll feed ye myself."

She took that for the threat it was and scooted to the edge of the chair. Taking up the wooden spoon, she ate. She hadn't realized how ravenous she was until she had that first taste.

"I think we should visit the tapestry room to see if anything has changed," he said.

Brianna didn't want to see if anything had changed. She didn't want to see if something was foretold in the woven fabric of the tapestries. The thought of walking into that room sent fear skipping through her. She clutched her spoon, her muscles tight as she peered at him.

"And then what?"

"And then we strategize."

But Brianna had another idea. "I think the three of us need to put the keystone back together."

Alarm crossed his features. "'Tis a dangerous idea."

"And the only idea that may give us the answers we need. We'll have to activate it with the blood magic, of course." Even as she said it, her bandaged hand throbbed.

"No," he said firmly. "I will no allow it."

Surprise flickered though her. His features were hard and unyielding. "But if it's the only way, then we should at least try."

He clenched his jaw, the muscles ticking along the edge as he considered her words. "Mayhap when yer stronger."

He was right about that. The two visions had left her in a weakened state. She polished off the rest of the bread bowl, her stomach full for the first time in days. There was something endearing about the way he fussed over her. She liked it far too much.

He was still too young for her.

She rose on unsteady legs, intending to return to the tapestry room to sleep and rest. But when she did, he got to his feet, too.

"Just where do ye think yer going, lass?"

"To my room."

She took one step toward the door and immediately crumpled to the floor with her utter exhaustion. He was there in a flash, though, his arm around her.

"Ye'll sleep here," he said.

"But—"

"I'll hear no more."

He swept her up, once again carrying her to the bed. When she was settled, she waved him off and kicked off her shoes.

"I don't suppose you have something I can sleep in besides my clothes."

She still wore her jeans and sweater from her world.

Jamie rummaged through an oversized chest at the foot of the bed and came up with one of his tunics. He offered it to her.

A strange sensation tingled through her as she looked at it, wondering if it would fit her. He was, after all, quite tall and broad.

"Thanks." She took it from him, clutching the material against her chest.

"I'll leave ye be while ye change, then." He started for the door, then paused and turned back. He pulled something out of his sporran. It was her piece of the stone. Once again, he'd picked it up for her. "Ye might want to look after this better, lass."

He winked as he said it. She plucked it from his hand and nodded. He was right, of course. Moira had told her to keep it safe and never let it out of her sight. So far, she'd left it behind twice. He left her alone so she could change.

CHAPTER FIFTEEN

IT WAS AN awkward feeling wearing Jamie's shirt.

Well, not exactly awkward. She'd worn men's shirts before but that was after sleeping together and it was a handy thing to pick up off the floor and slip on while she raided the refrigerator.

There was something *different* about wearing Jamie's shirt. Or tunic, rather, she supposed it was called. She wasn't sure why it felt different but it felt a bit scandalous.

They certainly hadn't slept together. Not that it hadn't crossed her mind. It had on numerous occasions. He was young and attractive, not to mention attentive in every way. She had a hard time forgetting that sweet kiss he'd placed in the center of her palm when they were standing by the loch. Or the way he'd held her in his arms and kissed her with a fiery passion that burned deep and hot through her.

Remembering it made heat wash over her body in a tidal wave for which she was unprepared. She huffed and shoved off the blankets, kicking her legs out and curling on her side to stare at the door. He hadn't come back yet.

She'd placed the jagged piece of keystone on the table beside the bed. Staring at it now, she was starting to resent that little rock. It had wreaked havoc in her normal, happy, quiet life. Something Moira had said haunted her.

Without you, all will be lost.

Add that to the two visions she'd had and she was not liking this prophecy one bit.

She huffed again and flopped to her back to stare at the overhead canopy of the bed. The thick curtains on each pole were made of velvet. When drawn, she supposed they would make the bed a cozy cocoon for—

She shoved that thought away.

There was no way she and Jamie were going to get *that* cozy.

The door scraped open and he reappeared. Her heart leapt into her throat. Delight skipped through her, as though she were a teenager again gazing at her first crush. She sat up, drawing her knees to her chest and watched as he closed the door. Their eyes met and something passed between them she tried hard not to acknowledge.

His gaze lingered on hers, then dipped as he examined her sitting there, her knees cradled against her chest. A sensuous light flickered through his devastating eyes and something told her she was not getting out of this bed anytime soon.

A grin crept up the corner of his mouth.

It wouldn't be wise to allow herself to be caught under his seductive spell but she figured it was far too late for that. She was ensorcelled.

"Yer no sleeping?" he asked at last.

"Not yet."

He went to the hearth and poked the embers, giving them some life.

"Have you ever been so tired you couldn't sleep?" she asked.

"I have."

"What do you do when that happens to you?"

He reached for a tankard of ale. "I drink." He raised it in a cheers motion and then downed it.

She giggled. "Maybe that's what I need, then."

Without asking, he poured her a tankard and brought it to her. She took it from him and downed it in one long quaff. The weak ale wasn't good but it would do. When she emptied it, she handed it back to him.

His eyebrows lifted as he peered into the empty tankard. He looked impressed.

"Another?" he asked.

"Better keep it coming."

"Ye best be careful, lass. Ye'll be as fou as a piper."

"Well, if it helps me sleep, then I'm all for it."

He laughed, a deep melodious laugh that rumbled around in his broad chest and it did something for her. A lot of somethings. She was certain it wasn't the ale that made her stomach flutter. It was Jamie.

"What does that mean—fou as a piper?"

"Means drunk." He granted her a wicked smile.

He handed her a full tankard. This time, she sipped it and allowed herself to relax. He lowered himself into the chair by the fire.

"Where will you sleep?" she asked.

"Here."

"In that chair?" she asked, unable to hide her surprise.

"Aye."

"No," she snapped. "You can sleep next to me." She patted the feather mattress beside her.

His surprised gaze lifted to hers.

"And don't tell me it wouldn't be proper," she added. "I can keep my hands to myself."

A devilish grin crossed his face. "Aye, lass, but do ye think I can?"

That sounded like a challenge. One she wanted to accept.

"Well," she said, slowly, a grin spreading, "I suppose we'll have to wait and see."

Brianna half hoped he would not be able to keep his hands to himself. There was a sense of curiosity about the young Scotsman as well as an attraction she was unable to deny.

He pulled off his boots and dropped them in front of him where he still sat in the chair. They eyed each other from across the room, which made her heart kick into a rapid beat. His gaze was unreadable. Slowly, he unfolded his tall frame from the chair and took long, methodical steps toward her. His gaze never left her face.

When he paused in front of her, she tipped her head back to look up at him. A shiver skipped through her. Not because she was cold, but because it was a shiver of need and desire.

"Did ye ken yer eyes are like the color of winter sky in the morn?" His voice was low, sultry.

Her breath hitched, pooling at the base of her throat. She was aware of the unusual color of her eyes. All her life, people had commented on them. They were a pale blue—giving her the look of cold calculation to her enemies. For those who were not intimidated by her eye color, they didn't bother to hide their fascination. No one, though, likened them to a winter sky.

"Are they?" she asked, trying to ignore the rapid-fire beat of her pulse.

"I've no' seen the likes," he said.

Handsome. The word drifted unbidden through her mind as she gazed up at him. His chiseled face was all sharp lines and rugged angles, as if carved from stone, and yet his eyes were a soft doe-brown that caught the light in a way that made her breath catch in her throat. And when he smiled, he showed off two deep dimples on either side of his oh-so-kissable mouth.

What was he doing to her?

"My mother had eyes this color." She didn't know why she told him that. It'd never mattered to anyone else before.

A dark brow lifted. "Aye?"

"She and my father were killed in an accident several years ago."

Sorrow flickered over his features. Why did she tell him that? She never spoke of her parents to anyone. She didn't want his sorrow or his pity. But something about the way he looked at her chipped away at her inner defenses.

"But you likely know that already from Evie or Chloe." She scooted away from him as she said it, reaching the top blanket and pulling it back.

"They dinnae speak of yer mam and da."

That stopped her cold. "They don't?"

"Not to me."

He walked around to the other side of the bed and pulled back the blankets on his side. Then he sat on the edge. She watched the muscles in his back as he removed the tartan, letting it pool on the floor beside him. Underneath he wore a tunic. He pulled this off over his head and dropped it to the floor with the tartan.

With her cheeks flaming, she turned away. She didn't need to see that expanse of golden skin or the way his muscles flexed along his back and biceps. Nope, she didn't need to see that at all.

She realized wearing his tunic was a huge mistake. Because now all she thought about was the way the soft material brushed against her bare skin underneath. Her modern clothes were in a neat pile on the chair opposite the one Jamie'd vacated.

After another sip of ale, she placed the tankard on the table next to the stone, the offensive stone that had altered her life and would, apparently, continue to alter her life.

She slid under the blankets and pulled them up to her chin, turning away from him in the hopes she would not be tempted by his hard, muscled body.

"Good night." Her voice was a bit more gruff than she intended.

The rustle of material next to her and then the bounce of the feather mattress indicated he got up from the bed. She snuck a glance in his direction to see him walking around the room and snuffing out the candles. The only thing that remained was the fire blazing in the hearth. He wore nothing but his birthday suit, which made her almost stop breathing. She stifled the gasp that wanted to erupt. He was glorious in every way imaginable.

He returned to the bed and settled next to her.

"Good night, lass," he said on a sigh.

As if he were disappointed she clung to the edge of the bed, afraid to get close to him.

She had never been afraid to get close to a man before. What was wrong with her?

She rolled to her other side. His back was to her, the blankets tucked under his arm. The firelight flickered over that expanse of perfect skin.

Without thinking, she reached out to touch him. Her hand landed on his upper arm. On reflex, his arm muscles tightened under her touch. Then he stiffened.

Whatever silent communication it was that passed between them, she didn't know. But he rolled toward her and reached for her, pulling her close.

Even in the shadowy darkness, she saw the smirk on his face.

"I thought ye could keep yer hands to yerself."

She grinned. "I guess I lied."

Her mouth met his in a searing kiss that was undeniable. His arms slid around her, pulling her even closer, if that were possible. Her mind screamed for her to put a stop to this madness, but her body was unwilling to listen to that nonsense. Her heart was already pounding so hard she thought it would burst through her chest.

She shimmied out of his tunic and tossed it off the side of the bed. The next to go was her modern lingerie—which was not her normal satin and lace. When she had gone on her shopping spree in Edinburgh, she'd opted for simple and comfortable cotton.

Not that any of that mattered to Jamie. He had never seen anything like that before and likely didn't care about what she wore under her sweater and jeans.

He kissed her with long, soft kisses. Impatience bubbled through her, but she sensed he wanted to take things slow. He wanted to savor her, to taste her, to bask in the glow of this one perfect moment.

"Jamie?"

"Shh, lass. I want to worship ye."

Worship?

The blood rushed to her head, making her lightheaded. It was, quite possibly, the sweetest thing a man had ever said to her. She wasn't sure how to feel. She wasn't sure *what* to feel.

The heat pounded through her, pooling in her abdomen. Normally, when she was with someone new, there was a frenzy that rose to a fever pitch. The men she had been with did not take their time and they certainly did not want to worship her.

"But—" she started.

"Shhh. I've waited for ye my whole life."

He kissed her again. He tasted like the weak ale and smelled like heather and woodsmoke. Her hand pressed against his chest. Below it was the frantic pounding of his heart, matching hers.

Ah, so he was as excited as she was. That was, at least, good to know.

His kisses moved from her mouth to her cheek, her earlobe, down her neck, and over her collarbone. With a gentle nudge, he pushed her to her back. She melted against the bed as he hovered over her, continuing to kiss her with those long, slow, drugging kisses. Her eyes fluttered closed. She reached up, letting her fingers tangle in his long hair.

He hummed his response against her belly.

Down the expanse of her body he went until he was at the apex of her thighs. Her skin erupted in gooseflesh, that tingling sensation shuddering through her as she anticipated his next move.

And he did not disappoint.

She bit her lip to keep from crying out the moment his tongue flicked over her. His mouth did magical, wonderful things to her, making every worry, every fear, every thought flee from her mind.

It didn't matter she was in the past.

It didn't matter he was younger than her.

All that mattered was him and this perfect, intimate moment.

She sucked in a cold breath, a moan escaping her as her hands tangled in his hair. She released her inhibitions. She allowed him to please her in a way she had never allowed before. And it was so liberating.

After long, drugging moments, he kissed his way back up her body. He paused to pay homage to the flat plane of her abdomen and then he worshipped her breasts. Their lips met in a frenzy as his long, lean body moved on top of hers. She opened herself and wrapped her legs around his waist. But he didn't take her right away. He kissed her, his long, lean body pressing against hers, warming her. She had never experienced the likes. Her previous experiences had been nothing more than carnal acts. This…this was something more. This felt like it meant something.

Finally, he slid inside her, taking his time with each thrust. Her hands tangled in his long locks as she clutched him to her, her muscles tightened around him. The climax was upon her before she was able to stop it. She was overcome. There was no holding back. His followed shortly thereafter.

And when it was all over, he stilled, peering down at her with a satisfied grin.

"I'm glad ye lied, lass."

Brianna was unable to stop the giggle that erupted.

AFTERWARD, THEY SLEPT. At some point, Brianna awoke cocooned in warmth against Jamie. The fire had long since died in the hearth, leaving the room chilled. It made her burrow deeper under the blankets, soaking up his warmth with her hand on his chest as it rose and fell with his rhythmic breathing.

He still slept which gave her time to think.

She allowed herself to be swept off her feet and succumb to his charms. She should have had more restraint but his kisses had drugged her senseless and made her fall for him hard and fast. She understood the first stirrings deep in her gut but refused to accept this was anything more than infatuation.

Certainly, it was not love.

She hadn't been in love in years. She had carefully built walls around her heart after her failed marriage to keep those feelings out. Instead, she'd found emotionally unavailable men with commitment phobias and allowed herself to be used until they were ready to move on. It suited her nomadic lifestyle as she'd traveled across the Caribbean.

What was her lifestyle now? It had crossed her mind she needed to find a way to return to her time, to her home. But then she didn't have a home to go back to, did she? Her childhood home sold years ago after the death of her parents. She had split the money with Evie and Chloe and then they'd gone their separate ways.

Now, here she was, stuck in the past prophesied as the one to "fix" the timeline. To make matters more complicated was Jamie. A medieval man who managed to rock her world and shatter all her resistance. A man who gave her adoring looks. A man who wanted to care for all her needs.

Those walls she had carefully constructed were beginning to crumble, the first few stones cracking and falling.

How could she have allowed this to happen? She hardly knew Jamie.

And yet, there was a part of her that sensed she had known him all her life. A part of her that found comfort in his arms. A part of her that wanted him forever in her life.

Next to her, he stirred. Her gaze traveled over his strong jaw to his face as his eyes blinked open. When he looked at her, a lazy, sexy smile tugged at his lips, showing off his two deep dimples.

"Yer still here." Under the covers, he reached for her, his hand sliding over her hip. "And yer still naked."

She flushed, hot. Why did him saying that to her make heat pound through her?

"So are you," she replied, her bandaged palm flattening on his chest.

The warmth of his body still brushed hers. He groaned his appreciation as he turned to her under the blankets, his arms sliding around her and pulling her close.

"What will we do about it, lass?"

She was powerless to resist. Her response was to plant long, slow kisses at the base of his throat, which he clearly appreciated. His arms tightened around her, his arousal evident between them.

"I have a few ideas," she murmured against his neck.

And just like that, she lost her head again.

CHAPTER SIXTEEN

B RIANNA AWOKE ALONE in the bed. She sat up on her elbows. In the fireplace, the embers glowed and smoldered. His boots were gone, which meant he was likely somewhere in them, along with his tartan.

She pushed off the blankets and swung her legs off the side of the bed. Her bandaged palm itched as though it were healing. She removed the bandage to see the slice was pink and almost fully healed.

How odd.

She tossed aside the strips of linen and then bent to pick up Jamie's tunic. As she pulled it on over her head, there was a knock on the door. It startled her. Her heart kicked into a frantic beat.

"Yes?" she called.

The door pushed open and Evie popped her head inside. "Oh, good! You're awake."

She grinned as she stepped inside carrying an armload of clothes.

"Am I disturbing you?" Her gaze took in Brianna's appearance. Her brows lifted as she gave her a knowing smile.

"I just woke up. Look." She held up her almost healed hand, trying to distract her from her obviously disheveled appearance.

Evie moved toward her to get a closer look, dropping the pile of clothes on the bed next to her. She took her hand in hers, her thumb grazing across the wound.

"It healed as fast as Chloe's."

"You've seen this before?"

She nodded. "I think it has something to do with the stone and the blood magic."

Brianna took her hand away and rested it in her lap. She wanted to pretend her piece of the keystone wasn't resting on the table, but it was impossible.

"I brought you clothes," she said.

"I have clothes," Brianna replied, nodding to the neatly folded pile in the chair.

"You'll want something warmer."

Evie held up a pair of woolen stockings. Brianna eyed the pile next to her with a suspicious eye. Her sister had abandoned her modern life altogether and embraced this medieval world. Chloe, apparently, had followed in her footsteps. Now, Evie wanted her to do the same.

Brianna wasn't convinced she was going to stay, though, despite her lovely night with Jamie. A lovely night that seemed endless and wonderful. The memories would not leave her alone.

"You're going to dress me like you, aren't you?" she asked, eyeing her medieval outfit.

"You need layers here. I had to convince Chloe, too. I can help you dress."

The last thing she wanted was her baby sister helping her get dressed. "I don't need help."

"Brianna—"

"I don't," she interrupted.

Evie held up her hands in surrender. "If you insist. When you're dressed, we have breakfast in the great hall."

"Fine."

Evie headed back to the door, then paused and turned back to her. "Don't hurt him, Bri."

She snapped her head up to look at her sister. "What do you mean?"

"Jamie. Despite his roguish attitude, he has a good heart." She clasped her hands in front of her round belly.

Heat flushed through her, pounding in her cheeks. It was clear Evie knew what they'd been up to last night. Of course, sitting on the edge of his bed in his tunic was the biggest sign of all.

"I don't plan to," she said. "And what makes you think I will?"

Evie shrugged, as if she had some secret knowledge she didn't want to admit. She headed back to the door and pulled it open. As she disappeared through it, she left Brianna wondering what, if anything, she knew.

A FRUSTRATING HOUR later, she made her way out of the bed chamber and down the curved stairs. She'd taken care to place the piece of her keystone in her dress pocket and not leave it behind. After her vision and talking to Jamie the night before, she had an idea about the stones.

Chloe and Evie were in the great hall. The men were nowhere to be found, perhaps tending to their manly, medieval duties. Both looked up at her as she made her way into the room and picked a chair. Evie sat near the head of the table, Chloe on the other side.

"Coffee?" Brianna asked, hope pricking through her.

"No coffee in this time." Evie motioned to the kettle on the table. "But there is my herbal tea."

"Herbal tea?" That must have been what she'd had earlier that smelled faintly like weak tea.

"Evie learned how to make herbal tea," Chloe said, accepting her cup. She sipped it, then held the cup between her hands.

"You did?"

Brianna tipped her head as she examined the younger twin. Evie had been born three minutes after Chloe, something she wasn't sure either of them knew. Color pinkened her cheeks as she took her cup and perched on the edge of the chair between them, like a proper lady.

"There are plenty of herbs in the garden," Evie said. "I learned by doing."

Brianna waved off the drink, disappointed as the need for a strong cup of coffee pounded through her. She reached for one of the little cakes on a nearby tray as Chloe watched in silence.

"I have an idea about the stone," she announced.

"You think we should put the pieces together," Evie said.

"I do."

"We don't know what will happen when we do," Chloe pointed out.

"We should find out then," Brianna replied. She gave Evie a pointed look. "But you should let me handle it."

"Why?"

"Because you're pregnant," she said.

"I'm fine." Evie waved away the notion.

"If the stone has the power I think it does, then you need to let me be the one to do it," Brianna said. If the vision she'd had carried any weight, then she was the one who needed the whole stone anyway.

"Are you expecting us to just hand over our pieces then?" Chloe's tone was less than friendly.

"I'm suggesting we give it a try," she said.

"And then what?" Chloe folded her arms over her chest, defiant.

"And then we see what happens." Brianna pinpointed her with her gaze.

"The stone will likely need blood magic to work," Evie said. "Your hand only recently healed."

"I can cut it again if I need to." Even as she said it, her palm tingled. "Has there been any change in the tapestries?"

"No." Evie gave a shake of her head. "Nothing has changed. I checked this morning."

"Is it true you saw them die?" Chloe asked, her voice echoing in the great hall. Worry creased her face.

"Yes." She broke a cake in half and popped it into her mouth.

She didn't want to remember that. It was a terrible, bloody scene. Even though it was a vision, she was still able to smell death and hear the screech of the winged creatures that poured in from the Realm of Chaos. She was the one responsible for stopping that and she wasn't sure how yet.

That's why she wanted to put the keystone back into one piece.

"We should try it," Evie said.

"It's too dangerous," Chloe said. "Remember what happened when we put the two pieces together?"

"What happened?"

Brianna looked between the two of them but neither seemed to want to talk. Evie wrung her hands together.

"Rory MacDonald kidnapped the two of us," Evie said. "He took us to his stronghold to try to force us to hand over the pieces of the keystone."

"Because he wants to use them for himself," Chloe added.

"Yes," Evie added. "When we tried to escape, we put the pieces together. And then something strange happened to the both of us."

"It was like we were seeing through our eyes, but...not," Chloe added.

"As though we *were* the Triple Goddess. Or at least the Past and the Present," Evie interjected. "They started to glow and somehow we knew the words to chant."

"A chant?" Brianna asked.

"Yes. I don't recall the words now."

Clearly, there was more to this story than she was getting. She had so many questions. The first being how were they kidnapped under the noses of two of the most fearsome Highlanders around? Callum and Malcolm were alpha to the core. But she didn't have a chance to ask anything as Chloe continued.

"Nor I," she said. "It was as though it'd happened to someone else. We were able to use the power of the stone to create a portal and escape from the MacDonald stronghold and return here." She cut a glance to Evie. "Should I tell her about Bruce?"

"Who the hell is Bruce?" Brianna couldn't help but feel as though they'd left out a lot of information.

Evie gave Chloe a solemn nod. Her emerald gaze shifted to Brianna, giving her the impression this was news she did not want to hear. Whatever it was.

"When I lived in Edinburgh, I dated a man named Bruce. Turns out, he had been using me to steal my piece. He and his brother, John, invaded my apartment one night. He followed me through from the future to here. I think he's helping the MacDonald clan."

A flash of heat washed over here as she stared at Chloe. "John MacDonald?" she asked.

Chloe nodded.

The blood drained from her head so fast, she saw dark pin-pricks. With a groan, she laid her forehead on the table in front of her.

"What is it? What's wrong?" Alarm sounded through Evie's voice.

"I know who John MacDonald is." She lifted her head and looked at both her sisters. "I visited your museum, Chloe, looking for answers. I talked to the director."

"You talked to Director Greaves?" Surprise etched on her features as though she could not believe Brianna would do something like that on her behalf.

"She was less than helpful." She pressed her lips together as she remembered the aloof woman who wanted nothing more than to shoo her away. "But it was the only place I knew to start. I knew Evie was at the gala that night. I thought maybe I could retrace her steps to see if I could figure out what had happened to the two of you. By that time, I'd already visited Mystic Treasures and received the piece of stone from Moira."

"What did the director tell you?" Chloe asked.

"She said your disappearance had nothing to do with the museum. That it was a personal matter I should let the police handle."

Disappointment flooded her face as she sat back in the chair, holding a half-eaten oat cake.

"You said you met John MacDonald?" Evie asked.

"Yes. In the museum. He said the stone called to him. We were on the terrace when he tried to take it from me. It was glowing and humming. That's when I activated it and ended up here," Brianna said.

"Bruce MacDonald said the same thing to me. He said it called to him. He didn't follow you, did he?" There was real concern in Chloe's voice.

Brianna shook her head. "I don't think so."

"Why would the pieces of the keystone call to the MacDonalds if they were meant for us?" Evie asked.

It was a question none of them could answer.

"Perhaps they have some sort of magic in their blood that senses it," Brianna suggested. Both of them looked at her as though she'd lost her mind. "It's the only thing that seems to make sense to me. Maybe it's tied to that glowing great axe somehow."

"There is clearly a piece of the puzzle we're missing," Evie said.

"And that missing puzzle piece should be as easy as putting the stone back together to see what happens," Brianna suggested.

Silence stretched between them. Evie sat rigid, her hands in her lap. Chloe fiddled with the half-eaten oat cake. Brianna was certain this was the right path. So certain, in fact, she reached into the pocket of her gown and brought out her piece. She placed it on the table in front of her.

After a moment of hesitation, Chloe did the same.

Evie's gaze skipped from Brianna to Chloe. She took a deep breath, expelled it. Then she brought out her piece of the stone and placed it on the table in front of her.

"Well," Evie said, drawing out the word. "I suppose there's only one way to find out."

CHAPTER SEVENTEEN

EACH OF THEM picked up their piece of the stone and moved into the center of the great hall. Brianna's stomach was in knots. The three of them faced each other: Evie to her left. Chloe to her right. None of the pieces were glowing or humming.

Brianna was the first to hold up her stone. Evie pressed her piece against it, then Chloe. They held the pieces together and waited.

But nothing happened.

After several long moments, Evie dropped hers and clutched it in her fist.

"Maybe we need the blood magic," she suggested.

Brianna glanced down at her freshly healed palm and winced. If the stone needed blood magic, she'd have to cut her hand again. A quick scan of the table showed nothing sharp enough to do that.

"We need a knife," Chloe said.

"For what?" It was Malcolm's deep voice that boomed through the great hall.

All three of them jumped. Chloe glanced at him, her cheeks turning pink as she gave him a sheepish grin. He took in the scene and quickly assessed what they were up to as he moved deeper into the room.

"What do ye think yer doing, lass?" His question was directed to Chloe but his gaze alighted on each of them.

"We're going to put the stone back together. Or try," Evie said, sounding confident.

But Malcolm was shaking his head before she finished. His gaze was fixed on Chloe. "Ye ken what it does to ye when using the stone."

"I do, but I agree with Evie. We have to try. It could give us the answers we need," she said. In an uncharacteristic movement, she batted her lashes at him. "Then maybe we can be rid of it."

His jaw clenched, the muscles flexing along the edge. Finally, he pulled the dagger from the sheath at his side. It was so well hidden, Brianna hadn't noticed he carried it.

"'Tis against my better judgment," he said with a hint of warning. "Mayhap I should get Callum and Jamie, too."

"That's not necessary," Evie said in a breezy tone.

"Och, aye, I think it is, my lady wife."

Callum must have overheard their conversation as he entered the great hall from behind Brianna. She cast a glance over her shoulder to see Jamie right behind him. Callum moved to stand next to Evie, his sharp blue-eyed gaze lingering on her. Jamie paused next to her, giving her a sense of warmth and comfort.

"What are ye planning, then?" Callum asked.

"We want to put the keystone back together," she said. "I think it's time."

Callum made no effort to hide his concern as he looked at her. Evie slid her hand over her round belly.

"I'll be fine," she said, her voice soft as she gazed up at him.

He looked unconvinced.

Brianna said, "Maybe it's best all of us are together. Since this prophecy names both our clans."

She sensed Jamie edging closer to her.

"Aye," Malcolm said with a nod. "I agree with Brianna."

"All right, then," Evie said, as though she were in charge. "That's what we'll do. But we need the blood magic to activate it, I think."

She held out her scarred palm. In the flickering candlelight from the candelabras, Brianna saw the silvery scar where she had cut herself. She glanced Brianna's way with a look that told her she wanted her to do the same. Brianna held out her freshly scarred palm. Next, it was Chloe's turn.

"I'm no so sure this is a grand idea," Malcolm said as he moved next to Chloe. "But I'll do it anyway."

She grinned her thanks at him as he placed the tip of the dagger in her palm. One quick swipe and her skin was cut. The blood seeped through instantly. Then he did the same with Brianna and Evie.

"Now what?" Brianna asked.

"Place the stone against your bloody palm and clench your fist," Evie instructed.

She did so and waited. A moment later, a low hum started. But not just from her. From all three of them. Light seeped through Chloe's clenched fist. Evie's followed next. Brianna lifted her clenched fist to see the light pulsing through hers as well.

She opened her fingers and held her hand out. Her sisters did the same, their fingertips brushing. Each of the stones were humming and pulsing light.

With her free hand, Evie picked up the stone smeared with her blood and held it up. Following her lead, she and Chloe did the same. After a moment of hesitation, Chloe pressed her piece against Evie's. They both looked to her. With her gut clenched into a tight knot, she pressed the final piece into place.

There was an audible *click* and then a flash of light that blinded them. Brianna squinted against the brightness, trying to make out the shape of the stone. It was whole once again.

White hot heat swarmed up her arm, then flooded her from head to toe. She cried out with the searing pain. Strong arms were on her—she assumed Jamie's.

Evie, too, cried out in pain, followed by Callum's deep voice growling, "God's teeth, woman."

Chloe whimpered, her body going limp, and Malcolm catching her before she hit the ground.

That was the last she recalled before the vision exploded through her mind.

The man wielded a great axe as he charged up the hill toward the castle ruins. The dilapidated towers were nothing more than jagged outlines as they stretched toward the darkened sky. Night flooded the area like spilled ink. There was only the waning moon to guide him but he forged on with his determination. Once he entered the crumbling castle walls, he halted, his breath seesawing in and out of him. Ahead, the roofless stone walls rose toward the night sky. Beyond, the cold sea nothing but a black chasm in the dark.

Standing before him in the center of the ruins were three women. Moira in the center. Athea to her left. Bridget to her right.

"We know why you have come, Morrogh MacDonald," Moira said.

His smile was a terrible one. "Do ye now, lass?"

Bridget said, her voice reedy and thin, "If you try to steal the Chronos Stone from us…"

"…you, your clan, and your descendants will be cursed for all time," Athea finished.

"If you try to kill us…" Moira said.

"…you, your clan, and your descendants will be cursed for all time," Bridget and Athea said together.

He laughed, a cruel sound echoing in the night through the ruins. "I havna come all this way to turn around and leave. I came for the power. I leave with the power."

Moira lifted her arms out to her sides. "Then there is no other choice."

The man charged, holding the great axe aloft. Together, the three women lifted their arms and repelled him with a burst of light. He stumbled backward but managed to maintain his footing. He shook it off, regrouped, and charged again.

Again, the women used a burst of light to drive him back. But he anticipated it this time and lifted his great axe to protect himself. The light—no, the magic—slammed into the steel of the axe. The weapon shuddered in his hand, vibrating up his arm with such a force it rattled his teeth. The weapon, though, absorbed the power and suddenly, it began to glow.

Athea sucked in a sharp breath. Bridget gasped with horror.

"The great axe!" Bridget cried.

"It was forged in the wilds of Éire." His face split into a wicked grin. "By the Tuatha Dé Danann themselves."

Moira's face remained impassive as she lifted her hands to the sky once more. But Bridget and Athea did not conceal their terror. It was unclear how someone like Morrogh MacDonald had obtained such a prized weapon.

"Hear me now, you of Clan MacDonald," Moira began. "By the light of the moon, and the gloom of shadows, I call upon the winds that whisper and wail."

Athea and Bridget stepped up next to her, lifting their hands to the sky along with her. The three of them spoke together, chanting the words that would forever seal the fate of Clan MacDonald.

"He who steals shall never keep. He who seeks what is not his will forever desire. His sons and daughters will eternally yearn. His sons and daughters will forever hear the call. Haunted by whispers. Blinded by fate. By our words, our will, our ancient law. So it is spoken. So mote it be."

A gust of wind blasted by Morrogh MacDonald, locking his destiny for all eternity.

From that moment on, his clan was cursed. He and his descendants would hear the call of the keystone while knowing it would forever be out of reach.

Moira dropped her arms to her sides and stared down at him with cold eyes. "Be gone, MacDonald. Never return. For if you do, it will be the end of your and your line forevermore."

He bared his teeth in a feral snarl, still clutching the glowing great axe. "One day, the keystone and control of all Time will belong to my clan."

"You may try," Moira said, her voice ice.

As the man retreated, the Triple Goddess watched.

"It is not over, sister," Athea said.

"He will return," Bridget added.

"Aye, my sisters," Moira said, her voice quiet in the night. "And we will be ready."

· · ·

CHAPTER EIGHTEEN

BRIANNA CAME BACK to herself. But it was difficult to open her eyes. The first thing she noticed was how badly her head throbbed with a deep, agonizing pain hammering her temples. She groaned. The second thing she noticed was her palm once again wrapped with linen bandages, as if someone had taken care to do that while she was unconscious. Her hand ached where Malcolm had sliced it with the tip of the dagger, where she had used the blood magic with her sisters to activate the stone and fall into the vision.

She wasn't quite sure where she was, but she felt strong arms wrapped around her, holding her close in a protective embrace.

The musky scent of leather and horses tickled her nose. *Jamie.*

"What—" Her voice was raw and raspy.

"Dinnae try to speak," Jamie said. He brushed a hand over her hair, which soothed her.

She cracked an eye open and looked into his concerned face. Beyond him was the wood-beamed ceiling of the great hall, which meant she was on the floor. A sudden pounding went through her as she thought of Chloe and Evie. She jerked, trying to push out of his arms.

"Stay still, lass."

"My sisters—"

"They're fine," he said.

But somewhere nearby, she heard a female whimper that

sounded like Chloe. And a sniff that might have been Evie. Her head rested against Jamie's broad chest as his arms tightened around her. She opened her eyes fully.

Across from her, Callum held Evie. Her face was buried against his chest as he cradled her in his arms.

Malcolm clutched Chloe, who still had her eyes closed and her brows drawn together as though she were in pain.

"Whatever the three of ye saw," Jamie said, his voice low, "it must have been something spectacular."

"It was…" Brianna began, but she wasn't quite sure how to explain it.

"The ancient past," Chloe croaked from her prone position in Malcolm's arms. "The true beginning."

"The curse of MacDonald," Evie added, her voice muffled against Callum's chest.

"A curse," Brianna agreed. "Morrogh MacDonald intended to steal the Chronos Stone from the Triple Goddess. In turn, they cursed him and his descendants to forever hear its call."

"His sons and daughters will eternally yearn," Chloe repeated.

And still Brianna had not shared with them that she was tied to the fate of the stone. Athea had told her she was the one to shift the timeline, to put things right again. But she still didn't understand how she'd do that.

It took some effort to turn her head and search for the keystone. She expected to see it on the floor. Instead, she saw nothing.

"Where's the stone?" she asked, her voice still weak.

"It broke again," Callum said.

"We retrieved the pieces," Malcolm added.

"I have yers," Jamie said, his voice soft in her ear. "'Tis safe, lass."

Jamie scooped her into his arms, then, cradled her against his chest. His body heat warmed her frigid bones.

"Put me down, Jamie."

"Nay," he said. "All of ye need rest."

She caught a glimpse of her sisters as Callum and Malcolm did the same. Jamie headed up the curved stone staircase carrying her as if she weighed nothing. As if this were the most natural thing to do.

"I can walk on my own," she said when he crested the top of the stairs.

"Aye," he agreed. But still he didn't put her down.

Not until he'd reached his bedchamber and kicked open the door with his boot. Once inside, he marched to the bed and put her on it, then returned to close the door. When he turned to look back at her, his assessing gaze swept over her.

Brianna scooted to a sitting position, pulling her knees to her chest and encircling them with her arms.

"Why are you looking at me like that?"

A tawny brow lifted in amusement. "Did yer sister make ye change?"

"Oh," she breathed, a flush creeping into her cheeks. "She insisted."

"I like it."

But she was uncomfortable in the borrowed clothes. She rested her chin on her knees as she peered into the flickering fire across from the bed. What she wouldn't give for a hot shower and a strong cup of black coffee.

It wasn't just the hot shower and the coffee she missed. She missed a lot of things. Warmer temperatures, for one thing. Sunny beaches. Frothy waves. A good long sleep. She was glad to be reunited with her sisters, even if it was under strange circumstances. But even still, she was tired of it all. The burden of carrying the weight of the strange little keystone was almost too much.

When all this was over, she decided she'd find a way back home. Even if Evie and Chloe refused to come back with her.

"What is it?" He moved to the edge of the bed, sitting next to her. Concern flickered through his eyes. "Ye have dark circles under yer eyes."

"When I had the second vision," she began, her voice low as she tried to choose her words. The sudden impulse to tell Jamie everything was urgent.

"Aye?"

"The third goddess, Athea…she told me something that I haven't shared with anyone."

"And it vexes ye?" he asked.

"Yes." The word came out as a whisper of ice. "She said I had the power within me to shift the timeline, to prevent or bring about certain destinies. That if I didn't, then all of us will die. She said I could change that outcome."

Jamie was silent as he reached for her, placing his hand on top of her bandaged one. His touch was gentle, reassuring.

"Ye dinnae tell yer sisters this?" he asked.

"No."

"What do ye think it means?"

"I think it means that I'm the one who has to fix the timeline. If I don't, then Rory MacDonald will use his magical great axe to open a portal to the Realm of Chaos and unleash hell. I can't allow that to happen."

"If you fix the timeline…" he asked, slowly as he considered her words. "Then what happens to this one?"

It was a question she, herself, pondered. If she fixed this timeline, as Athea suggested she should, then what would happen to her, Evie, and Chloe? Would they go back to their futures? Would everything be as it was before they traveled back into the past?

"I don't know, Jamie, but I'm afraid."

He scooted onto the bed to sit next to her, wrapping his strong arms around her and holding her. It was comforting.

"Yer safe here, lass. Dinnae fash yerself," he said.

Hearing him say this exact phrase sent a shiver of familiarity through her. She recalled he said that to her in a dream—one she'd had before she arrived here in the past. She wanted to believe she was safe here, but something told her there was inherent danger in what they—she—had to do.

But that was for another time. Now, she wanted to relish their time together. They were still alone, and though she was exhausted from the last few days, there was something irresistible about him. As though a slender, delicate thread of desire had formed between the two of them. Her gaze lingered down to his lips. He must have sensed what she felt because he wasted no time pulling her closer and kissing her.

His kiss was slow, thoughtful, with nothing hurried about it. It was the kind of kiss she dreamed of, the kind that took her breath away and made her weak in his arms. Gently, he eased her down on the bed. It sent currents of heat through her. He made her feel young again.

His hands explored the soft curves of her body. He took his time as he moved on top of her, as though their bodies were made for each other. She fit nicely into the hard contours of him, like a perfect match. Like two pieces of a whole finally coming together after being separated all their lives.

Now, skin to skin, they were one.

She told herself she didn't believe in destiny or soulmates or fate. But every moment she spent cradled in Jamie's arms made her rethink that. Maybe, just maybe, she *could* believe in destiny and soulmates and fate.

And maybe, just maybe, she could start to believe in forever.

As he moved against her, the world spun, careening on its axis. She drowned in a floodtide of emotion as they peaked together, yielding to that searing need that had built between them in only a matter of minutes.

Now that it was all over, he kissed her forehead, gathered her close and held her. His heart drummed a rapid beat under her ear as she rested her head on his chest. A contented sigh escaped her.

"I shouldna have done that," he said.

"Why not?" she asked.

"Because ye need rest."

While she didn't disagree, it was difficult to ignore how he made her feel and how she wanted to fall into his arms every time he kissed her.

"I should leave ye to that."

He nudged her gently off him and started to rise. He was right in that she needed rest, but the only way she was going to get that rest was if she found a way to relax.

"You know…what I'd like really is a bath."

He quirked an eyebrow at her. "I can have a tub brought in and filled."

"That would be wonderful."

A brightness beamed through her at the thought of a hot bath. For the first time in days, she cracked a smile as relief raced through her.

He kissed her cheek and rose from the bed. Before he left, he reached into his sporran and brought out her piece of the stone, handing it to her. She took it with a nod of thanks. Once again, he looked after the stone on her behalf. She was doing a terrible job of never letting it out of her sight.

"I'll be back soon."

After he left the bedchamber, she glanced down at the little jagged rock. Blood was smeared along the faded lines. She wondered then, if she shifted the timeline as Athea suggested in her vision, would it send her home? If it sent her home, then what of Jamie? What of her sisters? What of anything that had happened since Evie stepped back in time? Would it alter *this* timeline they were currently in?

There were too many questions. They all made her head hurt.

That and the thought of leaving Jamie sent a pang of longing with a hint of panic through her. Suddenly, she knew. She didn't want to leave Jamie.

And that was a problem.

She'd broken her own, first rule—never get attached.

Exasperated with herself, she dropped the small piece of stone on the bedside table just as the door scraped open. Jamie entered, standing aside to allow servants to bring in an oversized wooden tub. Several girls held kettles. Once the tub was placed in front of the fire, the girls filled it with steaming water.

Brianna was so happy to see the tub with steaming water, she nearly wept with joy. Even Jamie saw the happiness on her face and returned the smile, showing off those deep dimples of which she was so fond.

"I'll leave ye to it then, lass."

He granted her one last longing look as he reached for the door and pulled it closed, leaving her alone.

CHAPTER NINETEEN

THE WATER TURNED tepid and her fingers shriveled, a sure sign it was time to get out of the tub. Brianna finally pulled herself out and toweled off. She redressed, pulling on the woolen stockings, the shift, and the wool dress. The castle was drafty and—much as she hated to admit it—Evie was right in that she needed the layers.

She picked up the stone off the bedside table and held it a moment, gazing down at the fractured, faint lines. It was a wonder to her that such a small stone could hold so much power. Vowing to be a better keeper, she slipped it into the pocket of her dress.

Jamie hadn't returned yet. Likely he was giving her time to herself after the strange ordeal with the vision. A vision of the dark past the three of them had shared.

Her stomach grumbled, a reminder she hadn't eaten much that day. The vision had taken a lot out of her. Though her muscles were more relaxed than they had been in days, bone deep fatigue pounded through her.

She wasn't sure if she should wait for Jamie to return. The fire in the hearth was dwindling and the chill in the room spread. Unwilling to wait any longer, she pulled open the door and stepped into the hall.

There was a silent calmness to the castle. Something she hadn't noticed before.

As she headed down the hall to the stairs, a door scraped open. Evie exited into the hall. When she saw her, she stopped short.

"Bri…there you are." She waved her toward her, then rested her hand on the swell of her belly. "I was about to come get you."

"For what?"

"Chloe and I…that is…we think we need to talk." Discomfort flickered over her face, as though she were nervous to mention Chloe's name and that they all needed to talk. Then she added, "About what happened today."

"Where's Jamie?" Brianna asked, not wanting to acknowledge the invitation.

"He and the other men are out." She held her hand out in invitation. "Please, Bri?"

The imploring look she gave her made Brianna relent. She moved forward and took her hand. Evie grinned, happy that she'd agreed. She pushed open the door and led her inside the bedchamber.

A large four poster bed with curtains dominated the center of the room with an oversized chest at the foot of it. On one side, a wardrobe and a small dressing table with a mirror as well as a writing desk. Colorful tapestries hung along the walls to insulate the room. A crackling fire warmed the room. Near the hearth, a trio of chairs. In one of them, Chloe sat with her hands folded in her lap and a pinched, unreadable expression on her face.

Between the chairs was a small table hosting a tea kettle, three cups, and a tray of food that included fruit, cheese, bread, and dried meat. Upon seeing it, Brianna's stomach rumbled.

Evie motioned for her to take one of the chairs while she set about pouring the pale amber liquid into each of the cups. More of her herbal tea. She handed one to Brianna.

"Have some bread," Evie said, motioning to the thick slices that were still warm. Steam rose from the spongy center.

"Roslyn is teaching her to bake," Chloe said. "But she won't tell you that."

Baking and cooking was a skill Brianna had never mastered. Her meals—when she was in her own time—were usually chef-prepared. The chef, of course, employed by the wealthy bachelor she dated at the time.

"I'm impressed," Brianna said and meant it.

"Don't be," Evie said with a laugh. "I'm no good at it."

"That's not true," Chloe chimed in. She met Brianna's gaze and for the first time, granted her a weak smile. "She's good at it."

"Maybe you'll show me some time," Brianna said and sipped her herbal tea. It wasn't bad. It wasn't great, either. She wished it was something stronger. "So, tell me. What's this little family meeting all about?"

Chloe and Evie exchanged a look that said they'd already discussed it and were getting around to letting Brianna in on whatever decision was already made. There was no denying the wave of tension in the air between them all. She leaned forward and dropped her cup on the table next to the tray, then grabbed a slice of cheese.

"The vision we had today," Evie started. "I think I know what it means."

"Oh?" Brianna popped the slice of cheese in her mouth, interested to see what her sister came up with.

"We need to put the stone back together," Chloe said. "For good. We think it's the only way to stop whatever is coming."

"What's coming?" Brianna asked, her brows drawing together.

They exchanged another look, which told Brianna she didn't have all the information. She leaned forward, eyeing the two of them.

"Are you two going to tell me what's going on or not?"

"This afternoon, I had another vision," Evie said. "One of the present. At least one of all the outcomes of the possible present. Nothing has come to pass yet, of course, but I think something is going to happen."

"And I had a vision, too. Of the past as if it's already happened," Chloe added.

"Did you, by chance, have another vision?" Evie asked.

"No." Brianna sat back in the chair, her heart racing. "What did you see?"

"I saw a rip in time," Evie said.

"So did I," Chloe added.

"And," Evie said, "you were standing on the hill as these…creatures spilled out of the rip. You held the stone."

The future. She saw the future and mistook it for the present.

"I saw the same thing," Chloe said. "But in my vision, those dark creatures attacked and killed everyone and everything, allowing Rory MacDonald to take over all the lands of the Highlands."

She looked ill when she said all were killed. It was not unlike how Brianna felt when she awoke from that horrible nightmare, wrapped in Jamie's arms, when she saw the men's deaths. Now, she sat, numb, as she listened to them tell her almost the exact vision she'd had when Athea came to her and told her she had to be the one to shift the timeline.

"You both had a vision of the future," Brianna said. "I know this for a fact."

"How?" Evie asked.

"Because one of the first visions I had was similar to this."

She related to them how she had seen MacDonald use the glowing great axe to rip a hole in time, opening to the Realm of Chaos. She told them of the dark winged creatures pouring outand how all three MacLeod men were killed in the battle.

And all the while she stood on the craggy hill holding the whole keystone, her fist glowing.

"Athea came to me," she said, peering down at the tray, unable to look either of them in the eye. "She told me…" She paused as her mouth suddenly turned dry and swallowed hard. "She told me I had the power within me to shift the timeline. She told me I had the power to prevent or bring about certain destinies."

She braved a glance at each of them. Both stared at her with wide, round eyes. Chloe's face paled. Evie clenched the cup in her hands so tightly, her fingers leeched of color.

"What does it all mean?" Brianna asked when neither said anything.

Evie reached for a slice of bread from the tray and then sat back as contemplation flickered over her face.

"I think we need to put the stone back together," she said finally.

"How do we do that?" Chloe asked. "After that last vision, it broke apart again."

"I don't know yet," her sister replied.

"It's possible we have to try again with the blood magic," Brianna said as much as she hated the thought. "It might be the only way to mend the stone."

"But it wasn't enough," Evie pointed out. "There must be something we're missing. Something we need to do in addition to the blood magic to mend the stone."

"And if we do, then what?" Chloe asked. "What are we supposed to do with it?"

"Not we," Brianna said. "Me."

"You?" Chloe snorted. She put down her cup and swiped a piece of dried meat. "Why you?"

"Because I'm the one who's supposed to shift the timeline." Anger simmered under the surface at Chloe's incensed tone.

Brianna didn't have the reason as to why she was supposed to be the one to shift the timeline. Athea hadn't shared that information with her. She'd had enough of Chloe's snide remarks and hateful looks.

"Just what is your problem with me?"

Chloe glared at her from across the table. Evie's eyes widened as she opened her mouth to intervene, but her twin cut her off.

"My problem with you is you aren't interested in anyone but yourself and what *you're* doing. Even when you were taking care of us after Mom and Dad died, it was clear you wanted to be anywhere but there." Chloe folded her arms over her chest as she leaned back in the chair, as though she'd flung down the gauntlet.

Brianna took on the challenge. "I did everything I could to make sure you two were taken care of. Who do you think arranged the funerals? And dealt with all the endless paperwork? Went to probate court? Meanwhile, my then-husband was robbing me blind and charging up all our joint credit to the tune of thirty-thousand-dollars while I was trying to divorce his sorry ass."

There was a beat of silence between them. Evie sat ramrod straight. Chloe hadn't moved a muscle or relented her combative position.

"It was only after I was able to settle everything I could climb out of debt and finally kick that lousy man to the curb." Brianna's hands were shaking as she reached for the cup of tea. She peered into the pale liquid, wishing there was something stronger.

Without a word, Evie rose and walked to the other side of the room. She pulled open the door on the wardrobe and reached inside. She brought out what appeared to be a leather pouch.

Brianna watched her with interest as she plucked the cup from her hands. She poured the tea into the nearby chamber pot, then filled her cup with a splash of whatever was in the leather pouch. She did the same for Chloe.

Brianna sniffed the tawny liquid. It smelled like whiskey.

"What is this?"

"My husband's pride and joy," Evie said. "Drink. Both of you. God knows you both need it."

Brianna eyed Chloe, each of them staring at the other. Chloe was the first to take a sip. Brianna followed. It burned all the way down to her stomach.

"Now, you two will stop this incessant bickering." Evie's voice was calm, almost motherly. "We have to unite with each other if we're going to figure out what it means to shift the timeline."

"It means if we don't, we all die," she said. "I saw it as well as the two of you."

"I don't want to fight," Chloe said, her eyes downcast as she peered into her cup.

Brianna resisted the urge to ask her why she insisted on picking a fight with her then. She pressed her lips together and remained silent. Finally, her sister lifted her gaze. Her face was devoid of color and she looked as though she'd had a shock.

"I didn't know you were married."

"Neither of us did," Evie added.

Brianna blew out a breath. "Mom and Dad tried to talk me out of marrying him. But I wouldn't listen. You were both too young to remember."

She recalled the shouting match they'd had when, at seventeen, she announced she was running away with the older man whose name she long since buried into the dark recesses of her mind. She never wanted to think of him again and here she was having to think of him again. The last words between her and her parents had not been kind ones. It was something that had haunted her since the day of their horrible, unexpected death. Even now, guilt pounded through her as she regretted not being able to reconcile with them. Not being able to tell them how right they were. Not being able to say how much she regretted her decision.

She should have listened to them. She should have taken them up on their offer to send her to the local community college. But she had still harbored that deep resentment when they'd made her quit her riding lessons and give up her dream of being an Olympic equestrian.

"Anyway," Brianna said, her voice hollow. "It was a long time ago. I'll tell you the whole story someday. I'm sorry I wasn't more present for you both." She looked at them as she said it with meaning. "I never meant to drive a wedge between us. But I was dealing with a lot at the time and I didn't know how to handle it all."

Evie reached a hand to her. Brianna grasped it.

"I don't want to fight with either of you, either," Brianna said.

"We're family, after all. We need to stick together because you two are all I have left."

"We forgive you." She cut a glance to her twin, reaching out with her other hand. "Don't we, Chlo?"

Chloe looked resistant at first until she finally nodded, taking her hand, connecting the three of them together. The tension between them lifted for the first time in years. They sat like that for a moment, Evie smiling with elation. Chloe's face remained impassive but with a hint of relief. She released them and sat back.

"Now, about the keystone—" Evie started.

"Enough with the keystone." Brianna dropped her cup on the table. "I'm tired of talking about the keystone. I need a break from it."

"But—" Evie started.

"Later."

Brianna rose and left the bedchamber. There was one person she wanted to see the most and talk to him about finally reconciling with her sisters. She hadn't a clue where to find Jamie. She decided, though, she'd roam the entire castle until she did.

⌘

CHAPTER TWENTY

JAMIE KEPT HIMSELF busy in the stables, helping to brush the horses. It was the only thing he knew to do after Callum and Malcolm both had hustled him out of the keep. He'd left Brianna alone to soak in the tub and was pacing a hole in the rushes in the great hall.

While Callum attended to his laird duties, Malcolm was busy in the armory helping to sharpen swords and polish armor.

Not that they expected anything to happen in the future, but Callum insisted on being prepared on the off chance something *did* happen. He'd also been busy stocking the larder and making sure they had enough food for the inhabitants of the keep in case MacDonald decided to lay siege and starve them out. They'd have enough provisions for the next two years or so.

Mucking stalls was the only other thing he managed to do while he thought of Brianna. The lass had vexed him from the moment she arrived. It was as though she'd stepped out of the tapestries. Her visage was exactly like the magical woven fibers. With her pale, wintery eyes and her auburn hair, she sent his senses reeling.

At first, he told himself she was nothing more than an infatuation since he'd spent so much time in the tapestry room waiting for her to fully appear.

But when she arrived, she was more beautiful than he'd ever imagined.

He'd spent his youth chasing women and bedding them. He cared not for deep, amorous feelings. Only the thrill of the pursuit and the end result. It was the sole reason his uncle had packed him up and returned him from their journeys in Paris. He had consorted with the wrong noble's virgin daughter and managed to ruin her reputation.

He swore to Uncle Argyle he had no knowledge the girl was still chaste. At least not until it was far too late.

As it turned out, she was determined not to marry the man she was betrothed to and had used Jamie to ruin her reputation.

When he'd returned to Dundale, he'd made a silent vow he would never allow himself to fall for the charms of another woman.

And yet, here he was, vexed by the beautiful Brianna Sinclair.

Cursed by the curve of her full lips.

Charmed by her sweet kisses.

Bewitched by her soft skin.

Intoxicated by her sweet scent.

Most of all, he was enchanted by her impulsiveness and her strong sense of individuality. She knew her own mind. She knew what she wanted, even if she weren't able to fully obtain it.

And yet, she was vulnerable. Absent-minded when it came to keeping up with her piece of the keystone, something that endeared her to him more than he wanted to acknowledge.

He didn't want to admit those amorous feelings for her were starting to creep their way into his heart. He had fallen for her long before she'd stepped out of the tapestry as a flesh and blood woman.

"Hi, Jamie."

Her voice startled him out of his thoughts. He stood straight and looked out over the stall wall.

There she was, standing inside the stable doorway as though he'd conjured her by thinking about her. She clasped her hands in front of her, her gaze fixed on him and color high in her cheeks. She wore no cloak and, he could tell, she tried hard not to shiver in the cool afternoon wind. Her hair was long and loose, freshly washed, about her face. She tucked a wayward lock behind her ear, gazing at him with those adoring eyes. He loved the way she looked at him.

He dropped the shovel he was using to muck the stall and reached for a rag to wipe the sweat from his brow. He hadn't noticed the cool wind so much since he started working in the stable. He tossed aside the rag and walked toward her, the pain in his leg throbbing. He tried hard not to limp, but it was hard to ignore the discomfort radiating outward from his healed calf.

"Hello, lass."

He didn't want to show her how happy he was to see her. It took some effort to keep his face impassive. But inside, joy ignited through his chest, spreading warmth. He managed to stop the grin that wanted to erupt.

"Am I interrupting?" she asked.

"Och, no' at all. Ye look refreshed. Was yer bath satisfactory then?"

Refreshed really wasn't the right word. She looked relieved. Almost happy. When he paused near her, she hooked her arm in his and turned toward the door.

"It was great. Thank you for doing that for me." She hesitated a moment, as if there were something more on her mind. "Will you walk with me?"

"Aye."

As they stepped out into the pale afternoon sunshine coupled with the brisk north wind, he noticed the cold as it hit his sweaty skin. But even that wasn't enough to dampen his happiness at having her by his side. His heartbeat quickened. His pulse raced. And he knew, in that moment, that he would do anything for her. He would fight for her. He would die for her.

Such a strange, instant reaction to this woman whom he hardly knew and yet it seemed he'd waited for her his entire, disreputable life.

"Are ye well, lass?"

They took long, slow steps across the greenway. He tried to ignore his aching leg. He let her set the pace as she clutched his arm close to her. He suspected her slow steps were because she was aware of his limp and didn't want to push him.

"Yes, better than I have been."

"Ye seem to be." On impulse, he placed his hand on her still bandaged one.

"I think my sisters and I have finally reconciled," she said.

"Ah, I'm glad to hear it. I ken that troubled ye."

She halted, turning to him, pressing her chilled body against him. On impulse, he wrapped his arms around her, pulling her close. She snuggled closer.

"Jamie, thank you."

"For what?" He was unsure for what she was thanking him.

"When I first came, you said something that stuck with me. You said it in that beautiful language of yours, but what you meant was *blood warms to blood*."

"Aye…" he said slowly.

She tipped her head back to look up at him, her eyes bright and clear. "You were right. Family is everything. And they're all I have left."

"Och, lass. I dinnae think they're all ye have left." His voice was low and soft as he tilted his head down toward hers. His lips were a breath away from hers. If there were ever a time to tell her he loved her, now was it. Still, he hesitated.

She blinked owlish eyes at him, feigning ignorance. He spied the throbbing pulse in her neck and felt the jolt of her heart. "Who else do I have then?"

"Ye have my brothers and me."

And then he kissed her. His mouth landed on hers in a soft, sweet kiss. He didn't care that they stood in the middle of the bailey for all to see. He didn't care if everyone knew he wanted her in his arms for all time. He wanted them to know she was his and he'd never let her go.

His kiss was gentle at first, tasting her sweet lips that he had trouble forgetting. Then he moved his mouth over hers, devouring her softness. Her arms slid around his waist as they stood there, the north wind whipping about them and her hair fluttering around her head. She, like Chloe, had refused to braid her hair.

His hand slid up to those snarled tresses, his fingers tangling in the locks and then fisting them as he gently tugged her head back, breaking the kiss. A breath shuddered out of her as he trailed kisses down the long column of her throat. He pressed one long and slow kiss against that beating pulse. Smug satisfaction eased through him. He liked he was the one to do that to her. He realized then that this was not the time or the place to be kissing her, wanting her, seducing her.

Brianna Sinclair had ensorcelled him, forever changing him. He wanted to whisk her into his arms, take her to his chamber, and ravish her from head to toe.

In the distance, a rumbling that sounded like a war drum. She sucked in a quick breath and nudged out of his arms. The magical moment they shared suddenly shattered.

"What was that?" she asked.

A shout went up from the watchtower. Moments later, one of the guards ran down the steep steps and hurried across the bailey. He skidded to a halt when he saw Jamie.

"Where is the laird?" he asked, breathless.

"In the keep." Jamie nodded to the building behind them. "What is it?"

Before he answered, a war horn blared through the late afternoon air. Brianna stiffened, moving closer if that were even possible. Jamie tightened his arms around her. In the not too far distance, the thunder of hooves sounded, becoming louder and louder.

He understood then what was about to happen as the guard hurried away to find Callum.

"Jamie?" Her voice shook. She shivered against him.

Without a word, he took her by the hand and headed for the

stone steps at the wall. His limp hindered him as he tried to hurry, but he ignored the pain slashing through him. At the top of the wall, he paused. Brianna halted next to him, her breath see-sawing in and out as she tried to catch it.

Before them, there was a gap in space, similar to when the air had cracked open and Brianna had come through from the future. Through that hole men on horseback galloped through. Sitting to the left of the opening, holding his glowing great axe and dressed in full armor, was Rory MacDonald. Hundreds of his men poured through the portal he'd created. Foot soldiers pushed a trebuchet. Others carried a battering ram ready to do damage.

For all Callum's preparations, they were not prepared for an attack of this magnitude.

"My God," she breathed. "What…what is that?"

"That…" he said, his voice low as he tried to quell the fear, "is the MacDonald army. We're about to be under siege."

CHAPTER TWENTY-ONE

THE DECLARATION THEY were under siege made her face pale as she clutched him closer. She was a modern woman. She would not be prepared for what was to come. He had to send her away to safety.

He turned to her, gripping her by the arms. He saw the fear behind those wintery eyes.

"Yer piece of the stone…do ye have it?" he asked.

She nodded. "I have it in my pocket, but Jamie—"

"Good. There is only one clan who dares attack our keep and he comes for one thing."

"MacDonald." Her voice was ice.

"Aye. Ye need to get to safety, lass." He took her by the hand and started for the keep.

"I don't want to leave you." There was a note of desperation in her words.

While he didn't want to be parted from her, either, he knew the safest place for her was inside the keep. He granted her a reassuring smile, hoping it would give her a sense of calm.

"I'll be fine. Ye need to be with yer sisters."

Jamie tried to hurry, but his limp seemed worse this morning. The pain shot up his leg, making his knee throb. When he reached the great hall door, he shoved it open.

"I leave ye here, lass."

He started to turn away but she grasped him by the arm.

"Jamie, I—" She sucked in a breath. He saw the rapid beat of her pulse in the long column of her neck. Her mind worked as she tried to find the words she wanted to say.

He brushed the back of his hand over her cheek. "Stay safe."

Worry creased her lovely features. "But—"

"Dinnae fash yerself, lass. Ye'll be safe here with yer sisters."

He brushed her lips with a quick kiss before dashing off, leaving her standing in the doorway. He had to leave her now. His place was at the side of his brothers, fighting with them to protect the women they loved.

Jamie's first stop was at the armory where he found Malcolm handing out armor and weapons to the men. He stepped around his brother and reached for his favorite claymore.

"Where do ye think yer going?" Malcolm asked before he could slip out of the room.

"To fight." Jamie met his brother's gaze in a look of defiance.

He was aware the injury to his leg hadn't healed well. He was also aware it would make him a liability in battle. But he could not, in good conscience, let his brothers fight without him. He had to make a stand, too. He had a woman to protect as well as the two of them.

Malcolm looked as though he wanted to object. After a moment's pause, he finally nodded.

"Are the women safe?"

"I sent Brianna into the keep to find them," Jamie said.

"Good." When he handed out the last of the armor, he reached for his own claymore. "Let's go fight this blackhearted bane!"

THE DOOR TO the great hall banged closed behind Brianna, sealing her inside silence. Moments later, Chloe led Evie as they stepped off the curved staircase. Relief flooded Evie's face when she saw her standing there.

"There you are!" she exclaimed.

"We have to go." With her free hand, Chloe motioned for Brianna to follow her.

"Do you have your piece of the stone?" her other sister asked.

"Yes."

Everyone was so concerned with her piece of the stone. Perhaps they were right to be since she tended to leave it lying about. But today, she'd remembered to place it in her pocket.

Roslyn hurried into the great hall, her face white. "My lady, the castle—"

"Barricade yourself in the chapel with the other ladies, Roslyn. Don't let them see you."

Brianna was impressed with the authoritative tone of her younger sister. Roslyn wrung her hands together in front of her.

"What about you, my lady?"

The lady of the castle took a moment to grasp the woman by the arms. "We're going to the tapestry room. I need you safe in case something happens. I need you to be prepared."

She swallowed hard, her throat working. Though Evie didn't say *what* she needed to be prepared for, the woman seemed to understand. She nodded.

"Stay safe," she whispered.

"And you, too."

They bid each other farewell. Roslyn exited the great hall, disappearing into the kitchen while the three of them made their way to the tapestry room. Once inside, Evie closed and bolted the door. Chloe clutched her elbows as she stood in the center of the room staring at the tapestries.

"Are you sure this is the best place for us?" Brianna asked. "Maybe we should be in the chapel with the rest of the women."

"Chlo, what is it?"

She followed her sister's gaze and focused on the woven wall hangings. She understood then what Chloe stared at. The final tapestry revealed a new moving image showing Dundale under siege by the MacDonald army, led by Rory MacDonald brandishing his glowing great axe. Brianna moved to stand next to her as they both peered at it.

"It's happening," her sister whispered.

"We'll be safe here for a while," Evie said, unaware they were both entranced by the tapestry. "I'll build the fire and..." Her words trailed off. "What are you two staring at?"

"Eve...look." Chloe pointed at the wall hanging.

Evie moved to stand on the other side of Brianna. She sucked in a sharp breath when she saw it. The three of them were shrouded in silence as they peered at the horrific scene.

Callum, Malcolm, and Jamie stood on one of the curtain walls, each holding their sword. All the while a battering ram pounded the outer gate as a trebuchet flung massive boulders at the walls. One after another.

"Oh, God," Evie whispered.

"You never saw this in one of your present visions?" Chloe asked.

She shook her head. "No." She pressed her shaking fingers to her lips. "What are we going to do?"

"First of all, we're going to remain calm," Brianna said, trying to quell her own fear. "Panicking will get us nowhere. Have all the images in the tapestries come true?"

"Yes," Evie said with a nod. "All of them."

"Then we need a plan." She paced the small area of the room.

"Maybe it's time we figure out how to get this stone put back together once and for all," Chloe suggested. She pulled her piece out of the pocket of her gown.

Evie was still focused on the tapestry. "All this shows is the castle under attack. It shows nothing else. No outcome. We don't know that putting the stone back together will help."

"Isn't it worth a try?" Brianna held her own piece in the palm of her still bandaged hand.

Evie retrieved her piece of the stone from the pocket of her gown. "Maybe. But it would require the blood magic again."

At the mention of that, Brianna's palm itched, as though her blood stirred beneath her palm, ready to perform. Chloe clutched her stone in her bandaged fist, indecision on her face.

"It drains all of us," she said, still peering at the tapestry. "And I'd need Malcolm here with me to make it work."

She was right. Having him close to her was the only way to activate her part of the stone. They were connected somehow. Her power was different from the two of theirs, which made Brianna wonder if she was able to harness the power of the future to put the stone back together once and for all.

She thought of the vision she'd had with her standing on the craggy hill in the white dress, her sisters flanking her. In that vision, she'd held the keystone, which was whole again. Had she somehow mended the stone with her power and then used it?

Athea told her she had to shift the timeline if she didn't want to see the portal opened to the Realm of Chaos. She still did not know how.

"We need a knife," Evie said, glancing around the room. There wasn't anything suitable to use. "I can go back to our chamber and get one of Callum's daggers."

Her words were punctuated with a thunderous boom and the shuddering of the castle walls. It was the first large boulder crashing against the outer defenses. That would, likely, be followed by the battering ram.

"You can't go alone," Brianna said. "Not with the castle under attack."

"We'll all go," Chloe said.

Evie glanced between the two of them. "Maybe we should stay here and wait it out."

Another crashing boom as a boulder smashed into the walls. Brianna stared down at the small piece of stone smudged with her blood.

Something strange happened then. It was as though the world tilted on its axis—and not in the way it did when she was with Jamie. The sounds around her were as though she stood in a tunnel and her sisters were far, far away. She turned her head to see Chloe tilting sideways and, beyond, the strange enchanted tapestries.

Athea, the Goddess of the Future, appeared to turn her head and meet her gaze. And then something even stranger happened—the goddess stepped out of the tapestry. Her body was translucent—as though she were a ghost—and was outlined in shimmering light.

"You know what you have to do, Brianna of Clan Sinclair," she said, her voice soft and soothing. Her eyes flickered down to the stone she held in the palm of her hand.

"Do I?" Brianna asked.

"You do. Use the power within you."

"I don't know how." Her voice warbled on sudden unshed tears as frustration flickered through her.

This woman, this goddess, was telling her things she should know but didn't. She hadn't a clue how to use the power inside her. She had no idea what to do next.

"I told you once before you had the power within you to prevent or bring about certain destinies," she said. "You still have that power. Not only to shift the timeline, to save us from the Realm of Chaos, but to save the MacLeod men from certain death. For if you do not use this power within you, then they will all surely die in this battle."

The heavy burden of the goddess's words pounded through her.

"Tell me what to do!" she begged, hating how she sounded.

Brianna was never good at decision making, especially the hard decisions. It was why she'd returned to the Caribbean after she'd settled her parents' estate. She wanted to hide from the world and making the hard decisions. She wanted an easy life.

What she faced now was not easy. She didn't want the men to die. She certainly didn't want to see Jamie dead. He had become dear to her over the last few days. They had formed a sort of bond of understanding because they both had strife with their siblings. He understood her. She understood him. And it would destroy her if anything happened to him.

"Mend the stone. Use the power."

It was the last thing the goddess said to her before she disappeared in a poof of light and then the world righted itself. One of her sisters was shouting her name. Something cold and hard pressed into her back and she realized then she was lying on her back staring up at the ceiling.

"Bri!" Evie shook her.

"She's coming around." Chloe's voice hitched with worry.

Another mammoth boulder smashed into the walls. This time, it was close. Too close. The keep shuddered under the force.

"What happened?" She pushed herself to a sitting position, her head throbbing with sudden pain. She put a hand to her forehead as she winced.

"You fainted," Evie said.

"I know what we have to do," Brianna said. "We have to mend the stone."

"We assumed you'd had a vision," Chloe said.

She nodded, even though it hurt her head. "The Goddess of the Future came to me. She told me…"

She paused, her gaze alighting on both their youthful, hopeful faces. She knew they had to do this. She couldn't bear the thought of telling her sisters the men they loved would die if they didn't.

"Mend the stone."

As she struggled to stand, Chloe reached a hand down to help her. She was grateful for her sister's strength as she swayed a little on her feet.

"Let's go get that knife," Evie said.

CHAPTER TWENTY-TWO

EVIE LED THE way out of the tapestry room, Chloe on her heels and Brianna bringing up the rear. She couldn't stop thinking about Jamie and what the potential outcome of the siege would be if they didn't mend the stone. The thought of him dying at the hands of their enemy—albeit an enemy she had never laid eyes on—made her sick to her stomach.

As they entered the great hall, the sound of the battering ram bashing against the wood gate echoed through the keep. The sound was followed by the shouts of men and agonizing cries of pain. It was so close. Too close for her liking. She halted a moment, peering at the door, with her heart in her throat. It sounded as though any moment the oak door would crack and splinter and then they would be upon them.

Jamie.

What of Jamie? She tried to imagine him fighting, holding his own as he brandished his claymore and tried to keep his balance on the leg that pained him.

"Bri, come on!" Evie was at the foot of the stairs, ready to dash up them.

She glanced down at the piece of stone in her hand. The lines were glowing and it was faintly humming. The thrumming sound pulsed through her, vibrating through her hand and up her arm.

"My stone is humming."

"Mine, too," Evie said. "We need that knife." She turned,

ready to dash up the stairs, but something stopped her. She winced, pitched forward with her hand on her belly.

"I'll get it. You stay." Without waiting for her reply, Chloe dashed up the stairs.

Brianna moved to her sister, taking her by the arm and leading her to the nearest chair at the great hall table. Reluctantly, Evie lowered herself down.

"Are you all right? Is it the baby?"

"I felt a … twinge," she said, her voice hitching.

"You've been pushing yourself too hard. Maybe this blood magic thing isn't a good idea." Brianna's voice trembled, giving her second thoughts. Worry punched through her as she placed a hand on her sister's shoulder. "It will weaken you."

"We have to do it." Her dark brown eyes lifted to meet hers. "You said it yourself. We have to mend the stone."

"But at what cost?"

Chloe returned at that moment, panting, her face pink from exertion. Sweat dotted her forehead. She thrust the knife into Evie's hands.

"Here, Eve. It's the only one I could find."

"It will do."

"I don't know about this," Brianna said, suddenly getting cold feet. "What if this is a mistake?"

With an intensity that made her heart pound, the twins' gazes lifted to hers, their eyes blazing with a fierce and unwavering determination. Chloe held up her stone, the hum thrumming through the air, the lines pulsing and glowing. The bandage was already gone from her other hand, likely discarded while she retrieved the knife in preparation for what was to come. A faint pinkish line cut across the middle of her palm, bisecting the brand of the stone.

"We don't have a choice," she said.

"We don't," her sister agreed. She placed her piece of the stone on the table along with the dagger. Then she removed the bandage from her hand. She had the same pink scar across her branded palm.

Brianna knew without looking that hers would be the same. She pocketed her piece of the stone and then unwound the bandage Jamie had wrapped around her hand. The pale scar was there, just as she knew it would be.

"If you're sure," Brianna said, breathing the words.

But she was unsure even as Evie reached for the dagger and slashed her hand open. Chloe took the blade and did the same, then handed it to her. Brianna, taking a deep breath, cut her hand and watched the swell of blood in her palm.

Evie got to her feet, holding out her piece of the stone. Chloe pressed her piece to hers. Brianna slipped her third piece into place. That *click* sounded. The fully formed lines glowed and the humming increased.

At the great hall door, there was a bang.

"They're here," Chloe whispered, her emerald eyes wide with fear.

"What do we do?" Brianna asked. "This didn't work the last time."

"You said mend the stone," Evie replied. "How do we do that?"

Another bang on the great hall door. The wood cracked. Nothing happened other than the faint click of the stone. The lines continued to glow. The stone continued to hum.

"Blood magic," Evie whispered. "We need blood on the stone."

She squeezed her cut hand into a fist, then held it over the keystone. One drop of blood eked out and dripped onto it. Chloe did the same. It was up to Brianna then. She squeezed her hand into a fist, held it over the stone and watched as the slow trickle of blood dripped onto the stone.

When the last drop of blood landed, the stone hissed. The jagged lines of the stone emitted a bright yellow light. A strange sensation came over her as she peered at the glowing lines of the stone.

Suddenly, the words bubbled up and out of her.

"By our blood, mend this stone. What once was broken is now our own. Bound by magic, sealed in bone. Our destiny written, our power shown."

As she said the last words, the stone exploded in a blinding light. Evie and Chloe both cried out in pain and released it, stumbling back a step. She clutched the now-whole keystone in her fist. As she did, the great hall door cracked again and splintered.

A man barreled through, holding a glowing great axe in one hand. His face was a menacing mask as his terrible sharp-eyed gaze landed on Brianna. He was a large brute of a man with broad shoulders and a face that was nothing more than a map of wrinkles.

"Seize the lass," he ordered.

Two men shoved past the leader and grabbed her by her upper arms. She realized, too late, what was happening. Two more men entered the great hall. One with sharp, dreadful blue eyes who immediately pinned Chloe with his nasty gaze. She sucked in a breath when she saw him. The man following him looked familiar. Brianna, clutching the stone in her hand, recognized him as soon as he stepped over the threshold. He was the same man who had chased her across the museum terrace. The same man who tried to steal her piece of the keystone.

This man was John MacDonald from her future.

Her first thought when she saw him was *how?* How had he managed to come back in time when she was certain she'd left him standing on the terrace.

The second thought was panic skipping through her at the thought they had somehow got past Jamie, Malcolm, and Callum. Where were they? Had they been captured? Or—worse—dead? She didn't want to even consider they might be dead because that meant all of this was for nothing. Holding the newly mended stone in her hand hadn't done a damn thing to shift the timeline. She cast a quick glance to her sisters. They huddled together, the same look of worry creasing their faces.

John MacDonald walked right up to her, halting in front of her to give her a good once-over. His gaze drifted over her face and down her body in a way that made her want to cover herself. The vibes coming off him told her he was bad news.

"We meet again, lass." His face split into a smile she didn't like.

She said nothing, merely gripped the stone in her blood-and-sweat-dampened fist.

"I'm sure ye're wondering how I got here." He said it as though it was a pressing topic. As though it was top of mind.

She wasn't interested. All she was interested in was finding out where Jamie was. Her gaze flickered to the men behind him at the splintered door, but she saw no sign of him.

"Och, he's alive. Dinnae worry," he said, watching her intently. He knew she was looking for him.

"Where is he?" she asked, her voice strong and sure. She was proud of herself for that.

Movement caught her attention as the other man approached Chloe. She lifted her chin in defiance as he halted in front of her.

"I told ye I'd see ye again."

Her sister glared daggers and then spat at him. Her spittle landed on his cheek. Anger flared bright in his face as his fist clenched. He drew back his arm, but John stopped him.

"Leave her, Bruce," he snapped.

Ah, so *this* was Bruce MacDonald. The one who had followed Chloe through time.

John turned his attention back to Brianna. "Hand over the stone, lass. I ken ye have it. It calls to us."

As if in response, the stone buzzed against her palm. Like a warning. She clenched her fist tighter.

"Give it to me and I willna hurt anyone else." He held out his hand.

"No," she said. The stone buzzed again against her hand. "I know why it calls to you."

He said nothing as he continued to glare at her, then turned to one of his men. "Bring the lad."

Her heart thumped hard against her chest as she held her breath, waiting to see which of the MacLeod brothers they'd bring. Moments later, two of the men dragged Jamie in through the destroyed door. His defiant gaze met hers.

His face was dirty and sweaty. His clothes were splattered with blood. His hands were tied in front of him as he limped into the great hall.

Behind him, Callum and Malcolm followed in the same state. Chloe reached for Evie, grasping her by the hand as they huddled together when they saw their husbands were also captured. Evie whimpered.

John waved the two men holding Jamie forward. They stopped within an arm's length of her. Jamie was close. So close she smelled the musk and leather scent clinging to his skin. She kept her face impassive, pretending he meant nothing to her. It was that moment, though, she understood how much he really did mean to her. She hated seeing him as their prisoner.

"Hand over the stone, lass." There was a warning in his voice.

Brianna kept her eyes trained on Jamie. He gave an almost imperceptible shake of his head.

"It calls to you because you're cursed," she said. "Because your ancestor tried to steal it from the Triple Goddess. They cursed him and his descendants for all Time."

A feral smile crossed Rory MacDonald's face as he stepped toward her. "Ye ken yer history, lass. Ye also ken the prophecy, I'd wager. But what ye dinnae ken is how to break our curse."

Her defiant gaze flickered to him. "You think opening the Realm of Chaos with your fancy great axe will allow you to get what you want. You think controlling all of Time will give you peace. But the truth is…" She paused, taking a deep breath. "The truth is possessing the keystone will not break your curse."

It was a gamble. Honestly, she didn't know what would break the curse, but she wanted to seem as though she had more information than he did.

In her hand, the stone hummed and buzzed, as if urging her to take action. She cut a glance to her sisters hoping they would give her some sort of sign. It was clear neither of them knew what to do either.

It was all up to her now. She was alone in this. Or was she?

You have the power within you.

Blood warms to blood. Ye have my brothers and me.

Two bloodlines. One destiny.

The words echoed through her mind. Her gaze flickered from the MacLeod brothers to her sisters down to her enclosed fist where the stone continued to hum.

"Give me the stone!" John demanded.

"Dinnae do it, lass," Jamie said.

That awarded him a smack in the side of the head with the hilt of a sword. He winced. Blood trickled down the side of his face. Her fingers opened a bit to reveal the keystone resting against her bloody palm. The lines were pulsing and glowing in concert with the humming and buzzing.

"Blood warms to blood," she whispered.

There was a flash of bright light, blinding all who stood in the great hall. She looked at Jamie as he shielded his eyes against the light. The stone in her hand burned against her palm. A silent communication flickered between the two of them as she sent up a silent prayer for the safety of the keystone. It could not fall into MacDonald hands.

She lurched forward, stumbling on her own feet, causing her to fall into Jamie. She pressed her hand against his as their gazes collided. Question flickered through his, then understanding.

The power surging through her was more than she could bear. The moment their hands touched, the light exploded between them. She swayed backward, the light pulsing around all of them, followed by a loud boom. The last thing she recalled before she passed out was Jamie's face etched in concern.

CHAPTER TWENTY-THREE

Brianna awoke with a raging headache. Her tired body shivered against the cold pressing into her. Her hand throbbed from where she had sliced it open. Her arms were pulled behind her in an awkward, uncomfortable position. Something rough and sharp scraped against her wrists. Somewhere in the distance, she heard muffled chatter. Her mind tried to decipher where she was and what was happening to her. She finally managed to peel her eyes open.

Her head throbbed with a righteous pain that slammed into her as soon as she opened her eyes. She was tied to a chair in the great hall. Confusion settled in as her brows drew together and she tried to understand what she was seeing.

The remnants of battle lingered—splintered wood, shattered stone, the acrid sting of burning debris. Above her, a gaping hole in the roof yawned open to the night sky, moonlight spilling through in eerie contrast to the destruction below. The cool night air fluttered through the hole, chilling her to her bones.

Seeing the destruction sent a pang of sorrow through her. Their once lovely castle was now in ruins.

The destruction that was wholly her fault.

She clenched her hands into fists. Sticky, damp blood was still in her cut palm. The keystone, of course, was gone. She realized with some horror she was stuck inside the great hall, tied to a chair, and surrounded by the enemy.

The man she assumed was Rory MacDonald moved to stand in front of her, his thick forearms crossed over his chest as he towered over her and peered down at her with sharp, assessing, terrifying eyes. He no longer wielded the glowing great axe. His face was a map of wrinkles that had seen hard days and harder living. He wore the tartan of his clan. His well-worn boots were covered in mud and blood. His claymore rested in the scabbard on his hip.

Next to him, Bruce, his wicked blue eyes staring at her with a look she didn't like one bit. His hand was clenched into a fist at his side. They must still suspect she had the stone. Why else would they tie her to the chair?

"Well, lass, welcome back to the land of the living," the older man said. He smirked, as though he were happy to see she still breathed.

Or maybe he was angry she still breathed. Either way, it wasn't a good sign for her.

"Where is the stone?" Rory asked.

Now it was time to do her best actress routine. "Safe with me. Where else?" Her tone was haughty and full of annoyance.

"Tell us how to use the magic in the stone," Bruce demanded, his tone sharp and cold.

Good. They bought her routine. Now, to keep them guessing.

"Och, Bruce, give the lass a bit to come to her senses before ye go demanding such a thing."

Bruce MacDonald. Chloe's one-time boyfriend. She understood why Chloe was attracted to him. He was handsome, for sure, but there was something terrible glittering in his eyes.

The older man continued to stare at her, so she stared right back. "Are you Rory MacDonald?"

"Aye." A smarmy grin tugged up the corners of his mouth. "I've been waiting a long time to meet ye."

She ignored what sounded to her like a flirtation. "Where are the others?"

She didn't have to look around to know her sisters, Jamie, and his brothers were not with her in the great hall.

"Safe," Rory said.

"Where?" she demanded. She punctuated the word with as much venom as possible.

He lifted a tawny brow as he continued to peer at her. "In the dungeons. I'm sure Callum MacLeod will no' be fond of your handiwork here." He motioned toward the ceiling, the splintered door, the scattered charred debris.

She tried not to glance upward, but it was hard to resist. She had done this? The keystone must be more powerful than she'd realized. If she had blown a hole in the roof, what would it do when she tried to shift the timeline?

Rory said, then, "If you cannae give me what I need, then I will choose one of yer sisters."

And do away with her. That part was unspoken but understood. Like her death was nothing more than an eventuality. A fierce sense of protection pounded through her. That didn't bother her as much as the thought of this vile creature putting his hands on Evie or Chloe. She would sooner die than see that happen.

Bruce moved a step closer to her, looking her over with a critical eye.

"I can see the family resemblance between ye and yer sisters." He took her chin in his hand, turning her face one way, then another, as if examining her.

She jerked her chin out of his grasp. "Don't touch me."

Rory chuckled, a sound deep and rumbling in his chest. "She has a fire in her belly."

"She needs to tell us how to use the magic," Bruce said, his lethal gaze never leaving her face.

She wanted to punch him, if only to get him to stop staring at her. Behind her back, she twisted her hands in the ropes, trying to free herself. She did nothing but shred the delicate skin around her wrists, dampening the ropes with her own sweat and blood.

"I don't know what you're talking about," she said.

"If ye dinnae ken, then perhaps one of yer sisters will." Rory snapped his fingers to get the attention of one of his men. "Fetch me one of the other lasses. It doesna matter which."

The man nodded and started to hurry off.

"Wait." The word came out on a breath.

The man halted, gave a questioning glance to his laird, who motioned for him to remain where he was. Her heart beat a wicked tattoo in her chest. She inhaled a deep breath as she gathered her courage.

"Do ye have something to share with us, then, lass?" he asked.

"They don't know how to use it," she said, lying to save her sisters from this monster. "I'm the only one who knows how."

Her bluff would likely get her killed, but if she could keep them busy for a while, then maybe Jamie and the others could find a way out of the dungeon. It was a long shot, she knew but he was, after all, resourceful and in his own castle's dungeon. With the help of his brothers, there was hope yet.

She thought of the tapestry. The one of her standing on the craggy hill in the white dress and she wondered if that was a premonition. She wondered if that was part of the puzzle. The missing piece that would allow her to shift the timeline. Maybe she had to be standing on that craggy hill, wearing that white gown, holding the keystone.

She would have to find a way to get it back from Jamie. At least, for now, it was safe with him.

"Do ye care to share with us how to use it?" Rory asked.

She bit the inside of her lip, trying to work out a plan while she tried to pull her wrists free. She needed more time. She needed a way out.

"The keystone drained my energy when we put it back together." That, at least, was the truth. "I will need some time to regain my strength before I can use it again."

"How do ye use it?" he demanded, his patience wearing thin.

She saw the glittering annoyance swimming in his eyes.

"Only my blood will make it work." She hated telling him that.

His expression shifted as he realized he had to keep her alive and leave her sisters out of it. There was a long bit of silence as he continued to scrutinize her.

"At dawn, ye will use the stone again. Ye best have yer strength back by then, lass."

EVIE'S WHIMPER IN the dank cell was the only sound. She tried to keep quiet, but it was difficult when she woke up to find she was a prisoner in her own home. Chloe had yet to come to, which left her to her own dismal, terrified thoughts.

What was happening to Brianna if she wasn't in the same cell? Where were the men? Were they locked up, too?

"Eve?" Chloe's tentative voice reached out to her.

Chloe emitted a faint moan. She stopped pacing long enough to check on her. Her sister pushed to a sitting position, her brows drawn together and her face creased with pain. She kneeled next to her.

"Are you all right?" Evie asked.

"My head is killing me. What happened?"

"There was a flash of light and then nothing," Evie said.

She finally opened her eyes and gazed around the dark cell, confusion etched on her face. "Where are we, Eve?"

"I'd guess the dungeons. Chlo, they have Brianna."

"They?" She jerked to a straight sitting position as she glanced around. "MacDonald?"

"I can only guess. She's not here."

"Where are Malcolm and—"

"Locked up, too, I'd guess."

When Chloe struggled to stand, Evie grasped her by her arm

and helped her to her feet. She peered out through the cell door into the shadowy hallway, worry on her face. The same worry Evie, herself, felt.

"If they have Brianna, then that means they have the stone, too," Chloe said.

Evie nodded. "I have no doubt you're right about that."

"What are we going to do? How are we going to get out of here?"

When they were imprisoned in the MacDonald stronghold, Chloe had used her piece of the keystone and their combined blood magic to knock a hole in the back wall of the cell to get them out. Evie doubted there were secret passageways behind these MacLeod dungeons.

"I don't know," Evie said.

Her only glimmer of hope was that Roslyn had somehow managed to stay hidden and out of MacDonald hands. If she did, and she was brave enough, maybe she would find a way to the dungeons to let them out.

Beyond that, she had no idea what their plan should be. Once they were out, how would they rescue Brianna and get the keystone back?

"We'll find a way to get it back," Chloe said, sounding more sure than Evie felt.

She nodded, trying to remain positive.

But the situation seemed hopeless.

She turned back to the door and stared at it, as though doing so would present the answer.

"Now that they have the whole keystone, they can try to use it against us," Chloe said.

"Our blood is what makes it work." At least, she hoped that was the case. "They have to keep us alive if they want to use it."

Outside their cell, she heard a faint clink of a key. Chloe's gaze swiveled to the door as they both stared at it, waiting, holding their breath for the enemy to show himself. The lock to their door clicked and moments later it swung open.

But it was not the enemy standing on the other side of the threshold.

"Roslyn!" Evie breathed.

"Come, lassies." She waved frantically for them to step out of the cell while she checked the hallway.

They both hurried through the door.

"I dinnae ken what happened in the great hall, but there is no' much left of the room," the woman said.

"What do you mean?" Chloe asked.

"I mean there was a flash of light and a bang and then nothing. The room is in ruins. All of ye were unconscious when I found ye. I tried to wake ye but MacDonald's men came. So I hid again and waited as they rounded ye up and brought ye down here. They tied up Brianna. They want to make her use the keystone."

It was worse than Evie had feared. "We have to find a way back to her. We have to get her out of there."

"How did you get the keys?" Chloe asked.

"I took them off the sleeping guard. Here." She pressed the keys into Evie's hand. "The lads are just there." She pointed to a cell at the other end of the dungeon.

"Where are the MacDonalds?" Evie asked.

"They're camped outside the castle walls, scheming, debating what to do with the two of ye," she said, her voice tight with worry. A shadow of fear flickered across her face before she swallowed hard. "They intend to keep the other lass. They need her, they think. They want to kill the lads."

The words trembled into the air, heavy with dread, her eyes searching for some kind of reassurance, some promise that they still had a chance.

"Get to safety, Roslyn," Evie said. "You've done more than enough."

"Godspeed to ye all." Her voice barely carried above a whisper before she turned, feet silent against the stone as she hurried away. In an instant, she melted into the gloom, swallowed by the darkness like a wraith slipping between worlds.

"How are we going to get that stone back?" Chloe asked.

"We'll think of something."

Right now, she had something more important to do. Evie's heart pounded as she rushed to the cell door, fingers fumbling with the key in the lock. It clicked and she pulled open the door. Callum was the first one out. He swept her into his arms, cradling her against his chest, relief flooding his face. She whispered his name and buried her face there, reassuring him she was all right. It was a comfort to be in his arms once again.

Behind him, Malcolm wasted no time reaching Chloe and taking her in his arms. His grip was firm, protective. She fell against him, the tension dissolving from her features into unguarded, unrestrained solace.

Jamie was last to step through the doorway, hesitating for a moment. Blood crusted the side of his face, streaking through the dirt smearing his cheeks. His gaze flickered from Evie to Chloe and back again, his expression tight with worry.

"Where is she?" he demanded.

"They have her," Evie said, her voice quivering with her fear. "They want her to use the stone."

Fury erupted on his face as he clenched his fists.

"Well, they willna be able to do that without it." He reached into his sporran and brought out the stone, holding it up for them all to see.

Chloe hissed a breath of surprise. Evie gaped in shock. Words froze in her throat as questions flew through her mind.

"Well done, lad," Callum said. Pride showed in his face.

"God's teeth, man, how did ye get it?" Malcolm asked. "The last thing I remember was the flash of light. Then nothing."

"That's all I remember, too," Evie said.

"Aye," Jamie said. "But Brianna turned to me. She pressed the glowing keystone into my hand and though she said nothing, I ken she wanted me to keep it safe."

"Your hand," Chloe said on a whisper. "It's burned like ours."

Jamie pocketed the stone and held up his hand into the light to get a better look. There, in the center of his palm was the brand similar to hers and Chloe's and Brianna's. But it was *not* the same. This brand was the imprint of the whole stone. The Celtic triskelion with the circle going through it. He stared down at it as though trying to understand how it had happened.

"I took the stone from Brianna," he said. "It was hot to the touch. My hand closed over it. That was the last thing I remembered before I passed out."

"What does it mean, I wonder?" Evie asked.

"This feels significant somehow," Chloe said.

Jamie dropped his hand to his side. "We've tarried long enough."

Urgency was in his voice. He shoved past Malcolm and Callum both and headed for the exit.

"Wait, Jamie, it's no' safe," Callum called.

He spun to face his older brother, his eyes blazing with fury. "They have her. I mean to get her back. They dinnae ken I have the wee stone."

Callum released Evie to move toward his younger brother. He clapped a hand on his shoulder to calm him, reassure him.

"Aye, and we will. But we must have a plan first."

"Let's get to the armory," Malcolm suggested. "We can hide out there while we make a plan."

"Yes, we can't stay here," Evie agreed as she joined her husband, slipping her hand in his.

"Let's go, then," Jamie said.

He didn't wait for a reply as he headed out of the dank dungeon.

CHAPTER TWENTY-FOUR

DAWN APPROACHED.

Brianna had been tied to the chair all night without food or water. She had made no progress on getting her wrists free from the ropes. After numerous attempts, she had given up finally. Her hands were slick with what she could only imagine was blood and sweat.

She fought fatigue. Her eyes grew heavy. Her head drooped. When she realized it, she snapped it back up, trying to remain awake.

The shuffling of feet in the room caught her attention. Her senses went on high alert as she sat straighter in the chair.

The man stepped in front of her. The shadows concealed his features, but she had a sneaking suspicion she knew who it was. The question was why he had come to her. To taunt her? Threaten her?

He moved into the pale light enough so that she saw his face. John MacDonald peered back at her with his glittering, terrifying eyes. Eyes that bored into her. He clutched his hands in front of him and regarded her coolly.

"I bet you're wondering how I ended up here, aren't ye?" he said, his voice low and dark in the gloom.

She tipped her head up and peered at him. Though she couldn't quite make out his face, she tried on her best glare.

"No," she said, her voice flat.

She admitted to herself she was interested in how he'd ended up in the past, but not enough to want to have a conversation with him about it. Truthfully, she wanted him to go away and leave her alone.

He chuckled at her response as he circled her. Like a predator.

"When the portal closed, I thought all was lost. Ye left me there on that terrace with burns on my face."

He stood behind her. She sensed his presence close. Too close. The warmth from his body radiated outward, cascading over her in a way she didn't like one bit.

Even so, she smirked at the memory of that day. When she had thrown her hot tea in his face to get away.

"Yes, you screamed like a girl."

She didn't know why she'd taunted him back. It was likely going to get her hurt. Or dead. Neither of which she was interested in. A hot hand landed on one of her shoulders. He leaned down, his face a breath from hers.

"Ye think ye're funny, aye?"

Her mouth went dry at his furious tone of his voice. His hot breath whispered over her ear, sending a shiver of revulsion through her.

"I wouldna be here if it weren't for my brother."

His brother, Bruce. She remained silent with her eyes forward as he continued to hover over her in a threatening manner.

"Rory used his powerful great axe to bring me back. Because he needs me."

"Does he?" She tipped her head to one side to see the outline of his profile a breath away from her.

"Aye." His acrid breath whispered over her.

She turned her face away and peered once again into the depths of the shadows. She didn't know this man well enough to despise him, but she despised him.

Finally, he straightened and walked around to face her, his arms folded across his thick chest.

"Don't ye want to know why he needs me?"

"Not really," she replied. "But like any villain who wants to drag this out, you're going to tell me, aren't you?"

Even in the darkness, she saw the annoyance flicker over his face. Good. She wanted him annoyed. She wanted him angry. Being angry would cause him to make wrong decisions. Wrong decisions could lead to her escape.

"He needs me because once we have the Realm of Chaos open, it's up to us to use the keystone to control all of Time."

"Is that so?"

She had serious doubts they would get the keystone to work. But she pressed her lips together and said nothing more.

"Aye and you're going to help us with that."

"And how am I going to do that?"

He bent forward and pressed his face inches from hers. "You will use your blood magic to activate the keystone and then the two of us will take over from there."

Confusion settled in. How did they think activating the keystone for them would give them what they wanted? That was never the intended purpose of putting the keystone back together—it was keeping the Realm of Chaos sealed.

"You think it's that easy?" she scoffed.

"Isn't it?"

She didn't know but she was going to continue this ruse for as long as possible.

"If ye don't help us," he continued, "then we choose one of yer sisters to help. We will spill all her blood to activate the magic in the keystone. Maybe the pregnant one."

Brianna surged forward against her bonds. The ropes burned through her wrists.

"You stay away from her, you son of a bitch." The searing anger heated every word as she punctuated it.

"Ah, so ye do care about them. Good. We'll start with her. Unless, of course, ye want to cooperate."

Panic pounded through her. The last thing she wanted was for him to do something to one or both of her sisters. And where were the MacLeod men? Likely locked up, too. Her heart pounded so hard against her chest she thought it might burst through. She clenched her jaw until it ached as she looked up at him.

"I'll cooperate," she said at last.

An oily smile creased his face. "Good."

She pressed her lips together in a thin line. The last thing she recalled before she passed out was handing Jamie the keystone. The stone was hot when she pressed it, wordlessly, into his hand. Right now, this MacDonald assumed she still had it. She was going to let him continue to assume that. They couldn't force her to use the stone if she didn't have it in her possession.

She realized, though, that put her sisters in a terrible, dangerous position. Once the MacDonald realized she didn't have the stone, they would go after them. She had to think of some way to escape.

He walked around behind her. She stiffened as she waited, holding her breath. She felt the cold steel of a knife as he sliced through her bonds. She was free. Her arms had been pulled behind her for so long, when she was released and she was able to drop them to her side, the blood rushed to the tips of her fingers. The tingling sensation was so sharp, she winched.

Glancing down at her wrists, she saw they were raw and bleeding. Her cut palm still oozed.

John didn't wait for her to get her bearings. He grasped her arm and hauled her up from the chair, practically dragging her out of the great hall through the splintered doorway.

Outside in the bailey, the MacDonald clan had set up a crude camp. A campfire blazed brightly against the pre-dawn sky. The men were sitting around it, talking, laughing, drinking ale and whiskey from the MacLeod cellar. She heard the soft whicker of a horse. And smelled the acrid tang of cooked meat in the air. Her gut clenched tight as he led her toward the circle of men.

"She's ready," he announced.

Rory MacDonald, the clan leader, rose to his full height from the circle and turned to her. His piercing eyes met hers. Fear shifted through her. A shiver of dread skipped down her spine.

"We ride for the mountain, then." As he spoke, his gaze never left her face. "She'll ride with ye so ye can keep an eye on her."

"I can ride my own horse," she snapped, the ire rising through her despite the fear.

He lifted a tawny brow. He stepped forward, closing the gap between them. "Ye will ride with him." He jerked his head toward John MacDonald. "I cannae allow ye to have yer own horse. I think ye ken why."

Hope died right then. She thought if she got her own horse, she would be able to ride away from the group. Maybe even find Jamie and the others.

"Ye are no' so canny as ye think, lass." He reached for her then, taking her chin in his sweaty hand. "Even if ye are a bonnie one."

She jerked her head free. "Keep your damn hands off me."

Brief surprise flickered over his face and then he laughed. It was a deep rumbling sound in his broad chest. "And a fiery one, too, aye? Take her away."

John's hand tightened on her arm, his fingers digging into the fleshy part of her biceps. He dragged her away from the group toward the stables where the MacDonald clan had decided to use it for their own horses. He went directly to a large black warhorse that was already saddled.

There was a bustle of activity behind her. As John mounted the horse, she cut a glance behind her to see the other MacDonald men mobilizing to ride and leave behind the castle. Her heart thundered as she thought of Jamie and the others still locked up in the dungeons.

"Come, lass." John held his hand down to her.

A flash of defiance went through her and for a brief moment, she thought about making a run for it. But to where? Anywhere she went, she'd be captured and punished. As her pulse raced, she knew she had no choice. She reached her hand up and placed it in

MacDonald's. And then she was mounting the horse behind him. Moments later, they galloped away, leaving behind the ruins of Dundale Castle.

THE GROUP MADE it out of the dungeons and headed for the armory. There was an eerie silence that hung in the air. The hair on the back of Jamie's neck stood on end and he knew something was wrong.

Instead of going to the armory with the others, he headed for the tapestry room. There was something he had to see. He was aware of the weight of the stone in his sporran, as if it had become heavier the closer he got to the tapestry room.

"Jamie, where are you going?" Evie called.

He ignored her, though. He had one thought only—get to the tapestry room. He had a feeling that something was different, that something had changed. That feeling tingled in the middle of his palm where the stone had burned him.

The great hall was destroyed and deserted. Outside, nothing but silence. MacDonald and his camp had moved on, taking Brianna with them.

When he arrived, the door was slightly ajar. He pushed it open and stepped inside, the light from the corridor slashing across the threshold and sliding up the wall of woven wall hangings. In the half-light, they shimmered with their enchantments. Something was different about one of them. Something he was terrified to see.

As he approached, his heart in his throat, his gaze fixed on the one that was of the three women. The one where Brianna stood in the center, flanked by her sisters, wearing the white gown with the wind billowing through her hair. The one where she held the whole keystone as it pulsed and glowed.

The image shifted. Now, it was only Brianna standing on the

top of a flat boulder in the center of castle ruins with a glistening sea in the background. He recognized those ruins—Castle Caelnar was not far from Dundale, perched on a cliff overlooking the water. Her fisted hand lifted to the sky. Light seeped through her fingers, indicating she held the whole keystone. Her sisters were no longer in the wall hanging as before. Instead, she reached with her free hand for someone else. Someone whose appearance began to slowly emerge.

He watched, mesmerized, his heart thudding like a war drum, as he waited for the fully formed image. A hand reached for Brianna's. And then the shimmering threads shifted as a man emerged, reaching for her outstretched hand.

That man was him.

CHAPTER TWENTY-FIVE

J AMIE WAS STARING at the changed image when Evie entered the room. She paused in the doorway, hesitating, as if unsure whether or not she should enter.

"They changed," he said, almost as an invitation.

She moved to stand next to him and followed his gaze. She stared in stunned silence.

"It's you," she finally said. "Not us as it was before."

"Aye," he agreed.

"Those ruins were never there before," she said, eyeing the crumbling jagged walls in the tapestry.

"'Tis Castle Caelnar. It was built as a coastal fortress to guard against invaders and was once the stronghold of Clan MacRae. Local legend whispers the ruins are haunted by spirits cursed to roam the lands forever."

She shuddered, clutching her elbows. He'd never put much stock into the eerie legend, though now that he saw this place in the tapestry, he wondered if there was some truth to it. Mayhap the spirits of the Triple Goddess were the ones haunting the ruins.

"If the tapestry has changed, that means something else has changed." She turned to him, reached for his branded hand. He held his palm up to her. She traced the burned lines. "Because of this maybe."

"I dinnae ken," he said.

"Two bloodlines." Her glittering gaze lifted to his. "One destiny. It's the two of you now."

"What does that mean?" he asked.

She shook her head. "I'm not sure. But it appears you are the second bloodline that helps shift the timeline."

"I dinnae ken what to do." His voice was soft, shaking. And he hated that.

Most of his life, he had known what to do. He'd never backed down from a fight. But now, apprehension shifted through him. Aye, he knew he had to find Brianna—and he knew where to start. He had to get her away from the MacDonalds. But at what cost? Would he have to trade the keystone to do it?

Deep down, he knew he absolutely would trade the keystone for her life. He wanted her safe. He wanted her away from them. If it were the only way to save her, so be it.

"Yes, you do." Evie gave him a smile, her eyes shimmering with tears. "You have to go after her."

"I cannae give them the stone," he said.

"If that's the only way to save her, then maybe you do." She sounded so strong, so sure. She closed his fingers, making his hand into a fist. "I'm not sure what the brand in your palm means, but I suspect it has something to do with the power of the stone."

As if it heard her, the stone hummed in his sporran. Her brows lifted. She heard it, too.

"It's calling," she said.

"What does that mean?" he asked.

"It means, I think, you need to find Brianna."

"And then what?" His gut clenched with uncertainty.

"And then..." She paused, dragging her lower lip through her teeth. "And then you stop them from opening the Realm of Chaos. I think it's up to the two of you now."

She glanced back at the tapestry. The one where he reached for Brianna. Their hands were almost touching.

"What about ye and Chloe? My brothers?"

She shook her head. "I don't think we matter so much now."

"How do ye ken this, lass?"

Contemplation crossed her face as she turned her head and gazed back at the woven wall hangings. "I can't be sure," she said at last. "But something changed when she gave you the keystone. Some twist of fate or destiny that formed between the two of you, altering the prophecy. As though a bond formed. We know she has the power to shift the timeline." Her gaze flickered back to him. "But I believe you have the power to help her do that."

"How?" he asked.

"Blood magic," she whispered. "It's your blood and hers the keystone needs. Two bloodlines. One destiny." She clutched his hand in hers, squeezed, and gave him a small smile. "Go to her, Jamie. Stop the chaos."

He wasn't sure if Evie was right. Was she suggesting it was his blood and Brianna's that would help stop the coming war?

All he was sure of was that he needed to get to Brianna. He needed to find her before something happened to her. Before MacDonald realized she didn't have the keystone.

He squeezed her hands back and gave her a nod. He was going to find her and then they would do whatever was necessary to stop MacDonald from opening the Realm of Chaos.

"Tell the others," he said.

She nodded and released his hand. He started to turn away, to head for the door, but something stopped him. He turned back, leaned toward her and kissed her cheek.

"Ye keep my nephew safe, aye?" He glanced at the swell of her belly.

She flushed, her cheeks turning a pale pink as she cast her eyes downward. "I will. But, Jamie, how do you know it's going to be a boy?"

He flashed a wicked, charming smile. "I just do."

And then he hurried out of the tapestry room. He crossed the great hall, trying hard not to notice the destruction. Because if he did, it would tear his heart in two. This was his home. It hurt him to know that there was a gaping hole in the roof, charred ceiling beams and furniture, and a door that had been splintered by a battering ram.

He headed out the door into the early morning light and halted. He stared across the bailey where the men of their rival clan had set up camp and left behind a mess. He clenched his fists, hating they were on his land. Hating they invaded his home. The only home he had ever known.

He shoved aside those feelings and hurried toward the stables.

His brothers stood next to their own horses, which were already saddled and ready.

"What are ye doing?" he asked.

"We thought ye might do something like this," Callum said. "We cannae let ye go alone."

"This isna yer fight. It's mine," Jamie said, standing up to his big brother.

"We're going with ye, laddie," Malcolm said. "And if we're going to a war, ye'll need this." He handed him his claymore still in the scabbard.

Jamie took it from him, looking over both his brothers. They each had their own claymore strapped to their side, ready for battle.

"I can handle them myself," Jamie said as he placed the belt around his waist and tightened it.

"Och, can ye now?" Callum said with a smirk.

"Have ye faced real battle, lad?" Malcolm teased.

He was aware Malcolm was the warrior and Callum was battle hardened. But he wasn't soft, himself. He may not have faced a real battle, as his brother put it, but he was ready and willing to fight. He'd faced the MacDonalds alone when he was captured and injured. He'd made his way back to Dundale on a stolen horse.

"Leave off, brother," Callum said. Then to him, "Are ye ready, lad?"

"Aye," Jamie said as he headed for the stall that housed his horse. He was pleased to see it was already saddled and ready to go.

"All right, then," Callum said. "Let's get yer bonnie lass back."

THE JOSTLING OF the horse jarred her as they rode at breakneck speed away from Dundale castle. The morning air was cold and brisk and bit through her woolen gown. She hadn't a cloak and she shivered next to the man who was her captor.

Brianna had no choice but to wrap her arms around John MacDonald's thick waist. He seemed to enjoy it while she hated every second of it. The only perk was his body was warm. But not warm enough to keep her from shivering.

She suspected most of her shivering was from the fear and apprehension swamping her, though. She wasn't sure what would happen to her once they discovered she didn't have the keystone. It had been an impulse handing it off to Jamie and one that turned out to be the right decision. They had her, but they didn't have the keystone.

It was a short ride—no more than an hour. Ahead, someone shouted a command to come to a halt. Her rider pulled in the reins of his mount and slowed to a stop. She dared to peek over his shoulder.

Ahead were castle ruins perched on a craggy hill. Behind it, the glistening sea.

When they arrived, the company of men set about building a camp.

Her heart leapt to her throat as she stared at the ruins. She recognized it. This was the castle from her vision with the Triple Goddess and Morrogh MacDonald. They'd brought her to the place where it all began, where the MacDonald line was cursed.

John slid off the horse, then turned to her, holding his arms up to her with a grin on his face she despised. Ignoring him, she swung her leg over and dismounted without his help. Surprise followed by annoyance flickered over his features before he grasped her by the arm and dragged her away toward Rory MacDonald and flanked by Bruce.

In his hand, Rory held the great axe. The blade shimmered with its magic and she worried she was about to witness him opening the portal to the Realm of Chaos. She kept her gaze fixed on him, though, as they neared. They halted in front of him. He looked her over with a sharp, critical eye.

"'Tis time to give me what I want, lass," he said.

Her captor handed her off to him. He took hold of her, his fingers biting into her upper arm as he dragged her toward the slope leading up to the castle ruins. Bruce and John both fell in step behind them. Her heart drummed in her chest with every step. And with every step as they neared, her stomach twisted tighter and tighter into a knot.

"Do ye ken this place, lass?" Rory asked.

She pressed her lips into a thin line, remaining silent.

"'Tis where it began and where it will end."

He dragged her to the top of the slope where it flattened out, leading her through the crumbling stone walls. No roof connected them, leaving it open to the fading light in the indigo sky. She noticed the low stone—a round shape near the back of the ruins that stuck up out the ground about a foot. It had a flat top, as though well worn from wind and time. It seemed an odd place for it.

Here, within the open walls, the wind whipped through her, tangling her hair and chilling her to the bone. He gave her a shove forward. She stumbled a few steps, managing to keep her balance and turned to face the three expectant faces of the men.

She recalled this place with some clarity. It was the one from her vision, the one where the Triple Goddess had stood and cursed Morrogh for all eternity. Before her, Rory held his great axe that continued to shimmer. Next to him, Bruce and John held torches, their flames flickering in the violent wind.

"Well?" he asked, taking a step toward her.

She lifted her chin a little higher, her heart hammering hard. "Well, what?"

He scowled, his brow furrowing. But it was Bruce who spoke.

"Are ye daft? The keystone," he said.

She slipped her cut hand into the pocket of her dress in an elaborate show of reaching for the stone. Her fingers clenched into a tight fist, the pain pounded through her hand and up her arm from the cut. Her mouth had gone dry as her mind raced, trying to come up with a response. She had to tell them she didn't have it. And when she did, she had to be prepared to face the consequences.

Finally, she brought her hand out of her packet and unfolded her fingers showing her empty palm. "I don't have it."

They stared at her in shocked silence, the only sound that of the flickering flames of the torches and the whipping wind.

"She fooled us," John finally said. "All of us."

Rory moved toward her, rage creasing his face. When he reached her, he placed the edge of the glowing great axe inches away from her throat.

"Do ye think this is a game? Dinnae think I willna kill ye here, now."

She swallowed the fear clawing its way to her throat, remaining perfectly still. Her gaze stayed focused on his. "You can kill me," she said, slowly, quietly, "but then your curse will never be broken nor will you be able to control the keystone."

"She's right," Bruce said. "We need her and her blood." He moved to stand next to Rory. He placed a hand on his arm and pushed the blade away from her throat. "Where is the stone, lass?"

She smirked, pleased with her decision to give it to Jamie.

"She doesna have to say," Rory said then. "I ken where it is."

"Where is it?" John asked.

"With Jamie MacLeod, aye?" Rory said. "Or one of the other two lassies."

"You leave them out of this," she snapped.

Ignoring her outburst, Bruce said, "We should have brought them, too, instead of leaving them to rot in the dungeons."

Brianna winced hearing that. She hated they were imprisoned in their own home. She clenched her jaw and pressed her lips together tighter. Even though he guessed the truth, she didn't need to confirm it.

"Tie her up. Bring her. And then we will go after the lad and I'll kill him myself."

"Nay," Bruce said. "He will come for her. And then, when he arrives, we will capture him, too."

Rory smiled a toothy grin. "Aye, ye have the right of it, lad. That's just what we'll do."

Terror prickled the back of her neck, cold and relentless, her hair standing on end. She wished there was some way to get a message to Jamie, to warn him. But in his century, there was no such thing as cell phones or text messaging. She forced herself to breathe, to think. There had to be a way to warn him. Because if she didn't find one, then he would never see the danger coming and she might never see him again.

CHAPTER TWENTY-SIX

J AMIE WASN'T SURE the castle ruins would be where they'd take her, but it was the only place he had to start. He'd seen the image in the tapestries—the one of him and Brianna together. When he told his brothers that's where they were headed, neither of them objected. They took him for his word, nodded, mounted their war horses, and headed away from Dundale at a full gallop.

They had left both Chloe and Evie behind. Callum refused to let his lady wife come along since she was with child. Chloe didn't want to leave her alone in the near-deserted castle. So it was agreed the three of them would ride out to face their fate with the MacDonalds.

It was still dark as they made their way from Dundale toward the coast. He pushed his horse as hard as he dared for short bursts, the hooves pounding the ground, slipping slightly on loose gravel. He had to slow as the terrain became rocky and danger-ous, but that made his heart race and his sense of urgency no less.

As dawn pricked the sky, he knew it was too dangerous to continue to push his mount. Every thud of the hooves on the ground matched that of his beating heart and brought him that much closer to Brianna. Still, he cursed the slowness and the delay.

The sharp salt-tinged wind whipped past them and he knew they were nearing the ruins of Castle Caelnar. Ahead, he saw what remained of the castle as it loomed against the first faint signs of morning. With a moonless sky, there was nothing to light their way. But that was just as well. He wanted to arrive by the shadows with, hopefully, the element of surprise.

As they neared, they came to a slow trot and then halted. Callum pulled to a stop next to him on one side, Malcolm on the other. Ahead, they saw small orbs of flickering light. He assumed they must be torches. In the center, there was a huge bonfire casting yellow-orange light in a semicircle. The outline of tents dotted the area, indicating MacDonald had made a hasty camp at the foot of the ruins.

"What's yer plan, brother?" Callum asked. His blazing blue eyes were pinned on the camp ahead.

Jamie remained silent a moment as he considered all the options. They were far outnumbered. That much he knew. It would be unwise for them to charge in with swords swinging. They would quickly be overtaken and captured.

There had to be another way. And he thought he knew what that way was.

"I'll surrender to them," he said.

"Are ye mad?" Malcolm snapped.

"That's what they want," he said. "They want me and the keystone."

Malcolm snorted his objection. Callum made a motion for him to be silent. The eldest leaned on his saddle horn and peered at him.

"And then what, Jamie? Ye have an idea, don't ye?" he asked.

"Once I'm in the camp, they'll want the keystone. They'll capture me and take the stone to give to Brianna. Then, they'll make her use it," Jamie said.

A broad grin spread on Malcolm's face. "And that's when we attack. Aye?"

"Nay," Callum said. "We need a diversion." He cut a glance to Malcolm. "Like before."

"I'm afraid the lasses are no here to create that diversion," Malcolm said.

Jamie knew they referred to the fire at the MacDonald stronghold. That was the only thing that had helped them escape, while he was still a prisoner. But Callum was right. They needed a diversion.

"Aye, brother," he said. "We need a diversion. While I surrender myself, the two of ye can set fire to the camp."

"More fire, eh?" Malcolm chuckled.

"'Tis effective," Callum said. "All right. We'll leave the horses here. Malcolm, ye take the left. I'll go right. Jamie, ye will surrender yerself and when ye do, that's when we take the torches and light it up."

"Then, when the camp is in chaos, I'll find Brianna," Jamie said.

"Sounds easy enough." Malcolm dismounted and pulled his horse toward a copse of trees. "When ye have her, make haste for the horses. Then we'll get back to Dundale."

The plan was easy and that's what worried Jamie the most. Anything and everything could go wrong. But he was willing to risk it to save Brianna. Once he had her back and away from the MacDonalds, then they'd figure out how to shift the timeline.

He and Callum both dismounted, tying their horses next to Malcolm's within the shadows of the trees. He hoped this worked. And if it didn't…he shoved away those thoughts. Callum placed a hand on his shoulder and squeezed. In the faint light of the new day, his brother's eyes were nothing more than dark orbs.

"Good luck and Godspeed, brother," he said.

"And to ye," he replied.

He cut one last glance at Malcolm who gave him an encouraging nod. He turned toward the camp, took a deep cleansing breath and expelled it. He slipped his hand into his sporran, wrapping his fingers around the cold keystone and relief sputtered through him. It was still there. Not that he had any doubt, but it was always good to check.

He started down the slope of the hill toward the crude camp, his eyes pinned on the bonfire glowing in the center of it all. There, MacDonald held Brianna. There, he would find her and release her.

He focused on one step after another as he went down the hill, his lungs and calves burning with the exertion. His heart thudded against his chest as his eyes skipped from one tent to another, looking for signs of light. For signs of *her*. But he didn't see her. Likely, MacDonald would keep her close to him. She was his prized possession at the moment. He'd never let her out of his sight.

Behind him, he heard the soft swish of steps in the heather. One to the right. One to the left. He knew this was his brothers headed for the camp to carry out their plot. The moment the camp was in chaos was his one and only chance to find her, grab her, and get out.

He was at the edge of the light now. He stepped into the camp, within the circle of light, and paused. No one seemed to notice his arrival. He would have to make his presence known before his brothers torched the place.

He moved deeper into the camp, shuffling his feet. When he was close to the center bonfire, he pulled his sword with a *shing* that finally got the attention of the men MacDonald had left to guard the camp.

They leapt into action, pulling their own swords and pointing them at him. He dropped his and held his hands up in surrender.

"I'm Jamie MacLeod," he announced. "I want to see yer laird."

Two of the men came forward and took him by the arms, dragging him away from the edge of the camp without a word. Good. His plan had worked. Now all he needed was to find Brianna. They took him through the camp to a large tent on the other side of the bonfire. There, two men guarded the entrance.

"Tell the laird we have a gift for him," one of the men holding him said. "Tell him we have Jamie MacLeod."

BRIANNA HEARD THE commotion outside the tent. Her head snapped in the direction of the man's voice. She bit down on the gag as she peered at the flap, trying to see through the canvas. But all she saw were the shadowy outlines of the men. Her hands were bound behind her once again.

Rory was not in the tent, though. She was left alone with Bruce and John. Bruce rose to his full height and stepped toward the tent flap. He shoved it open, poking his head out and saying something. His words were muffled.

And then she heard the words that made her die a little inside. *We have Jamie MacLeod.*

Oh, God, no. They'd captured Jamie. And he had the keystone. Now they were all doomed. There was more talking outside the tent, but she couldn't make out the words from the hushed men's voices. Bruce backed into the tent, turning to face them, his eyes gleaming with triumph.

"We have him," he said.

"That means we have the stone," John replied. "Bring him."

"No," Bruce said. "We need to find Rory."

"Forget Rory," John said. He rose to his full height and advanced on his brother. "Bring in MacLeod. He has the stone, aye?" The last was directed to her. "Doesn't he, lass?"

She said nothing. Merely glared back at him. When she didn't respond, he backhanded her. Her head snapped to one side, and she tasted blood.

"Answer me," he snapped.

"John, we haven't time for this. We know he has the stone. We can finally get what we want." Then to the men outside, "Bring him."

Brianna blinked her surprise as she snapped her head toward Bruce. What did it mean—they could get what they wanted? Did he and John plan to double-cross Rory MacDonald? If that was the plan, they were stupid to think they could use the keystone for themselves.

Two men stumbled inside the tent. Between them was Jamie. His eyes instantly landed on hers and in his expression she read something strong and defiant. Had he surrendered himself to get to her? If he had, did he truly have the keystone on him?

She hoped he'd had the good sense to leave it behind with Callum or Malcolm.

"Search him," Bruce ordered. He appeared to be the one in charge.

One of the men reached for his sporran. Jamie jerked his arm free and batted his hand away. "Dinnae touch me," he said, his tone one of warning.

Bruce chuckled. "Ye have the stone, don't ye?"

For a brief moment, she saw the guilt flash through his eyes. Oh, God. He'd brought the stone with him.

"Your silence tells me ye do," Bruce continued. To the guards, he said, "Leave us."

That didn't bode well. Jamie stood his ground, his jaw clenched. The two men who'd brought him ducked out of the tent. When they were gone, Bruce turned his attention back to him.

"Hand it over."

Brianna wanted to scream at him not to do it, but the look he gave her told her he intended to hand it over. It was clear in that moment he was willing to give up the stone *for her*. If she hadn't been so angry about that, she would be touched.

Surely, he had another plan up his sleeve. He didn't intend to hand over the keystone—the very item that had brought her here, the one the MacDonalds wanted, the one that had cursed the clan for generations.

Shouts outside the tent caught their attention. Her heart thudded against her chest, her breath fluttering in and out as she looked at Jamie. His face remained impassive, but she thought she saw a hint of smug satisfaction there.

"Go see what's going on," Bruce ordered.

"Are ye ordering me now, brother?" Fire flashed in John's eyes.

Another louder, more urgent shout. Bruce pulled a dagger from his belt and pointed it at Brianna.

"Just go check. I'll keep an eye on these two."

Scowling, John ducked out of the tent, leaving the two of them alone with Bruce. The moment he was gone, Jamie lunged for the dagger. Brianna yelped a muffled surprise as he shoved Bruce backward. The two of them struggled, each one vying for control of the weapon. They were locked in battle. Bruce stumbled backward toward her. She stuck out a foot and tripped him.

Down he went, tumbling to the hard ground with a muffled oof. As he did, Jamie snatched the dagger out of his hand and pointed it at the man.

"Stay down," he warned.

A fine sheen of sweat was on Bruce's face. He glared up at Jamie as he shoved to a sitting position, clutching his elbow.

"I know you have it. I can hear it calling to me," he said.

Jamie ignored him as he scurried behind her and quickly slashed the rope binding her hands. She shoved off the gag and then she smelled it.

The acrid tang of smoke. Her eyes flew wide as she looked at Jamie.

"We havena much time." He grabbed her by the hand and dragged her toward the tent flap.

Bruce was getting to his feet, sniffing the air. "You bloody fool. You killed us all."

He charged toward Jamie, a snarl on his face, as he reached for him. Jamie ducked. Brianna spun in the tent, looking for something—anything—that could be used as a weapon, but the tent was sparsely decorated. She heard a sickening thump and realized Jamie had knocked him out. He lay sprawled on the dirt floor of the tent.

He reached for her hand, taking it, and pulling her to him. There was an urgency in his eyes as he looked at her. Then he held up his hand, showing her his burned palm. A burn that resembled hers.

"What—how?"

"When ye gave me the stone. The tapestries changed. I'm the one on the hill with ye. No' yer sisters."

"I don't understand."

"We have to go."

He tugged her out of the tent. The camp was in chaos. The fire spread from both ends of the camp, heading for the middle, where they'd been. Flames licked the pale dawn sky, turning it into a chaotic inferno. Men shouted, running for water.

Worst of all was Rory MacDonald running for the tent wielding his great axe. Thankfully, the weapon wasn't glowing. Yet.

The moment he saw them, his lips curled into a cruel snarl of a smile. Before they realized what was happening, they were surrounded. Jamie was ripped from her, their hands yanking apart. Someone grabbed her from behind while another one of the MacDonald men punched Jamie in the gut. He sputtered a breath as he doubled over.

His surrender was supposed to save her. Instead, it had doomed them all.

Rough hands wrenched her arms behind her back.

Figures emerged from the smoke and in the distance, she heard familiar voices shouting. Callum and Malcolm. Their plan to set the camp on fire had unraveled quickly. A blade was pressed to her throat as she stood rigid against the man holding her.

From the corner of her eye, she saw Callum and Malcolm fighting their way to them. One of them fell but she didn't see who, as they were driving in retreat from the camp inferno. Smoke billowed into the sky and tumbled through the tents. She tried to hold her breath but she started to cough and sputter.

"Bring them!" MacDonald shouted.

He turned and fled the camp, heading away from it and toward the slope that would lead up to the castle ruins. The man holding her wrapped a meaty hand around her arm and dragged her along. She stumbled and tripped over the edge of her gown, nearly falling face first. The only thing that kept her on her feet was the man.

It was hard to see through the smoke but as they headed away from disaster, she saw Rory MacDonald hold aloft his great axe.

It was glowing.

CHAPTER TWENTY-SEVEN

EVIE PACED THE length of her bedchamber, biting her thumbnail. They had barred themselves inside. Panic settled into the center of her chest. Her back ached. Her feet hurt. But she refused to stop pacing. She refused to rest until her family was home.

"Eve, you'll wear yourself out."

Chloe sat in the chair by the fireplace, her hands clasped in her lap. She seemed far too calm.

"How can you sit there like that? Aren't you worried about Malcolm?"

"Of course, I am." Her voice cracked with emotion.

Evie halted. Her sister's face was creased with worry and fear. But still she managed to sit there, rigid and stiff, her hands clenched in her lap.

"I'm terrified my baby will grow up without a father," she whispered.

Her mouth went dry as surprise flooded through her. Hot pinpricks danced up her spine as her sister's words sank in. Then she hurried to her, dropping to her knees in front of her, and taking her cold hands in hers.

"You're…pregnant?" Evie asked.

Chloe's big green eyes were glassy as she looked up at her, nodding. "He doesn't know yet."

"Oh, Chlo. Why didn't you tell him?"

"I didn't want him to stay because he felt he had to. He's a warrior at heart, Eve. He *wanted* to fight with his brothers. And now I don't know if he'll make it back."

She squeezed her hands. "Of course, he will. And so will the others. I have to believe that."

A knock sounded on the door. Chloe sucked in a breath as Evie's gaze flew to the door. They stilled, each one holding their breath.

"Who could that be?" Chloe asked.

Evie shook her head to indicate she didn't know.

Another knock. Then, a shout. "My lady, are ye in there?"

"Dougal!"

Evie shot to her feet and hurried to the door. She shoved aside the bar and flung it open. Then she fell into his arms, hugging him tight.

"I thought you were with the others," she said.

"Och, aye, I was, but Roslyn made me stay behind to make sure ye were all right."

"Stay behind? What do you mean?" Her brows drew together in question.

"When she released ye all, she rode to clan Sinclair for help," he said. "She dinnae want ye to know because she knew ye'd try to stop her."

Hot tears sprang to her eyes. "She's going to send them to help."

"Aye."

She hugged him again. Behind her, Chloe whimpered. When she turned to face her, she saw tears slipping down her cheeks.

"They're going to be all right," Chloe said, her words wobbling with relief.

Though she wasn't too sure, Evie nodded, praying Angus and his men made it to the ruins before it was too late.

⚛

THEY MADE IT to the top of the slope, entering the crumbling walls of the castle ruins. Rory's great axe glowed with a fierceness that did not bode well for what was to come. Brianna's heart was in her throat, her nerves shot. Next to her, Jamie. His hands were bound in front of him. She chanced a glance in his direction. His eyes met hers. In them, she saw the despair and regret and a silent apology.

He didn't need to apologize for trying to save her. It was the single most romantic thing that had ever happened to her before, even if they were going to die together on this hill, in these ruins. She would forever love Jamie for that.

The thought banged into her with such force, she swayed on her feet. The guard behind her put a hand in the center of her back to keep her steady. His palm was hot, searing through her woolen gown.

And while she tried to ignore that, she could not ignore the thought of loving Jamie that insisted on beating against her head. She loved the way he smiled at her with his deep dimples. She loved the way his eyes glinted with adoration when he looked at her. She loved the way he doted on her and took care of her, even when she tried to shove him away and insisted she was an independent, strong woman.

She loved him with her whole heart.

She had never loved anyone that way. Not even the man she'd married under the neon glow of a Las Vegas chapel.

As she stood there, basking in the glow of her love for Jamie, she also faced fear. Fear they would not survive this night. Fear she would fail. Fear she could not alter the timeline. Fear she would never be able to tell Jamie how much she loved him.

And fear she would never be able to stand in front of their kin while their hands were bound together and they pledged their lives to each other forever.

Because every piece of her wanted that. She'd longed for the fairy tale. Now, as she looked at him, with tears threatening, she understood the moment she'd landed here, in this time, she was *living* the fairy tale. He was her knight in shining armor. Her prince. Her soulmate. And she may never have the chance to tell him.

"Jamie, I—"

"Bring her to the center," Rory said.

He halted in the center of the ruins and turned to face them. The guard still had a hand on her back and gave her a shove. Jamie objected to that by surging forward, jerking against the men holding him. Brianna forced her feet to walk, moving toward the enemy. The one man who insisted on destroying all that she had come to love. This land. That man. Her sisters' husbands who had become her family as much as the twins.

She lifted her chin and gave him her best defiant glare.

"Now, lass, 'tis time to use that wee stone of yer's."

"You have to untie me first," she said, her voice strong and sure. She was proud of herself for that.

He jerked a nod to the man standing behind her. She felt him tug at the knot and then the ropes fell away. She dropped her hands to her sides, the feeling returning in a whoosh and sending pinpricks to her fingers and palm.

"And I need a knife," she said.

His eyes narrowed in suspicion. "Why?"

She held up her scarred palm. "Blood magic."

He stared at her in contemplation, as if trying to decide if he should hand over a dagger to her or not. Finally, he pulled a dagger from his belt and handed it, hilt first, to the man behind her.

"Do it," he ordered.

"Brianna—" Jamie started, and then a muffled thud.

She turned in time to see one of the henchmen smacking him in the side of the head with the butt of his sword.

Fury burst through her.

The guard behind her moved to stand in front of her. She held up her hand, ready for the slice across her palm. But something caught the man's attention. The shuffling of feet at the entrance to the ruins. More of MacDonald's men brought Callum and Malcolm.

A smile creased Rory's face. "MacLeod," he said in greeting. "Are ye ready to see the end of yer clan?"

Callum's face was impassive as he peered at the man, concealing all his emotion. Malcolm, too, remained calm and expressionless.

"'Tis no' the end," Jamie said.

"We shall see," Rory said. Then to his man, "Get on with it."

"Wait," she said, seconds before the dagger sliced. "It won't work without the stone."

Rory waited. She stalled. She cut a glance to Jamie. He gave an imperceptible shake of his head as if to say, *don't do it*. But she had to.

"She doesn't have it. He does," Bruce announced, pushing forward from the back of the crowd. He had a lump on the side of his head as he glared at Brianna and then Jamie.

"Bring him forward." Rory used his great axe to point to Jamie.

The men shoved him forward. Her heart raced as he stopped next to her. She tried hard not to look at him but it was nearly impossible. His imploring expression said everything he couldn't. She knew he didn't want to give her the stone, but at this point, he had no choice.

"Release him so he can give me the stone," she said, using her best demanding tone.

Rory continued to glare at her until finally he gave the go-ahead nod to one of his henchmen. He cut the ropes off Jamie's wrists. She turned to him. He reached into his sporran and brought out the now whole keystone. The lines were faintly glowing and she thought for sure she heard the soft hum.

Their eyes met for a long moment. He placed it in his palm— the one with the brand—and lifted it to her.

As she reached for it, he said in a low whisper, "One destiny."

The words pounded through her as she plucked the stone

from his hand. Something he'd said in the tent came back to her.

The tapestries changed. I'm the one on the hill with ye. No' yer sisters.

She grasped the stone in her fist, her gaze never leaving his. "Two bloodlines?"

He nodded.

Her heart leapt to her throat as she turned back to the man holding the knife. Everything clicked into place then. He was the one on the hill with her—he was the one who was part of her destiny. He was the one who had to help her shift the timeline.

He would also need to slice open his hand.

Blood magic.

But not just her blood. His, too.

"Now, lass," Rory said. "It's time to give me that power."

She clenched her jaw so hard, her teeth ached. She held out her hand with the newly healed cut.

"Do it," she said.

She hadn't a clue what would happen once her hand bled and she placed the now glowing, now humming whole keystone in her fist. With her stomach in a knot, she held her breath as the man sliced open her skin.

Blood welled as she sucked in a sharp breath. The humming of the stone grew louder.

But before she closed her fist around it, shouts rose up from the foot of the hill. Shouts and the thunderous pounding of horses. One of Rory's men burst into the castle ruins, out of breath and red faced.

"It's the Sinclairs!"

Rory roared his frustration. The great axe flared to life. In one swift motion, he sliced open the air between them. The seam sparkled and shimmered and then pulled apart, bursting with light long enough to blind them all.

Rory MacDonald had unleashed hell.

"Now, Brianna!" Jamie shouted.

She was frozen in place, unable to move as she held her hand open with the stone sitting neatly in the middle of a pool of blood.

Everything happened so fast, she was paralyzed with indecision.

Dark winged creatures spilled out from the Realm of Chaos into the air, attacking anyone and everyone in their path. The three MacLeod brothers went into action, somehow avoiding the attacks, as they fought the MacDonald men.

A man screamed behind her. She turned to see a winged creature sink its claws into his back, pick him up, and fling him over the side of the ruined castle wall.

Someone slammed into her from behind. She pitched forward and fell, the stone tumbling from her hand. She watched as it landed in the dense grass. Frantic, she clawed her way toward it while the creatures continued their assault on the MacDonald men and beyond.

"I'm here, lass."

Suddenly, Jamie was there. He snatched the stone out of the grass with one hand and reached for her with the other. She scrambled to her feet as he wrapped an arm around her shoulders and darted off toward another part of the ruins. The boulder, well-worn with age, was before them, glowing and pulsing. Carved on the top of the stone was the exact same symbol as the one on the keystone. She sucked in a sharp breath of surprise.

"Jamie, look!"

"Aye, lass."

He said it as though he already saw it and knew it was there. He must have seen it before he got to her.

"Ye have to stand on it," he said.

"How do you know?" Her heart rammed hard against her chest as she tried to regain her breath.

"Trust me."

He pushed the stone into her bleeding hand. With her heart in her throat, she stepped onto the flat boulder and closed her hand around the keystone. The moment she did, it vibrated so hard it sent tremors up her arm, to her shoulder, all the way through her.

"Jamie?"

He whipped a dagger from his belt, sliced his hand, and reached for her. "Take my hand. We must hold the keystone together."

But as she reached for him, an arrow thunked into his shoulder making him fall back a step. A shriek escaped her throat as he watched him nearly fall, then regain his footing. He turned toward the assailant, rage on his face. Without blinking, he snapped off the shaft, emitted what sounded like a war cry, and lifted the dagger.

A sudden wind whipped around her, tangling her hair. The portal remained open, the creatures pouring in, and all around her the sounds of swords clashing, men screaming. The smell of death and blood permeated the air. And, strangest of all, the black creatures seemed to ignore her standing on the boulder with her fist glowing.

She didn't understand that. Light seeped from between her fingers as her entire body hummed in concert with the keystone. Then, the light pulsed. The low hum grew louder and louder until it vibrated from her throughout the ruins.

Some instinct told her to lift her hand to the night sky. She punched it upward, a scream of terror ripping from her lungs.

And then a warming presence was behind her, surrounding her. The Triple Goddess appeared in a shimmering form. Athea to one side, Bridget to the other, Moira in front.

"Close the portal, Brianna," Moira said, her words drifting to her on the wind.

"I don't know how!"

She heard her name on the wind. Her eyes filled with tears— from the wind or her emotions, she didn't know which. She blinked them away, searching through the melee for Jamie. And then, she saw him. He'd stabbed the man he'd been fighting and then bolted for her. His brothers were right behind him, fighting all those who tried to stop him. Fighting the dark creatures trying to attack them.

When he was within reach, he stretched out his hand, bloody from the cut. She held her bloodied hand out to him, the keystone resting in the center. He clasped his hand over hers, sealing the stone between them.

A surge shot through her to him and up his arm. His face contorted in momentary pain as he acclimated to the strange sensation cascading through him. He clenched his jaw, the muscles ticking along the edge.

"The portal," he said through clenched teeth, his words nearly lost on the wind.

"How do I—"

But she never finished. The Triple Goddess moved before her, their hands clasped forming a shimmering, bright line as though a barricade existed between the two of them and the Realm of Chaos belching its evil. Their images swirled into one, spinning into a glistening vortex. That vortex twirled toward her and then punched through her with such violence she wobbled on her feet, nearly tumbling off the boulder. Jamie's grip tightened on her and then...then she was overcome with a strange sensation.

She heard a mellifluous voice in her head.

Blood warms to blood. A maiden's grace. A warrior's heart. By the light and will of ancient power, I command this chaos gone forever.

A pause, then Moira's voice. *Say the words, Brianna. Close the portal. Shift the timeline.*

But if she shifted the timeline...what, then, would happen to her? To Jamie and to her sisters?

"If I do, then what? Will they be safe?" Her voice was raw and ragged, the wind taking away the words the moment they left her lips.

All will be as it was once before. Before the Night of Shadows. Before the Shattering. Chant the final words and save this world from Chaos.

She repeated the words. Before her, the portal began to stitch back together, the seam of light closing.

The battle continued to rage around her as indecision flashed through her. Ahead of her, she saw Malcolm and Callum fighting alongside another man she didn't know. But when he turned just so, he had eyes the same color as hers. He had a shock of red hair, reminding her of Evie. His face was covered in a faded red beard. His tartan pattern was different from that of the MacLeods or the MacDonalds.

Was this, then, the laird of Clan Sinclair?

"It's working, lass!" Jamie's words were battered in the raging wind. Still, she heard him.

Now, shift the timeline, Brianna.

She glanced at Jamie, who was focused on the closing gap in front of them. She squeezed his hand to get his attention.

"Jamie, I—"

"What? I cannae hear ye, lass!"

Her hand tightened on his as she angled her body toward him. "Jamie, I love you. I will always love you no matter what happens."

But the wind stole her words. He didn't hear her. She didn't have a chance to say it again, as she turned back to close the portal and watched as the last few dark creatures tried to squeeze through to wreak havoc on this world.

The words came to her mind in a flash and she knew this was it. This would forever alter Time.

"Threads of time I weave together as Past and Future stitch forever. Now shift this timeline to what once was; forever mended with no more flaws."

Her hand never left Jamie's but before her, the earth's rotation spun faster and faster and faster, until there was nothing but a smear of light before her. The black, evil creatures that had come from the Realm of Chaos disappeared in a puff of onyx smoke. The sounds of the battle dimmed. The walls of the castle ruins changed and shifted.

What have I done?

It was the last and only thought she had before the earth cracked beneath her feet as though an earthquake rumbled. Jamie was ripped away from her. She no longer felt his hand in hers. The shimmering light of the Triple Goddess jerked out of her, the images of the three women hovering over her, and then Brianna tumbled to the ground. The last thing she saw were the spinning stars overhead and then nothing at all.

CHAPTER TWENTY-EIGHT

DARKNESS SURROUNDED HER. Her head throbbed with a massive headache between her eyes. It swept back over her scalp. It felt as though a hot poker was jabbed into the base of her skull. She was uncertain where she was, but she felt the soft cushion of a mattress beneath her body. A groan rumbled in her throat. Her eyes did not want to open even as soft light pressed against her closed eyelids.

"Oh, she's coming around." That was Evie's voice tinged with hope.

There was a shuffle of feet, the rustle of fabric indicating movement in the room. Her arm rested against her side. There was a coolness to her surroundings and she sensed she was inside the castle. Dundale? Or somewhere else?

"Can ye hear me, lass?" The familiar voice was warm and encouraging near her ear.

Jamie.

He was still with her. A hand slipped into hers. A calloused hand that was all too familiar. She cracked her eyes open and looked up into his handsome, youthful face. The moment their eyes met, he grinned, showing off those deep dimples on either side of his kissable mouth.

On impulse, she shot upward from the bed and wrapped her arms around him, pulling him close and burying her face in his neck. His familiar heather and leather scent was there, lingering on his skin. His arms slid around her waist, hugging her back, holding her close as though he would never let her go.

But the movement cost her. The blinding pain relentlessly pounded her head. She squeezed her eyes shut again as she clung to him, reluctant to let go.

"I thought I lost you." Her words were muffled against the warmth of his skin. She pressed a kiss against his neck and felt the fluttering of his pulse.

"Nay, lass. Ye dinnae."

Relief flooded her. And though every part of her body screamed in pain, she refused to let him go. She turned her head, resting it against him, as she gazed out to see her sisters standing there with worried expressions on their faces.

"Is it over?" she asked, her voice cracking on a whisper.

"Is what over?" Evie asked.

"The battle."

"What battle, lass?" he asked. He stroked the length of her hair.

Confusion pressed through her. They didn't know? How could they not? He was there. So were his brothers. She stared at Evie, who rested a hand on the small swell of her belly. Chloe was nearby, gaping at her with her wide emerald eyes.

"Ye hit yer head hard when ye fell," Jamie said, his voice rumbling against her ear pressed against his neck.

The last thing she remembered was passing out and looking up the night sky. She must have landed so hard she smacked her head on the ground and then passed out.

"Where's the keystone? Did we do it? Is everything fixed?" she asked. "Where's Callum and Malcolm?"

Silence in the room. No one spoke or moved. Jamie's hand stilled on her hair.

"I dinnae ken what ye mean," he said. "Yer talking nonsense."

Either he was in denial or the timeline really had shifted and she was in an alternate reality. She had many more questions that needed answers. She needed to know what had happened to the dark winged creatures that had attacked and to the others who'd came to their aid.

"Jamie, could you give us a moment?" Evie asked.

With reluctance, he released her. She remained sitting upright despite her raging headache and watched as he moved away from the edge of the bed. He cast her one last glance as he headed for the door and slipped out, pulling it closed behind him. Brianna glanced down to see her hand had completely healed from the cut. The brand from the stone in the center of her palm faded. Evie reached a hand toward Chloe. She took it. Together they approached the bed.

"Bri, this is going to be somewhat difficult to explain."

Her brows drew together. "What's going on?"

"You did, in fact, shift the timeline. And something changed within this time," Evie said.

Heated fear flashed through her as she lifted her gaze to her sister's. Evie held out her once-branded palm and saw, like hers, the lines had faded. Chloe moved to stand next to her, also extending her hand to show the faded lines on her palm.

"You sealed the portal, too," Evie said. "But the men...they don't remember anything."

"What?" The icy word slipped out of her on a breath.

"We remember, though," Chloe added. "We remember everything. Do you?"

Brianna thought back to the moment she had taken the piece of stone from Moira in the antique shop, to escaping John MacDonald by traveling back in time, to falling in love with Jamie, and, finally, to the battle in the center of the castle ruins. She nodded.

"I remember it all. Moira, the keystone, sealing the portal. Everything."

Evie blew out a breath as though she had been holding it. "Thank goodness."

"But what do you mean the men don't remember?" she asked.

"They don't recall anything about a prophecy or a time-controlling keystone. They don't know we traveled from the future," Chloe said.

"How could they not remember any of that?" Brianna lifted a hand to her throbbing head and rubbed her temple.

"We think when you shifted the timeline, it wiped their memories but somehow allowed us to stay behind," Evie said.

"With our memories intact," Chloe added. "Like I recall everything that happened to me from the moment I arrived to now."

"And so do I. We don't know what happened to you in the castle ruins. They couldn't tell us, of course, because they don't remember. But we felt a shift happen," Evie said.

"Yes," Chloe nodded, taking up the story. "As though the world tilted on its axis. It was the strangest thing to see the great hall mended while the world spun around us in slow motion."

She sucked in a breath and raked a hand through her tangled hair. There were snarls from the wind that'd take a lot of patience to get out. "It was the same for me. Somehow, Jamie's hand had the brand of the keystone—the complete Celtic symbol and the circle."

Nodding, excitement lit Evie's eyes. "When you destroyed the great hall—quite by accident—and you gave him the stone, it branded him. Then, the tapestries changed."

She told her about the images in the tapestries changing from the three of them to showing Brianna reaching for Jamie in the castle ruins.

"That's how he knew to use the blood magic," Brianna said. "He sliced open his hand. Together, we held the keystone between our bleeding palms. And…" She hiccupped a breath. "The Triple Goddess was there and they…spoke…through me."

Chloe's head snapped up to Evie. "Like when we were trying to escape the MacDonald keep?"

"It happened to you both, too?" Brianna asked.

"It did. And it was a strange feeling. Like they were within us and we were speaking for them."

"Yes." Brianna's heart pumped as she nodded emphatically. "There was a chant. Something about mending time forever. I can't remember now. But at the time, I *knew* the words. I said them and watched the portal to the Realm of Chaos close."

She bit her lower lip, trying to recall. Evie started to say something, but Brianna lifted her hand to stop her.

"Oh! I remember now. *Threads of time I weave together as Past and Future stitch forever. Now shift this timeline to what once was; forever mended with no more flaws.*"

Chloe pressed shaking fingers to her lips as she stared, wide-eyed at her. Evie remained perfectly still.

"The brand on our hands. That's why the lines are faded to almost nothing," Evie said.

Brianna held up her hand to show her the same. The two stared at it for a long, quiet moment.

"Then the world started to spin. I don't remember much after that. How did I get here?"

"I don't know," Evie said. "The same happened to us. We woke up on the great hall floor."

"And the roof is mended?"

"As if there never were a hole in it," Chloe said.

With Jamie's and the others' memories erased, how was she supposed to go on? Did he remember their relationship? Or was that gone, too?

The crushing weight of it pressed down on her chest. Was this it? Was she supposed to accept this was her life now—stranded in the past, bound to a future that wasn't hers to choose? She pulled in a slow, shaky breath, but it did nothing to ease the raw ache inside her.

Everything was gone. Erased.

Jamie. Callum. Malcolm. Every moment, every battle, every whispered word between them—ripped from their minds as if it had never happened. As if she had never happened. As if there had never been a prophecy at all.

Her voice wavered as she broke the silence. "Do they… remember us?"

The quiet stretched between them before Chloe answered. "That's the strangest thing of all. Malcolm remembers we're handfasted. Callum remembers Evie is pregnant with their first child."

Her pulse pounded, a painful, desperate rhythm in her ears. And Jamie?

Did he remember the nights they spent tangled in each other's arms, the way he whispered her name like a prayer? Did he remember the fire between them, the love that had bound them together, stronger than time itself?

Did he remember her standing in the wind, shouting that she loved him?

Or had that, too, been lost to the void?

"And Jamie? Does he…?" Her words trailed off.

She was never the type of person to share her feelings freely with anyone, even her sisters. But it was hard to deny the love she had for Jamie. She could not imagine her life without him.

The twins exchanged a knowing glance.

"He has feelings for you. Of that I'm sure," Evie said. "He kept a vigilant watch over you since the moment we found you in the middle of the bailey. He refused to leave your bedchamber for his and only took meals once in a while."

She paused, as if there were some unspoken exception hanging in the air.

"But?" Her insides jangled with nerves.

"But he's promised to Margaret MacDonald," Chloe added, her voice low with a twinge of sadness.

A sort of numbness slammed into her. "They're sworn enemies."

Evie shook her head. "Not anymore. It's like that part of the memories—the prophecy, the keystone, the clan feud with the MacDonalds, all of it—was plucked from their minds and tossed aside," Evie said.

"And yet, our memories remain," Brianna mused.

More questions pounded through her. If they were no longer sworn enemies, then how was her and her sisters' presence explained? Why did Jamie think she was here?

"Perhaps a parting gift from the Triple Goddess," Chloe suggested.

Silence wrapped around them, heavy and thick.

Evie reached out her hand, her fingers warm and steady as they closed around Brianna's. Then Chloe's hand joined, firm and grounding. Brianna grasped Chloe's other hand, completing the circle. A quiet understanding passed between them, unspoken but undeniable.

They held on, their hands locked together, as if bracing against the unknown. No words were needed. The weight of everything settled between them—the memories lost, the world unfamiliar, the path ahead uncertain.

They were in a strange new world. And they only had each other.

"Have you heard from the Triple Goddess?" Brianna asked.

Evie shook her head. So did Chloe. Whatever happened, then, the Triple Goddess wasn't going to make an appearance and offer an explanation.

"But we will never forget what happened," Evie whispered.

"Blood warms to blood," Brianna said.

Time had truly mended. And so had her relationship with the twins.

CHAPTER TWENTY-NINE

IT WAS SOME time before Brianna was ready to leave the bedchamber. Exhaustion and fatigue hit her hard and she slept for what seemed like days. She was vaguely aware of Jamie's presence coming and going, the bounce of the bed as he lay next to her or got up.

She woke up once in the middle of the night, ravenous. But she was still too tired and too cold to climb out of the bed and leave the warmth of the covers and send Jamie to find food. Instead, she burrowed deeper and slept some more.

While she slept, she dreamed of the battle she'd witnessed at the castle ruins, the battle that had seemed to rage on around her with the strange winged dark creatures that poured out of the Realm of Chaos to destroy any and all life.

After days, morning light pressed against her eyes. When she opened them, she found she was alone in the bed. The hearth hosted a cheerful, flickering fire. Jamie's tartan was draped over one of the chairs in front of the fire. His boots were on the floor in front of it. But he was nowhere to be found.

Perhaps he was wandering the keep.

She was glad to wake alone so she could think. She did not know what had happened to Rory MacDonald or his glowing great axe. Nor did she know what had happened to Bruce or John MacDonald. Were they still here in the past? Or had the shifting of the timeline sent them back to the present where they belonged?

And what of Clan Sinclair? She was certain she had seen the laird fighting against the MacDonalds and the dark creatures moments before she grasped Jamie's hand and chanted the words.

They'd fled her mind. And though she recalled standing on that stone, sensing the Triple Goddess's power deep inside her, she did not remember the words.

Brianna pushed to a sitting position, gazing around the bedchamber. It was a mess. Clothes were strewn about. Hers. His. She glanced down to see she wore a simple shift. Her modern clothes were gone.

She slid to the edge of the bed, draping her legs over the side, trying to get the energy to stand up, to find the rest of her clothes, and to escape this room. She needed food. Her stomach rumbled and cramped. As her feet hit the cold stone floor, the door opened and there, standing in the doorway, was Jamie.

He paused to gape at her, clearly surprised to see her up and about. She admired his handsome, youthful features. She liked his chiseled face with the sharp lines and the rugged angles. His doe-brown gaze softened as a smile tugged at the corners of his mouth.

Those dimples did things to her.

Once she had thought he was far too young for her. Now, she was certain he was perfect for her. And yet he was promised to another.

"Good morrow, lass." He pushed the door closed behind him and stood a moment, as though admiring her. "I'm glad to see ye up."

"Me, too," she said and her voice was raw and raspy from nonuse. She cleared it, gazing about the chamber but saw nothing to drink.

Sensing her need, he stepped to a table near the fire and poured a cup of water. He brought it to her. She took it, grateful for the cool liquid against her inflamed throat.

"Thank you," she said.

She held the cup between her cold hands, watching as he kneeled, and set about rekindling the fire. She watched the way the muscles worked in his back underneath his tunic.

"Evie tells me you never left my side."

She didn't know why she said it. But she had to find out his true feelings for her. She was uncertain how to proceed with questions about Margaret MacDonald. The cold, frigid bitch, as he'd called her.

He stilled, his back going straight and rigid. Then he dropped a bit of peat on the fire and brushed the nonexistent dirt from his hands.

"Aye, I did." His voice was low, sultry.

"I'm glad you did."

He rose to his full height and turned toward her. She realized then he stood barefoot. His pants were dirty and his tunic was sweat-stained, as though he'd just completed a workout. He reached for his tartan to wrap around his waist.

"Ye gave us all a fright when we found ye in the bailey."

Her hand tightened on the cup, her fingers cramping. "How long ago was that?"

"Four days."

So, she had been in and out of consciousness for four days. She had no idea how she ended up there but she assumed the Triple Goddess dropped her there when the timeline was altered.

"Do ye recall what happened?"

He moved closer to the bed, perching on the edge an arm's length away, as though he wanted to keep his distance, yet still be close. She wished she knew how their relationship had changed in light of the new events. Were they intimate as they were before?

She shook her head. "The last thing I remember was falling to the ground and then nothing. I must have fainted."

It was as close to the truth as she was willing to get.

"I'm glad yer all right," he said, his words sincere.

Her gaze met his and something deep inside her twinged. She realized she was desperately in love with him. But now was not the time to tell him that.

She thought of the ruins where everything happened. They weren't far from Dundale. Only about an hour's ride.

"Jamie, do you think we could go for a ride later?" she asked.

"A ride?" He lifted a tawny brow, the corner of his mouth tipping into a half smile.

"Yes, I need some fresh air." And the best way to get that was to ride out from Dundale. Plus she had an ulterior motive—she wanted to see the castle ruins on the beach where everything went down.

"Of course, we can. I'll have yer horse saddled."

At least that was still a thing for her in this time. But his face creased with an expression that told her something was off. Worry lines appeared at the corners of his eyes. He plucked the cup from her and set it aside, then took her hands in his, shrouding her in his warmth. She relished the way his roughened hands gripped hers.

"There's something ye should ken, though, lass."

Hope bloomed in her chest. "Yes?"

"On the morrow, things will change for us."

Her brows drew together. "What do you mean?"

"I have behaved badly." He wouldn't meet her eyes. Worry clanged within her. "But I found yer charms to be irresistible." Glancing up, he gave her a sheepish grin.

"Oh." She stared at him, her heart throbbing madly.

So that must mean they *had* been intimate and now he had to confess his sins. She decided to go easy on him. "I know about Margaret MacDonald."

His head snapped up, his eyes wide and round. "Ye do?"

"Evie told me." Now was her chance. She had to tell him how she felt about him. "Jamie—"

"I shouldna have led ye to believe we had a future together, when I ken the lass was my betrothed."

"Oh," she said on a breath.

"I dinnae have a choice, though."

Fire flashed through her. "You do have a choice. You don't have to marry her. Break off the betrothal."

He looked at her as though she'd lost her mind. "I cannae."

He didn't offer an explanation and truthfully, she wasn't owed one. The back of her throat burned hot with tears and threatened her eyes. She swallowed hard to keep them at bay.

"I understand."

"If ye dinnae wish to ride out together—"

"I still do."

Because she wanted to relish every last free moment she had with him while she still had the chance. Tomorrow, everything would change.

AFTER HE PICKED up his things and departed, Brianna pushed herself out of the bed and dressed. She wasn't all that good at it, but at least she got the woolen gown over her head. She pulled on woolen stockings and her shoes and then took a comb to the tangles in her hair. She wasn't having much luck.

A knock sounded on the door. She called for them to come in. Roslyn poked her head in a moment later. When she saw what she was trying to do, she entered the room with a huff.

"Och, lass, ye'll rip out all yer hair doing that. Let me."

She took the comb from her hand and pointed to a nearby chair. She sat and waited while Roslyn took her time removing tangle after tangle, heaving heavy sighs all the while.

"Roslyn, do you know Margaret MacDonald?"

Her hand stopped moving for a moment. Then, she said, "Aye."

"What do you think of her?"

She snorted. "A bit of a snob, if ye ask me. And ye did."

Brianna smiled as the woman continued to pull knots from her hair. "I understand she and Jamie—"

"Och, aye. I dinnae like it one bit. She's no' the lass for him. Even if she is bonnie."

There was that hope again, blooming in her chest.

"Too high and mighty for our Jamie," she continued. "He needs someone grounded, smart, and, o' course bonnie, too. Someone who can calm him. He's a bit of a rogue."

She wanted laugh, but kept it in. "Sounds like you have someone in mind."

Roslyn stopped combing and stood still behind her. The only sounds in the bedchamber were that of the crackling fire and Brianna's breath. When the woman didn't respond, she tipped her head back to look up at her.

"Do you?" she asked.

"It's no' my place to say, lass." Then she went back to removing the last of the tangles. "But…" She paused again. "If I were to say, 'tis only one lass who can give the young lad the balance he needs."

Her mouth went dry as she waited. Roslyn leaned down and dropped her voice low.

"Tell him before it's too late, lass." She straightened and put aside the comb. Then, with a smile in her voice, "Now, let's get this mess of hair under control."

ONCE ROSLYN WAS finished braiding her hair, she sent her out of the room while she tidied up and changed the bed linens. She ventured out of the room and found it was on the same level as Jamie's and the others'. She followed the curved staircase down to the great hall. That's where she found Evie and Chloe. The men were nowhere about.

Evie jumped to her feet. "Bri, there's something you need to see."

Without waiting for a reply, Evie took her hand and dragged

her from the great hall. Chloe fell in step behind them. She led her straight to the tapestry room where the door was ajar. Evie pushed it open to allow the light from the hallway to slash inside, illuminating the walls and the four-poster bed that dominated the center.

"We came in here for the first time today," Evie said. She stepped aside and motioned her inside.

"What is it?"

Brianna moved into the room and immediately her heart was in her throat. She glanced around the walls at the tapestries. They were nothing more than woven textiles with a damask design.

Gone were the enchanted images that shimmered. No more Evie, Chloe, or Brianna within the silken threads showing their arrival in the past. No more Triple Goddess standing on a craggy hill. No more threat of MacDonald and his glowing great axe. No more Night of Shadows. No more Shattering.

Just as the world had shifted and changed, so had the tapestries.

Brianna stared at the hangings. She glanced down at her hand with the fading lines from the keystone.

"So. It really did shift."

"Yes," Evie said.

She and Chloe moved to stand on either side of her, staring up at what was once their past, present, and future.

"I don't know why I'm surprised," she added.

"We were surprised, too," Chloe said.

"I guess we can't call it the tapestry room anymore, can we?" Brianna said.

Evie laughed, but it was a humorless sound. "No, I guess not. Hamish brought me here when he wanted to convince me about the prophecy and the magic of the keystone. Callum remembers his father dying of natural causes. I remember him dying of a deep wound from MacDonald's great axe. He was insistent that I convince Callum the prophecy was real."

"It *was* real, Evie," Brianna said. "For you, me, and Chloe. It was real for us. Nothing can take that away from us."

"I only wish the Triple Goddess would have explained this to us before…" Chloe motioned toward the blank tapestries. She puffed out a breath as she dropped her hand to her side.

"Me, too, Chlo," Evie said.

"But would it have changed anything?" Brianna asked. "The timeline still had to be shifted if it were to save this world and the men we love."

"I suppose you're right," Evie said, though she sounded as though she didn't like the thought one bit.

She hooked her arm in Brianna's. "Come on. Let's get something to eat. I'm starving. And so is the baby."

She grinned brightly as she placed her free hand on her round belly. She was getting bigger. Soon, they would welcome a new baby into this world.

"And me, too," Chloe added. She pressed a hand against her abdomen.

Brianna blinked surprise. "You, too?"

With a sheepish grin, Chloe nodded.

Brianna hugged her hard. "I'm so happy for you. For you both."

Unbidden, tears sprang to her eyes. She blinked them away furiously, but her eyes still burned with them. Once again, Evie hooked her arm in hers. They started out of the room they once called the tapestry room.

"You should tell him how you feel, Bri," Evie said.

"Yes, before it's too late," Chloe added.

The same thing Roslyn had told her. Her only response was to nod. Though she wanted to, she was also afraid to tell him. The last thing she needed was a broken heart.

CHAPTER THIRTY

AFTER SHE AND her sisters had had their fill of food, Brianna retrieved her cloak and headed out of the keep to the stables. She wrapped the cloak tight around her shoulders and was grateful for its warmth as she crossed the green. Overhead, the sky was overcast with heavy white and gray clouds. The wind was still cold and, despite the warmth of the woolen cloak, chilled her to the bone.

As she entered the stable, she saw Jamie talking to one of the stable hands. When he saw her, his face lit with joy and he gave her his famous knee-melting smile.

"Ah, there ye are, lass."

He examined her for a long moment as he approached her, looking her over as though decades had passed since he'd laid eyes on her.

"Your hair…" he said.

She reached up and ran her hand down the thick braid Roslyn insisted on. "Yes, Roslyn did it for me."

He started to reach for her, but then dropped his hand.

"You don't like it?" she asked.

"I'm no' used to seeing it like that," he said.

"Roslyn said it would keep my hair from being snarled with tangles."

The woman was right, of course. Standing there, the wind whipping around her, would surely cause more gnarled knots.

"I like it better the other way. Long and loose."

She flushed, the heat rising to her cheeks as her mind went utterly blank. Thankfully, she didn't have to think of a response. He motioned to the two horses he had saddled and ready to go.

"Are ye ready to ride?"

"Yes."

Though he tried to help her, she didn't need it as she stuck her foot into the stirrup and hoisted herself onto the back of the horse. He looked impressed as he then mounted his own horse. Then they were away, heading out of the castle gates.

Brianna gripped the reins tight in her hand as she peered across the expanse of land. The wild, untamed landscape still took her breath away. And though she missed her sun-drenched beaches and her Caribbean breezes, she knew that was not her life anymore. That was her old life—her old self—and here, now, she had been renewed. She was in love with this land, not to mention the man riding next to her.

"Jamie, there are castle ruins not far from here. Maybe an hour's ride. Do you know it?" She cut him a glance.

"That's Castle Caelnar," he said.

"Could we ride out to it?"

Confusion etched his features. "Why do ye wish to see ruins?"

She shrugged. "I just do."

Of course, there was no way she could tell him the truth. He would never understand because he didn't remember.

When he looked as though he would refuse her request, she hastily added, "Please, Jamie. It would mean a lot to me."

He relented. "All right, then. If it means that much to ye, let's go."

Jamie turned his horse in the direction she knew to be the ruins. She had ridden there once—on the back of a horse with John MacDonald—so she only remembered the way the direction felt as they headed there. It was definitely into the wind, the wind that now whipped through her.

They rode on, making small talk, as though they hadn't

shared a near-death experience with each other. She wondered if he still had the scar across his palm. She hadn't noticed when they were together in her chamber. All she noticed was how wonderful his roughened palm felt against hers.

In the distance, she saw the ruins perched on the cliff, reaching for the sky. Her heart tumbled around in her chest. When she chanted the words and altered the timeline, she'd thought she recalled seeing the walls return to normal. But the castle on the cliff was still in ruins.

Excitement burned through her. She wanted to hurry. She wanted to see if that flat boulder was still there with the symbol of the keystone carved into the top. She cut a glance to Jamie, who rode at a normal pace, his gaze forward. She recalled the day she'd raced him to the keep, when she'd kicked her horse into a full gallop and headed over the rocky terrain. It was exhilarating to ride like that. And it would be again.

"The ruins are ahead," he said.

She gave him a wicked grin. "I'll race you."

Before he had a chance to reply, she kicked her horse into a full gallop.

"Brianna—"

But his words were lost in the wind. She hunched down toward the neck of her horse as its hooves pounded the ground, sending up dirt clods in its wake. She snuck a glance over her shoulder to see that he was closing in fast. He was grinning from ear to ear and loving every second of the chase.

When they were near the slope leading up to the ruins, she slowed the horse to a walk and then a halt. She was windblown. Her cheeks were chilled but she found she couldn't stop smiling. He pulled to a halt next to her.

"I win," she said, sounding breathless.

He laughed. It was a glorious sound deep in his chest.

They left the horses to graze in the grassy area at the base of the slope and headed up to the ruins. Jamie was beside her, keeping pace with her hurried steps. Her legs burned with the exertion. Her breath see-sawed in and out of her. Her nerves jangled through her, her palms breaking into a cold sweat.

The moment she stepped through the crumbling wall, her heart stopped. She stood there staring around the ruins and remembering the horrible, ugly battle with MacDonald and the strange, dark creatures pouring out of the opened portal from the Realm of Chaos. That night was terrifying.

"Are ye all right?" he asked, his voice soft near her ear.

"Yes," she said on a breath.

Even though it was only days ago, the ruins showed no signs of a battle. No red-stained earth. The ground was not littered with bodies. It was as if it had never happened.

But it had. And the two of them were there together.

She moved deeper into the ruins. One peaked wall stretched toward the sky. There was no roof here. She recalled every moment from that night with such clarity, it was as though she relived it.

Then she saw it. The low boulder with the smooth top. She hurried toward it and dropped to her knees in front of it. Though she saw no lines, she stretched her hand out to touch it. The stone was warm—a strange sensation on such a cold day. There was a groove. She traced it and realized, though she couldn't see it, the Celtic symbol with the circle through it was there.

"I was here. It really happened," she whispered.

She flattened her palm on it—the one with the fading burn lines—and closed her eyes and smiled. It was enough for her to know the boulder was there with the symbol. Enough to know what happened that night really did happen. Enough to know the Triple Goddess allowed her to keep her memories of that night, of Jamie, and everything else that had happened here in the past.

"Thank you," she said again.

"Lass?"

Jamie's voice was right behind her. Then his hand was on her shoulder. She removed her hand and stood, turning to him. Question burned deep in his eyes.

"What is that?" He nodded toward the flat boulder with the Celtic symbol faded in the stone.

"I…" She turned her head to look at it, wondering how to explain it to him. "Maybe I'll show you."

She clasped her hand in his and, on impulse, pulled him toward the boulder. She stepped up. He dutifully followed. The moment his second foot landed on the top of the flat surface, the wind gusted around them, lifting her braided hair. She heard voices on the wind. Hers. His. Voices from that night when everything changed. When the wicked breezes had pummeled them and the dark creatures invaded. And she chanted the words that had closed the portal.

It's working, lass!

She gripped both his hands, hard, looking deep into his mesmerizing eyes. There, she saw the confusion with a hint of fear as he tightened his hands on hers. She saw he heard his own voice on the wind and he didn't immediately understand. And then their last words echoed back to the both of them.

Jamie, I—

What? I cannae hear ye, lass!

Jamie, I love you. I will always love you no matter what happens.

The wind howled through the ruins, whipping around them in a ghostly wail before dying as suddenly as it came. Silence settled over the ruins, thick and humming with something unseen, something ancient. Yet, they still stood there, their hands locked together, the heat of his palm anchoring her, tethering her to this moment.

Her breath caught as she saw the flicker in his gaze—the sharp glimmer of realization, of memory returning like a tidal wave crashing over him. His fingers twitched against hers. His pupils widened. Then, with a sudden jolt, he stumbled back, his hand raking down his face, leaving a bloodless trail as if pushing away the impossible truth clawing into his mind.

"Och, God's teeth," he said, his voice low and urgent. Then he spun back to her with an expression that told her he saw, he knew, he *remembered*.

He rushed toward her, taking her in his arms. His lips found hers in an urgent desperation that seared through her. A kiss that sealed forever between them. A kiss that said he understood, he heard, and he would never let her go. Tears sprang to her eyes and she was unwilling to wipe them away. A sob broke from her as she let them slide down her cheeks with happiness and pure joy, and when they broke, she gasped for air and clung to him.

"I remember. I remember it all," he said with his face buried in her hair. "The portal. The keystone. *You.*"

She buried her face against his strong chest, inhaling the sweet leather and heather scent that was all him. Her arms were tight around his waist, holding him as though he were the only thing tethering her to this world. He pressed a kiss against her temple.

"You love me." His words were deep, rumbling against that broad chest.

"I love you," she whispered back, though she wasn't sure he'd heard her muffled words.

He pulled back, cupping her face in his hands and looking down at her with unfathomable love and quiet tenderness. It rendered her speechless. He smiled, then, those dimples carving into his cheeks like she'd seen so many times before but never quite like this.

"Since the moment ye appeared in those tapestries, I waited for ye." He whispered the words against her lips, featherlight. "I loved ye from that moment. I'll love ye until my last moment on this earth."

His vow was sealed with a kiss. Deeper this time. They tumbled to the ground, their arms tangled together and bodies pressed close. And there, in the shadow of the ruins, he pledged his love forever to her and she to him. There would be no more parting. No more lost moments. Only this. Only them.

Always and forever.

EPILOGUE

I T WAS SPRINGTIME in the Highlands, a time of renewal and subtle beauty as the rugged and windswept land shook off the cold grasp of winter and embraced the coming warmth. The days were getting longer. The sun was getting warmer. The winds were turning breezy with hints of salt and heather.

Within the stone walls of Dundale keep, life had resumed its rhythm. Fires still burned in the hearths to keep the damp chill of night at bay. The scent of roasted meats and fresh baked bread filled the air. It was a time of feasting and celebration, ushering out the season of dark and ushering in the season of light. Mead and ale flowed freely. Boisterous laughter rang out through the great hall. Tales of the long, hard winter were shared over a trencher.

Angus Sinclar and his lady wife, Fiona, were in residence, invited by Callum. Chloe lounged in one of the chairs, her feet propped up in Malcolm's lap as she rested a hand on the large swell of her belly. Her face glowed, a faint smile of contentment on her features. Evie sat next to Callum holding their newborn son whom they named after his da, Hamish.

Brianna watched and listened to it all as it buzzed around her. She never thought she would have a sense of belonging. Until now as she sat next to Jamie, holding his hand while he talked and laughed with the others.

For a while, she'd missed her Caribbean beaches and her life of leisure. But now things were different. She didn't miss that life any longer. She had come to love the wild, untamed landscape of the Highlands and the rogue who had captured her heart now and forevermore. Her nomadic, isolated days were behind her. She had roots. She was settled. And she would never take her sisters or her found family for granted.

Jamie lifted her hand and kissed it. "Are ye happy?"

She grinned and pressed her forehead against his. "Of course, I am. Are you?"

"Aye," he said. "Happy to call ye my lady wife."

"And I'm happy to call you my husband."

He lifted her hand and kissed her fingers, his lips warm and soft and perfect. He still stole her breath and made her swoon.

"Tomorrow, we'll take Callum and Malcolm to the ruins," he said.

"Do you think it will work for them, too?" she asked, eyeing the men sitting on the other end of the table.

"We can only try."

It was something she and Jamie had kept to themselves. When they'd arrived back at the keep that day, the MacDonald laird and his daughter had arrived a day early.

Rory MacDonald was less than happy to hear he broke the betrothal to his daughter. Thankfully, everything worked out when Margaret announced she was in love with the stable boy and intended to marry him. Her father, however, was less than amused by this announcement.

Then things moved quickly as Jamie announced he intended to marry Brianna. The planning was a whirlwind. It was enough to send Evie into an early labor, which put the wedding on hold until she was strong enough to attend at her insistence.

Brianna was finally living her own fairy tale. She was content and happy. She watched as Jamie eyed the baby Evie cradled with the light of hope in his eyes. And it made her happy to see that because there was one last bit of news she had yet to deliver. She squeezed his hand to get his attention.

"Jamie, there's something I want to tell you."

He turned her, giving her his full attention. "Aye?"

She smiled, then, her heart swelling with love for the man. She lowered her voice so only he heard. "We're going to have a baby."

He stared at her for a long, quiet moment, his expression unreadable. And then a slow grin spread across his face.

"A bairn?"

She nodded. Understanding dawned in his eyes, followed swiftly by joy. He barked out a laugh, then squeezed her hand as he leaned over to press a kiss on her forehead.

"A family all our own." He whispered the words as he pressed his forehead against hers. "Aye, lass, 'tis what I've wanted."

"I know."

Warming spread through her as she leaned her head on his shoulder. Laughter and chatter filled the great hall around them. A sense of contentment went through her. This was her home now. Her life. And for the first time she felt as though she truly belonged.

Outside, the wind carried the promise of a new season, and with it, a future full of love, adventure, and endless possibilities.

THE END

About the Author

Michelle Miles believes in fairy tales, true love, and magic. She writes heart-stopping urban fantasy, young adult and adult fantasy, and paranormal romance with an action/adventure twist that will leave you breathless. She is the author of numerous series that includes everything from angels and demons to fairies, dragons, and elves.

She is a member of Romance Writers of America (RWA) and Science Fiction and Fantasy Writers Association (SFWA). A native Texan, in her spare time she loves reading, listening to music, watching movies, hiking, and drinking wine. She can be found online at Facebook, Instagram, Pinterest, and more!

Website & Blog: www.michellemiles.net
Facebook: MichelleMilesAuthor
Instagram: MichelleMilesAuthor
Threads: @michellemilesauthor
YouTube: MichelleMiles
TikTok: @michellemilesauthor
BookBub: bookbub.com/authors/michelle-miles